IFON Academy

EMILY ROSS

ISBN 979-8-88540-229-3 (paperback)
ISBN 979-8-88540-230-9 (digital)

Christian Faith Publishing
832 Park Avenue
Meadville, PA 16335
www.christianfaithpublishing.com

Printed in the United States of America

Contents

happy summer

Pencils scratched against papers in excitement as the last minutes ticked down. I leaned back in my chair to relax, while everyone else was still writing their three paragraphs. Everyone except Kaylani. I looked across the classroom to see my best friend relaxing just as much as I was. We never struggled in science.

"All right, class, let's get those papers in," Mr. K eventually said, and students excitedly walked up to turn in their papers. We were to write how we felt about the last day of school and how science would impact our summer. Thankfully, the report wasn't for a grade. Nothing for the past two weeks had been graded, which was one of the best benefits of finishing junior high.

"Jessie!" Kaylani whispered, leaning across the aisle. "It's three forty four." I glanced at the clock that hung over Mr. K's desk to see that it was, in fact, three forty four. Summer break started in a matter of seconds.

I rubbed my hands together in excitement and sat up high in my chair. The other students grew excited and checked their phones to see the exact second of the minute it was. Lion and Michael came over to Kaylani and me.

"It's almost summer break," Lion announced. He and Michael were grinning so wide from excitement, and I felt myself smile as well.

1

"Ten!" Some kids started counting in the back of the class. "Nine!"

My eyes widened, and I grabbed my book bag from underneath my chair. "Eight! Seven! Six!" Kaylani and I went with others to the front door and then started to join the countdown. "Five! Four! Three! Two! One!"

"Happy summer!" Mr. K called just as the bell rang. Someone blew the door open, and everyone piled into the hall. Kaylani grabbed my hand so we wouldn't lose each other, and we raced with the crowd heading for the front doors. The halls were filled with laughter and calls of joy. I glanced behind me and saw a lot more kids running from their classroom doors. Kay pulled my hand, and a large group of kids began to emerge into the school lobby.

We picked up speed, making a pointless effort to be the first people out of the front doors. Principal Reeves said something on the intercom as we approached the front doors, but I didn't hear. Not because it was inaudible but because it was the last thing I was worried about.

Especially since the lobby was filled with armed policemen.

*****

The heat was overwhelming, but I was too scared to move. I felt the blazing sunlight on the back of my neck and was relieved when I got to move up in line. I looked at the boy in front of me. He was a ginger, with a green top and green shoes that I'd seen my brother wear. The officer pulled him forward and started to pat him down. I turned my head left and right, looking for Kaylani, but she was nowhere in sight.

"Next!" My head jerked back to face the officer. The ginger who had just been checked ran toward the street to meet with his friends. Kaylani had to be there as well. I walked up to the officer who removed my backpack and handed it to another. The officer with my backpack used his pistol to examine the inside. The other officer patted down my arms and legs. Being surrounded by a lot of guns made my stomach turn. Even though the people holding them were supposed to protect me, I didn't feel very safe.

"Clear," said the officer with my book bag. He handed it to me and motioned me away. I swung my bag over my shoulder and went in the direction I'd seen the boy in front of me go. On the pavement were the kids who had already been checked—at least a hundred students. It wasn't too hard to find Kaylani, who was sitting on the curb by the streetlight. I rushed over and sat next to her.

"There you are." She smiled. "Ready to go?"

"I guess." We stood and waited for the pedestrian signal to allow us on the crosswalk.

"Do you know what all that was about?" I asked.

"Apparently, some kid took a gun to school or something." She shrugged.

I scrunched my eyebrows and turned around to face the school, which now seemed like a death zone. "How are you so chill about that?"

"Because we're alive. And we're fine."

I wasn't fully surprised that Kaylani was so relaxed. She'd never shown fear since I'd met her, which was basically since we were born.

The pedestrian signal conducted us to cross the street again, where we met up with Michael and Lion at the next streetlight.

"You guys all right?" asked Lion.

"Yeah, we're fine," Kaylani responded. "Are we still on for ice cream?"

"Definitely," Michael said.

I tried to shake off the fact that something so dangerous had happened at school and reminded myself that I wouldn't have to ever return.

"I can't wait to get some vanilla," I said.

Kaylani nudged my arm. "You're so basic," she complained.

We kept discussing ice cream flavors until we reached the corner that we'd split up at.

"Ice cream in an hour—don't forget!" Michael told everyone.

Michael and Kaylani crossed the street to the left and headed for their neighborhood. Lion went straight down the street, and I turned right on the pavement.

I took out my phone, plugged in my earbuds, and listened to music for what would be the next four minutes heading home.

One of the tall buildings came more and more into view as I approached. Miles, my older brother, was walking toward the apartment complex from the other way. We raced to the front door of the building, but he made it before I did.

"Slowpoke," he said before leaning over to catch his breath.

"At least I'm not as tired as you," I joked. I went into the lobby and waved to the doorman, who waved back. Miles came up behind me, and we stepped into the elevator heading for the third floor.

The elevator soon stopped, but the hallway was full of kids talking outside of their rooms. Miles and I went to ours, where he unlocked the door and we went inside. As soon as I closed the door, our living room was much quieter than the hallway full of laughing teenagers.

"Mom! We're home!" he called into the living room.

"Stop yelling, child. I'm right here." Mom was sitting on the couch and typing on her laptop. Temmie, our Pomeranian, was asleep at her feet. "How was the last day of school?"

"Great for me," said Miles, plopping down next to Mom. "I'm going to a friend's house later."

"That's nice." She smiled before looking at me. "And how about you, Jessie?"

I closed the front door before answering. "It was pretty good. I'm going for ice cream in an hour."

Miles grabbed the remote from the coffee table and started to flip through television channels.

"Where's Dad?" he asked. I went into the kitchen for a snack but still listened for Mom's answer.

"He's having to work late. Not all adults have summer break like you kids."

"That sucks," said Miles.

I reached into the cabinet for a box of animal crackers and felt my phone buzz in my book bag. After setting down the snack, I reached for my phone to see that Kaylani had texted me.

4:20 p.m.
Kay: Hey Jess
Get your bike
Michael had something to do last min so
we're meeting up early if its ok

I responded, typing "yeah that's fine" before telling Mom that I'd be leaving earlier than I thought. After instructing me to stay safe, I was free to excitedly go back to the elevator.

There were tons of kids celebrating their first day of summer break in the lobby, and I could hear them before the elevator doors opened. The tall windows covering the front wall in the lobby allowed me to see Kaylani on her bike, riding toward the complex.

I'd always admired her bike: chrome white with sleek black handlebars. It was always kept clean and prized by my best friend herself. She was steadying my bike with one hand, its chain wrapped around the handlebars, and pulled it along as she rode. She'd already used the key I'd given her years ago to unlock my bike from the racks outside.

At the sight of me, Kaylani motioned me over. She took her scrunchie from her hair and redid her ponytail while I raced outside.

"Hey!" She smiled.

"Hi," I responded. "I'm surprised we're meeting so early."

"Me too. But we wouldn't want Michael to not be able to go."

"Yeah. He'd miss out on the vanilla!"

Kaylani rolled her eyes and turned her bike around. "You're vanilla-obsessed," she told me.

My bike steadied under my climbing onto it. One of my feet pushed against the ground while the other started to pedal. My bike took me past Kaylani, and I turned my head to say, "Can't catch me!" She obviously was up for the challenge.

We sped up on the pavement, Kaylani just behind me. I pedaled faster across the street and could hear the wheels of her bike catching up. My hands squeezed on the brakes that hung beneath the handlebars, and I turned left. Cars were going the opposite way on the street, and the wind from the momentum started to lift my hair.

The ice cream parlor was just a block away. The wind made my eyes water as my pedals turned faster, and my bike rolled down the sidewalk that led to the parlor. My hands squeezed on the brakes that led me to a stop, and I climbed off the bike. Kaylani came rolling behind me, stopping to my right. A few more cars drove by.

"You got lucky." Kaylani smiled, rolling her bike toward the parlor.

We pushed our bikes into some open racks next to the building. My bike looked like garbage next to hers. The blue paint had begun to peel off the handlebars, and the wheels looked like plastic in the sunlight. Kaylani and I used our chains to tie the bicycles to the racks. I asked her for the copy of my key that she had and used it to lock my bike to the rack. Finally, we were ready to enter the parlor. Kaylani took my hand in a grip just as tight as when we were barreling down the school hallways not too long ago. I shivered at the thought of going back.

As we approached the parlor and pushed the door open, a bell rang overhead. Patricia, who we called Pat, was standing at the front counter and was delighted to see us. Pat was a junior in high school and had always worked at the ice cream parlor part-time. She was super funny and cheerful, and her personality was admirable.

"Good afternoon, guys!" She smiled brightly. Kaylani and I walked up to the counter to greet her.

"Good afternoon!" we said.

"If you're here to meet up with your friends, they're down at booth 8." Patricia pointed to her left. I looked where she'd directed to see Michael and Lion laughing at one of the booths by the far window.

Kaylani rested her arms on the counter. "How was the last day of school for you?"

"Pretty great, honestly. I can't believe I'm going to be a senior next year."

"Congrats," I told her.

"We better hurry up before all the ice cream melts in this heat," Kaylani said to me.

I nodded and told Pat, "Have a nice day!"

We went down the aisle and waved at Michael, who could see us approaching. Michael tapped Lion, who turned around and smiled. They were sitting on opposite sides of the booth, and each moved over to make room for us.

I slid into the seat next to Lion and leaned onto the table. "What are we getting?" Kaylani asked.

"You know what she's getting," Lion said, pointing his thumb sideways to me.

"Vanilla is great, okay?" I defended myself. The others laughed.

"I think I'll have chocolate...with sprinkles of course," said Michael.

"Yeah, me too," Lion agreed. "How 'bout you, Kay?"

"I'm sorta inclined to try that vanilla," she said, pursing her lips and looking at me.

"Do it," I told her. "It'll change your life."

"Yeah, might kill you." Lion laughed, and Michael joined in.

A tall woman with a white T-shirt, white pants, and a brown apron wrapped around her waist came up to our table. As she approached, I continued my habit of looking at the name tag on the shirts of every waiter or waitress I'd met; hers said *Carson*. She said the typical line we'd heard all the waiters and waitresses say to every table, that always ended with "How can I help you?"

The boys ordered their chocolates first. She wrote down the orders on her notepad. "I'll have vanilla ice cream," I said. "No toppings."

"I'll have the same," Kaylani chimed in.

The boys' eyes widened in surprise. "What?"

Kaylani shrugged. "It might be good."

I looked sideways at Lion, who rolled his eyes playfully.

"Your orders will be here soon," Carson said, writing a couple more things on her notepad before heading off.

"That's a pretty big risk, Kay," Lion told Kaylani.

"Oh my gosh," I groaned, turning away. The others laughed again.

"On a *serious* note," Kaylani said, eyeballing Lion. "What are you doing later, Michael? I mean, you had us come here early for some reason."

"Yeah, right." Michael shifted in his seat. "I'm going to Southern California for a while."

I raised my eyebrows and leaned forward. "Southern California?" I echoed. "That's epic."

"And far," Lion added. "How long is a while?"

"Not sure. I think for the whole summer."

Kaylani's mouth dropped, and she lowered her voice. "My cousin lives there. What city are you going to?"

"I'm not sure about that either," answered Michael. "I just heard I'd be leaving in an hour or two, and I wanted to meet with you guys."

"Well, when were you gonna tell us all this?" Lion asked.

Michael shrugged. "I was going to wait until after we were back outside, but it doesn't matter much now, does it?"

"I can't believe you're going so soon." I frowned. Michael nodded but didn't say anything.

We started to talk about other things that weren't about Michael's trip, mainly to ensure he didn't feel like he'd be missing out while away. Mid-conversation, Carson returned with a tray of holders for ice cream cones. She handed Kaylani and me our vanilla ice cream cones first and then handed us the chocolate ones to pass down. As she walked away, Kaylani examined her ice cream cone.

"It's not a bomb." I laughed, taking a bite of mine. She drew a deep breath and took a bite, gazing off toward the booth across from us. I leaned forward as she turned to face me and smiled.

"Okay, it's not that bad."

"Told you guys." I turned to Lion and Michael. Michael rolled his eyes, and Lion started to dive into his ice cream cone.

"I'll try it someday," Michael told me before diving into his own ice cream.

After more talking between sweet bites of ice cream, we'd devoured our treats and were ready to head out. Michael had brought enough money to pay for the ice creams, but when he offered to also buy us candy to take home, we politely declined. Kaylani and I went to the bike racks while Michael and Lion grabbed their skateboards.

8

"Guys think they're so cool with skateboards," Kaylani scoffed, looking toward Michael and Lion. She used the key to unlock my bike, which I took off the rack and wrapped the chain around the handlebars.

"To be fair, skateboards are pretty cool," I told her.

"Bikes are better."

We rolled our bikes to the pavement where Michael and Lion were talking. Michael's phone rang, and he dug it out of his pocket. He raised an eyebrow as he looked at the screen.

"Guys, I gotta go. Apparently, I'm leaving sooner than I thought."

Kaylani pulled us in for a group hug, and it was saddening to think that we'd be missing someone from our group hugs for the whole summer.

"Be safe, man," Lion told Michael, giving him a separate "bro hug" as I'd heard Miles call them.

"Have fun, Michael," I said.

"Thanks, guys," he said. "I'll text y'all a lot, trust me. Bye, Kay, Jess, Lion." He made a show of looking to each of us. "Don't miss me too much." He dropped his skateboard from his hand and pushed off down the pavement.

Lion dropped his to the ground as well and set one foot on the board. "Have a g'day, ladies," he said in an accent, tipping his non-existent hat. He started to go the opposite way Michael had. Lion flipped his board horizontally and stretched out his arms to balance himself as gravity pulled him back down. He landed perfectly, gaining speed.

"Showoff!" Kaylani called after him. I could hear him laughing as he got farther away.

"I'll miss Michael," I admitted. I turned around to set up my bike and prepare to head home.

"Same," Kaylani agreed.

I pulled myself on the bike but stopped as Kaylani tapped my shoulder.

"You see that?" She pointed slightly down the pavement. I pushed down my kickstand and left my bike before following

9

Kaylani. There was a shiny charm that was shaped like a cross. It was silver, just like Michael's favorite one. "Oh no." Kaylani sighed, picking it up.

"I can take it to him," I offered. Kaylani turned to me and raised an eyebrow as if to say, *You sure?* I nodded and took the cross, examining it myself. "Must've fallen off his necklace," I observed before looking back up to Kaylani. "I've got it. Don't worry about it."

We returned to our bikes, and I slid the charm in my pocket. "Get it to him before he leaves," she told me.

"I will," I assured her. We kicked up our kickstands and rode down the pavement, her ahead of me this time.

The breeze felt great, especially in such heat. I drifted across the street and smiled at Kaylani, who parted left. I had to keep going straight in order to get to Michael's house. The neighborhood looked a lot different than mine. All the houses were at least three stories, and most people had beautiful front yards. A lot of kids gathered in various places on the sides of the road or outside a house.

Nobody seemed to care that a new girl was riding a bike down their neighborhood. Then again, the neighborhood was massive—so much so that I doubted people would notice if there was someone that didn't live there. I could spot Michael's house nearby, which was a bright royal blue and had a large moving van parked outside.

I used the brakes to stop, hopped off my bike, and leaned it against the front fence. As I went through the front yard, I fished for the charm in my pocket. I knocked on the front door a few times and waited for an answer.

"Michael?" I called. "It's Jessie. I have something for you." No answer.

I turned around to face the moving van. *Was Michael not home yet? Did they already leave?* Despite my conscience advising against it, I opened the storm door and reached to turn the doorknob. As I did, the door opened. Since there were people nearby and I didn't want to seem like I was debating on breaking in, I slid inside the house.

The foyer felt much larger than it had the last time I was there. That was probably due to the lack of furniture. I closed the door and called out for Michael but heard no response. The chandelier in the foyer was beautifully polished, and the wood flooring was shinier than before. There was plastic wrap hanging from each doorway.

Entering the living room, everything had vanished. The coffee table, the television, the electric fireplace. The curtains were gone, and the windows were sealed tightly with silver locks. Carefully approaching the far wall, I saw a note hanging where Michael's old family painting used to be. I pulled the note off the wall and squinted to read the formal writing.

> It is with our greatest apologies that we leave on such short notice and will not return until the summer is over. Do not take much from this adjustment, rather, focus on staying cool during this season—that's a note for you *and* me! Despite the dreadful hot weather, continue to be active, especially in swimming. Continue in your studies as well, especially science and math. Overall, make the best of your summer even with our absence so this summer may be a time we will never forget!
>
> Happy Summer
> The Brown Household

The writing looked like Mrs. Brown's, Michael's mother. Messy but admirable, yet this time there wasn't much admiration in the words written. I folded the note and gripped it tightly in my hand before starting to leave. I didn't want to stay in the house any longer than I had to. As I emerged into the foyer, an engine started outside the front door.

I raced out the door, leaving it wide open and ran toward the moving van, which was taking off. There'd be no time to race after it, unless I had something that could go multiple miles an hour. My bike was the closest thing to it.

The van started to move faster as I climbed onto my bike and started to pedal. I steadied as well as I could with one hand on the handlebars, while the other took my phone from my pocket and tried to swipe to the camera. My feet pedaled faster to try and get a close look at the driver. Whoever they were obviously didn't want to be seen. I finally reached the camera and started taking pictures of the sides of the van.

The side I was on had the name *Kasheille's Moving Company* and a phone number. The truck picked up speed, and I couldn't go any faster considering we were going uphill. I started to slow down but spammed the photo button to capture the license plate as many times as possible. The bike became just as worn out as I was and came to a stop. I got off and drew in deep breaths and then swiped on my phone to ensure I'd gotten enough pictures.

There were enough pictures, but my brain was too fried to piece things together. I turned my bike around and saw kids about my age playing with a basketball on the pavement. More kids emerged from a house, gathering in my way. It was going to be a long ride home.

innocent...maybe

"That's kinda creepy, but I don't know what you really want me to do," Miles said, fiddling with Michael's cross charm.

"I didn't know anybody else to tell," I admitted. He scrolled through the photos on my phone as I retold the story. "I would've told Kaylani, but she underreacts sometimes."

"Yeah, she does," he agreed.

Miles had just finished his sophomore year and went to a science academy downtown. I'd always found it amusing that he went there since he'd never liked science. From what our parents said, it was very expensive to send him to the school, but my family was proud that he'd been accepted and wanted to give him the best education.

He usually stayed on a campus, which was rare for high schools in our area. Nonetheless, he would come home sometimes, and one of those times was today. He went to summer school alongside regular school, and summer school started next week. That meant that he'd be living at home until Monday, and I could tell him in person about everything that had happened earlier.

"Oh!" I dropped my book bag that had hung over my shoulder all day. Fishing between books, I found the note buried at the bottom. Miles set the cross down on his desk before receiving the note and examining it carefully.

13

"Where did you say your friend was going?" Miles asked.

"California."

"How'd you even get in the house?"

"The door was unlocked," I recalled aloud. "I went inside, and everything was gone. The windows were locked shut."

"And the door wasn't?"

"Yeah."

He handed the note back to me and picked at his hair the same way he did whenever he was focused. I decided it might be best to give him some space to think, so I looked around his room.

At the other side of the room, Miles's soccer trophies sat on a shelf above his cluttered bed. His sheets were never laid properly, but he hadn't been back in a while to clean his room. Outside the window beneath the shelf, I could see cars driving in front of Alexis's house. I squinted my eyes to see Alexis, my old classmate, heading toward her house.

Why was she coming back so late?

I reasoned with myself that I should mind my own business and sat down on the bed before sitting the note on the pillow next to me. My feet rhythmically tapped on the rug until Miles finally spoke up. "Maybe you should just call your friend and see how he's doing," Miles suggested.

"I did since I got back. Four times. I'm worried."

Miles sighed and gazed out the window closest to him.

"Wouldn't you know how to track him or something?" I asked, approaching the desk Miles sat at.

"What makes you think that?" He turned to face me.

"Well, they teach you computer science at school, don't they? I'm sure you've learned coding or hacking or stuff like that."

"I'm not a stalker. And even if I did know how to do things like that, I wouldn't. He's fine, trust me. You just need some air."

I hated that Miles didn't see things the way I did but gave in regardless. Miles helped me get my things, and I stepped out into the hallway, closing the door behind me.

Temmie was running around the living area when I entered, and Mom was still doing work. Temmie barked after seeing me and rushed to the door. She scratched at it, and Mom looked up at me. "Take Temmie out please," she said. I grabbed the leash from the couch next to Mom and placed it on Temmie before going into the hallway. The teenagers were still talking and laughing, and some of them greeted me as I passed by.

After reaching the main floor, Temmie started to pull against the leash, leading me outside. We walked to the bench off the tower block premises. I dropped Temmie's leash to let her roam freely while I checked my phone and scrolled back through the pictures from earlier that day. *Maybe I should call the number from the truck.*

My hands swiped to another app and dialed the number from the picture. I held my phone to my ear while Temmie ran back over and sat by my feet. The phone stopped ringing and was silent for a few seconds.

"Hello! Thank you for calling Kasheille's Moving! We are out of service today. Please try again later." I cringed at the loud talking in my ear before the answering machine hung up.

"Hey, Jessie!" When I looked up, Alexis was approaching me from her house across the street. She'd changed out of her school uniform and seemed happier than ever.

"Hi, Alexis," I greeted her as she took a seat next to me.

"I was about to head down to the park," she told me. "Wanna come? Some other girls will be there as well."

"I'm good. I've gotta look at some things."

"What things?"

"Confidential."

She raised an eyebrow and turned to me. "Only spies say stuff like that."

"I am a spy." I tried to keep a straight face at the lie, but when Alexis started to laugh, so did I.

"That's a really good poker face." She laughed. "Like you'd be a spy."

"I could if I wanted," I defended myself. She noticed me sitting up and quickly agreed.

"No, I didn't mean it like that! I'd never be a spy either. Too much life-or-death stuff."

15

I nodded in agreement. "I'm actually just trying to call this number." I turned the phone to her, and she read the contact name.

"*Trying to?*" she echoed. "What's stopping you? Are you moving or something? I don't want my only neighbor from school to go."

"I'm not moving," I promised, glad I could get a sentence in. Alexis had always been talkative. "I'm calling because I wanted to bring Michael something and I thought I could contact him with their number."

"Is he moving?"

"He's just leaving for the summer. To Cali."

"Sounds cool."

I set my phone beside me, and Temmie brushed against my leg. I picked her up and set her on my lap. Alexis softly groomed her back. This was exactly how it'd been last summer. Alexis and I met outside on the last day of school to relax and talk like we always did. But this school year, we hadn't talked much, and I realized how little we knew about each other now.

"You know, I think I will go to the park," I said. "Maybe get my mind off this."

"That's great!" Alexis smiled. She rose from the bench and helped me up.

"I'll be right back," I told her, gripping Temmie's leash and rushing back toward the complex.

After entering my apartment, I took Temmie off her leash, and she sat down by the television. Mom had instructed me to be back in an hour once I asked to go to the park. I turned to exit back outside when I realized I was missing Michael's charm. I went down the hall toward Miles's room and opened the door without knocking, expecting my brother to scold me. To my surprise, he wasn't there.

When I looked at his desk, the charm wasn't there either. Wind against my side and I turned to see the window open. *Did he sneak out?* Miles used to always sneak out, not to do something sneaky, but just for the fun of exploring without others knowing. I was surprised he'd done it again though as he hadn't for a few years now.

"Jessie? Are you going yet? That hour on the clock is still ticking," Mom said from the living room.

"Yeah, give me a sec!" I responded. I looked through the mess of papers on the desk, forgetting about trying to keep things the way they were. Miles really did take the charm.

Alexis was still outside, and it'd be rude to make her wait much longer. As I turned again, I caught a glimpse of a sheet of paper on Miles's bed—the note. I grabbed it and slipped it into my pocket before finally rushing toward the front door. If I was going to give Michael his charm, I had to find out where he was. And that note might've been how to do it. I said a quick "goodbye" to Mom before slipping into the main hallway and dashing toward the elevator.

Alexis was now in the lobby waiting, as it was hot outside. "Sorry for keeping you so long," I apologized, jogging to the chair she was in.

"It's all right," she said, standing up. "Let's hurry. I think Kaylani will be there too." It was a good thing I was going. I just really hoped I'd get the courage to tell her about everything going on. After all, not only did I have to find Michael, but now I had to find Miles as well. And nobody I knew was better at finding things—or people—than Kaylani.

*****

"Those swing seats were *hot*!" Tori fanned her backside with her napkin, making the rest of us break into laughter. She knelt down next to me on the grass and set her hot dog in front of her.

"Don't let the ants get to your food," Alexis told her. Tori rolled her eyes and set it in her lap.

"First day of summer." Kaylani sighed, almost to herself. "First day away from school. I honestly don't know what to do with myself."

"Same," Lacy agreed. "If anything, I just want to study for next year so I can be ahead."

"Of course you do," Tori shook her head.

"How about you, Jess?" Kaylani nudged my arm. "You're quiet."

I thought about the note I still had in my pocket. Bringing up the note in front of Lacy, Alexis, and Tori wouldn't have been smart as they weren't close to Michael. Kaylani and I needed a moment alone.

17

"I'm kinda nervous," I admitted. They turned to me to explain. "There'll be a ton of new people in high school. And I'm still…shook too about what happened at school."

"Yeah, it was surreal," Lacy agreed.

"Not surprised about any of it," said Tori. She leaned back on her forearms. "Kids are crazy, and school sucks."

"We're not crazy," Alexis said.

"Not us, but most are crazy. I love our neighborhood, but at this point, downtown might be safer."

"I heard it's a war zone down there," I said, hoping to take part in the conversation.

"It's not that bad," said Kaylani. We all looked at her.

"I went there for camp last summer. The city is really admirable. The small bits I saw at least."

"You must've been on the northside, then," said Tori. "Everywhere else is as dangerous as Texas."

"Hey, I'm from there!" Alexis said.

"Exactly." Tori laughed.

Alexis swiped Tori's hot dog and bit into the end she hadn't touched. "Hey!"

"What? It's good?" Alexis defended, her mouth full of the relish that it'd been topped with.

"Ew, relish!" I cringed, which made Lacy and Kaylani laugh.

"You don't know real cuisine," Tori scoffed. She snatched back the hot dog.

"I'm basically done anyways." As she rose from the grass, Alexis stretched out her hand full of trash.

"Take this with you," she said.

"You do it yourself," shot Tori.

Lacy stood up and waved her trash in her hand. "Slowpokes!" she teased, racing toward the garbage can across the park. Alexis and Tori took off after her, trying to get there first.

I realized that Kaylani and I were alone. *Should I tell her about the note?*

"I guess neither of us care for hot dogs." Kaylani smiled.

"Yeah," I agreed, doing my best to smile as well. Unfortunately, fake smiles don't work on best friends.

She turned to face me and leaned forward. "Tell me what's wrong."

"Nothing," I lied.

"I can tell something's off," she said. "No point in telling me there isn't."

I glanced to my left and saw the other girls laughing by the trash can. I wondered who had won the race.

"Alexis won," Kaylani said, reading my mind. "Gotta give it to the girl. She's pretty fast. But Lacy was her only competition. Tori's not one for running."

"Especially with her 'designer shoes.'" I made air quotes around the words which had Kaylani laugh. Tori had always been fashion obsessed.

Kaylani touched my arm and I turned back to face her. "You gonna tell me what's goin' on?" she asked again.

I sighed, looking at the girls, then at Kaylani, and back at the other girls again. They were arguing and talking, but they'd be coming back soon. My hand reached into my pocket and pulled out the crumbled paper. I unfolded it and flattened it against my leg before handing it to Kaylani. She took it and began to read. Her face grew with concern—something I'd very rarely seen her express.

"What's wrong?" I asked. I leaned over her shoulder to see if I'd missed a clue.

"Nothing," she said, returning to her calmer self.

I felt terrible that she could tell when something was wrong with me but I couldn't always tell that about her. She *had* been good at hiding her emotions a lot, which made the fact that she'd been visibly worried just now even more scary.

"Where'd you get this?" she finally asked, carefully handing it back to me.

"Michael's house," I told her. "I went to give Michael his charm, but nobody was there. The windows were locked, but the front door wasn't."

Kaylani's eyes lit up as I said that, and she wanted to hear more.

"There was a moving van outside his house," I continued. "I had a suspicious feeling, but they kept driving off even when I went after them. I called their phone number, and they're apparently out of service."

"What's the number?"

I took out my phone and showed her the image of the side of the truck. She zoomed in on the number and read it aloud.

"That area code doesn't exist," she said matter-of-factly.

When she saw me look at her in confusion, she clarified. "I studied them at camp. All the ones in the states. It doesn't exist."

I wasn't surprised she'd memorized all the area codes in the country. She'd learned a lot at camp—apparently much more than I'd thought.

"But somebody picked up," I recalled. "Well, an answering machine. It said the service wasn't working any longer for that specific company. Which means they used that number before. Why would Michael be moving with a company that doesn't even exist anymore?"

Kaylani thought about what I'd said for a few seconds. "Might just be an old number," she said.

"Didn't you say the area code doesn't exist?" I asked.

"It doesn't. Not here anyways. Maybe in another country."

"So why would the company be in *this* country?"

Before Kaylani could answer, Lacy came racing back, tripping over her own feet. She caught herself before she hit the grass.

"Don't try so hard," said Alexis, jogging from close behind. "We all know I'm the fastest. You're not proving anything."

"You're so stuck up," Lacy joked.

I looked to my left and saw Tori approaching calmly, from much farther behind.

"Hey, Tori!" Kaylani called over her shoulder. "Why so slow?"

Tori smiled and shook her head. "I'm retiring!"

stealthy

Temmie was already barking loudly before I even reached the door. Maybe she had a good sense of smell. She's cool like that.

"Hush!" I heard Mom scold her from inside the living room. I knocked on the door and waited for Mom to let me in. Temmie brushed up against my leg when I entered. Comfort was probably what I needed most.

"How was the park?" Mom asked, tightening the apron around her waist.

"Fun," I told her. I looked to my left where the kitchen area was to see what she was making.

Instead, I saw something else. "Miles?"

"Hey," he responded without looking up from the salad he was making.

"Don't forget to check the cupcakes," Mom told Miles.

"Cupcakes?" I perked up at the word.

"Not for you, baby," she set her hand on my shoulder. "For my coworkers on Monday. There's pasta heating up for dinner, and your father's here as well."

Temmie followed me to the couch where I started to sit down before hearing Mom's voice.

"Go and help your brother with the food," she said.

21

Normally, Miles would protest against having me help with anything. This time, he didn't say a word. I felt uneasy having the house be so quiet. He would only be staying here until Monday, but before he'd left for school, he would be very loud around the apartment, so much so that the neighbors would ask him to quiet down. Now that was different, and I missed the playful side of him.

Temmie didn't follow me to the kitchen. She must've felt the tension between Miles and me.

"What should I help with?" I asked.

"You can get the pasta off the stove," he responded. "Season it too, if you don't mind."

If you don't mind? Since when is he polite? "I don't," I responded, turning off the stove. When I took the lid off the pot, the aroma of basil and tomato sauce seemed to surround me. I set the pot on the counter and opened the spice cabinet, which smelled even better.

"Don't add too much," Miles said. I turn around, surprised he'd said much to me at all.

"I'll only add a few things." I shrugged.

He raised an eyebrow playfully as if to say, *You better*. While browsing the salts and spices, I wondered how to bring up his sneaking out. I also wanted to know why he'd taken Michael's charm and if he'd give it back.

I added seasoning salt and paprika to the pasta before looking for dishes.

"Paprika?" Miles looked at the pasta. "Just great."

"Don't hate it 'til you try it," I told him, pulling out bowls to place the food.

"I've got the plating," Mom said from behind me. "Miles, check the cupcakes."

I washed my hands and sat down at the table with four seats—one for each of us. Temmie's food and water bowls were by my chair, and she was waiting patiently to be served. *Spoiled.*

Mom set bowls in front of each chair and motioned Miles to come take his seat across from me.

"James!" Mom called down the small hallway. It hadn't been one minute before Dad emerged from his room and took a seat at the table across from Mom's seat. She took Temmie's food and water bowls into the kitchen, filled them, and then brought them back to Temmie, who dug in right away. *Seriously spoiled.*

When Mom took her seat, Dad started to say the prayer. I didn't even notice the bowed heads and closed eyes until Mom snapped in front of my face. I lowered my head but couldn't take my eyes off the shiny gold slightly rising above the hem of Miles's shirt pocket. *Michael's charm.* "Amen," was the only part of the prayer I'd heard before picking up my fork.

Dad asked Miles about his day, but I wasn't listening to the answer. I kept staring at the charm, wondering what had pressured Miles to steal it in the first place.

"How about you, Jessie?"

My family looked to me expecting a great answer about the last day of school, but I couldn't tell them everything, which took most of the excitement from my answer.

"It was good," was the first thing I said. I didn't dare mention the police coming to our school and be scolded for not mentioning it sooner. "Classes were a lot easier and I had fun at the park."

"That's good," Mom said, visibly unsatisfied with my vague response. Mom and Dad talked about their day as I started to eat the pasta. Usually I'd be rambling about how good it was, but I was too preoccupied with everything else that'd happened earlier. Suddenly, Miles took the charm from his pocket and fiddled with it in his hand. *That's it.*

"Where'd you get that charm from, Miles?" I asked over my parents' discussion.

Mom not confronting me about talking over others was a miracle. Miles looked at me and chuckled. "A friend gave it to me," he lied.

"Who?" I pressed.

"His name is Michael," he responded.

The rest of the meal, neither Miles nor I said a word. Miles kept holding the charm for the whole time yet didn't bother to even glance at me.

After what seemed to be an hour, Mom stood up and started taking plates into her hand. It *was* Friday, which meant I could pull an all-nighter if I wanted. I rose up and headed to my room, sensing Temmie walking behind me. I held my door open for a second longer to let her rush in before closing it.

"How dare he," I said to Temmie, lifting her into my arms.

I sat on my bed and pulled her close, wondering how to ask Miles for the charm back. Michael still hadn't answered my calls, and I had no way to find him. Temmie leapt from my lap and set her paw on the door. I sighed and opened it for her, letting her out into the hallway.

I grabbed my phone from my desk and scrolled through the pictures of the truck. *I should've taken pictures of the house.*

Michael, Lion, Kaylani, and I had a group chat that was usually flooded with gossip and stories after school. Today it was silent. No notifications, no gossip, no stories. I'd never known silence to be so loud.

"Can I come in?" Miles softly opened the door and looked inside. He scanned the room like he always did as if judging it of its organization. Not that his room was any better.

"Yeah," I told him.

He came in and waved Michael's charm in his hand before making a show of setting it down on top of my dresser.

"Why'd you take it?" I asked. "Or should I say, *where?*"

He closed the door and leaned against it, arms crossed. "I was trying to get it cleaned," he told me. He noticed my expression of "I don't believe that for a second" and tried to defend himself. "It's better than it was." He picked it up again and brought it to the lamp. "See? When you get with your friend, you can tell him you took good care of it."

I took the charm from his hand and examined it. In all honesty, I hadn't looked at it before to see how presentable it was. I was more focused on finding Michael. So there was no way for me to know if he was lying or not.

He took back the charm before sitting it on the dresser again. "I should've asked you first," he told me. "Sorry." He smiled and left the room, closing the door behind him.

I laid down on the bed and closed my eyes. Michael had rushed home so quickly after getting a text message, and now his house was practically abandoned. He hadn't been too far gone when I'd gone to find him. So another possibility came to mind... What if he'd never made it home? Or what if he was in the truck that drove off? I reasoned with myself that it wasn't worth worrying over at the moment. There'd be plenty of time tomorrow to call Kaylani and talk more.

My brain would've rambled on with more worries, but my exhaustion took over, causing me to drift off to sleep.

Moving in and out of consciousness, I heard the door slowly creaking open. I softly buried my face in the sheets more. It felt like four in the morning, and Mom would've told me to go to sleep if this had been her. I heard rattling on the other side of the room. After a few seconds, the floorboards slowly creaked closer to the door again. Whoever had been in made a rush to get out, as the door closed once again. I cautiously opened my eyes just enough to see in front of me.

Nobody was there.

My curiosity led me to sit up and place my feet into my slippers at the end of the bed. I hadn't even changed since I'd fallen asleep. I could hear a door down the hall close, and it sounded like the door closest to me. *Miles.* Either Mom or Dad was going through our rooms to make sure we were asleep, or Miles had come into my room. I hesitantly bet the latter.

I went over to my lamp on my table and turned it on, careful to avoid creaky floorboards. Whoever had come in went to the opposite side of the room and had gone through my things. My dresser was open, and my clothes were out of order. The disorganization had caused me so much discomfort that I almost didn't notice Michael's charm was missing. Almost.

My shoes shuffled against the wood as I went to open the door and slid into the dark hallway. Miles's door was locked. I glanced behind me to make sure nobody was there, which wasn't easy to do in the dark. My hand raised to my bun and moved around until I felt my hair pin.

Picking locks was something I'd never done urgently. I figured out the concept at six but never used it again. It was a miracle I still had the talent.

The pin shoved toward the back of the doorknob until it slid in neatly and turned to the right. I snatched it out and turned the handle, but the door barely budged. Miles was obviously up to something because his chair was lodged underneath the doorknob. I shoved the door open a bit more before taking a peek inside. There wasn't enough room to see.

I looked behind me once again, praying that I wasn't making too much noise. All my strength went into pushing the door, the chair legs scraping against the floor. I slipped inside the room and closed the door again.

A draft of wind chilled my arms, and I noticed the window was open. *Did he sneak out again?*

Cars audibly drove by, occasionally honking. I approached the window and saw the busy road, but no sign of Miles.

I squinched to see a car pulling up by the front of the complex. A tall figure climbed into the passenger seat, the streetlight shining above them. I couldn't see where they'd come from. The car drove off, turning its lights on again as it got farther down the road, but only to the red light a couple feet away.

After taking one last glance behind me, all of my brain said to go back to sleep, but my actions did the opposite. I opened the window more, slid out onto the railing of our neighbor's balcony, and reached for the tree in front of me. The wind slowed down, and I felt the humidity of the air. *Heat rises*, my brain mocked Mr. K.

The lowest hanging branch wasn't too far a reach, but once I'd gripped on, it took all of my brainpower to convince myself to leap from the porch. My hands lowered me down the branch more, and when I got to the trunk, I started to slide down. The cars were still stopped, and I took off running toward the bike racks.

"This is so stupid," I taunted myself aloud. "No phone." I yanked my bike from its port harder than I'd intended. "No charm." Riding onto the pavement, I went alongside the curb, heading for the car that I'd wanted to follow. "No idea if this is even Miles." I stopped a bit behind it to read the tag. *L, B...*

A couple cars behind me honked as traffic started to pick up. "No, no, no." I pedaled as fast as I could, a bit ahead of the car now.

If Mom and Dad found out I'd left, they'd punish me for half the summer. But there was no going back now.

The car gradually started to speed up, and I pedaled even faster, not wanting to fall behind. My head leaned back, trying to see the tag again. I could only see the last letter, *C*. The car turned the corner in front of me, making no effort to slow down. I squeezed the brakes and stopped with my foot, breathing heavily. They knew I was following them and wanted to get away fast.

Starting back up again, a car stopped to let me cross the road. I kept going straight. If they were to go back the way they were heading, I'd run into them again. The sun started to rise above some buildings to my left and practically blinded me.

Loud cars were honking to my right, and I turned at the next corner. A car in front of me sped down the road noticeably faster than the others, some honking for it to slow down. I pedaled harder through the morning's heat and ignored the pain in my legs. When I turned the corner, the car stopped at a traffic light close to the pavement. I rode closer to it, reading the numbers again as I approached. *L, B, 10, M, M, C.* I sighed in relief and repeated the license plate number in my head as the traffic picked up again.

I turned my bike around and started to go back the way I'd come. The only motivation for pushing through the pain in my legs was the shoved-back thought of how I'd be grounded for the summer if I didn't get home. *LB, 10, MMC.* I recited it in my head like a poem, refusing to let it slip my memory until I was able to write it down. I got on a familiar road that I'd remembered when departing the complex.

What if that wasn't even Miles? I wondered, breathing too heavily to think it out loud. The thought along with other doubts got shoved away until the license plate was the only thing giving me reason to get home.

LB, 10, MMC.

amplified

"*Great! Back to you, Shawn,*" news lady said.

"Thank you, Tracy." Shawn smiled. "We're gonna take a quick commercial break and come back to talk about yesterday's game. Stay tuned!"

"You know the longer you wait, the soggier it gets," Dad nudged me. I looked down from the television at my bowl of cereal and mushed it around with my spoon.

"Why so tired, sweetheart?" Mom asked from the kitchen. She raised a glass from the sink and scrubbed it with her sponge.

"No reason," I lied. It wasn't like I'd broken into my brother's room (and the neighbor's porch), climbed down a tree, rode my bike toward the city in the middle of the night, came back, struggled to scramble back up the tree, and got in bed for three hours in which I couldn't even sleep. That'd be bizarre.

Dad's phone dinged, and after a few seconds, he stood up and went toward the coat rack. "I'll be going to work." He grabbed his cap and placed it on backward.

"Over the weekend?" Mom asked. She picked up a bowl from the sink and scrubbed it harder than the glass.

"System issue," he said, still looking at his phone. "I should be back in an hour."

28

Mom sighed and nodded. "Hurry back, and stop by the grocery store on your way," she told him. "I'll text you a list."

"Bye, Jess," he called to me.

"Bye," I called back, less enthusiastic than I'd wanted to be.

Mom turned to me. "I can't have that negativity here," she half-joked. I tried to smile, but she could see through me. "Make yourself useful and take that box to the post office." She motioned to the small cardboard box on the kitchen island. Usually I'd complain, but she was right—I wasn't being useful to anyone, including myself. While verbally complying, I approached the package.

The box was sealed with duct tape and a delivery label on the side. I thought of asking what's inside but decided it's best not to. A door down the short hallway audibly closed, and Miles quickly entered the living area.

"Morning, Miles," Mom said.

"Morning." He plopped on the couch, not even bothering to get breakfast. I eyed him sharp, wondering if he could tell someone's staring. If he could, he wouldn't show it.

I picked up the box and headed toward the door. I would've left to deliver the package if I hadn't heard the typical intro for a new segment on television. I'd always loved the news, so I just had to wait a minute or two longer.

"This just in, the armed student of Symson Middle School has turned himself in to authorities. The male student claims he didn't plan on using it on anyone but himself. This tragic statement has sparked on social media and is holding us all tenderhearted. The boy claims his friend was the hero who called the police, although he managed to leave the school without anyone else knowing he had the weapon. Plenty of heartfelt letters have been sent to him, and encouraged discussion about mental health in students, as well as safety measures in public schools." The television seemed louder than before, and Mom turned her attention from the news to me.

"Were you there when that happened?" She had a look of concern that told me not to dare lie.

"Yeah, I didn't see him, though," I admitted.

She put down a dish so hard, I feared it cracked. "And you didn't think to tell me?"

"I didn't want you to worry."

Wondering if my friends were watching the news too, I thought about how they would've reacted. Kaylani would've shown sympathy. Tori would've blamed the school, saying a famous line of hers: "School does nothing but deteriorate the mental health of students."

Miles's phone beeped loudly before he said, "Sorry, Mom, I have to get to school. There's a project that my friend needs me to work on."

"Since when are they open on weekends?" Mom questioned him.

"They always are," he said, but I was sure he's lying. "They just don't usually have students there. Always someone at the front desk, though." He started heading to the door.

"Can I go too?" I asked. "After I drop off the package?"

"I'll be quick. Plus, you'll slow me down." He left the room with the door open.

"Jessie," Mom said. I turned to face her. "Be careful." She separated her words to convey her concern.

"I will," I promised, though what was coming to mind didn't prove it. I steadied the box in my hands and went out into the hallway.

The neighbors were quieter than usual, especially on a Saturday. I rushed toward the staircase, not willing to wait for the elevator. Going down the last set of stairs, Miles was leaving the lobby and heading outside. I held the box under my right arm and chased after him, who was already racing down the pavement. Miles stopped at the traffic light where he quickly opened the door of a car next to him—a car I wouldn't have recognized had he not climbed to the passenger seat.

The light changed, and the car turned the corner, but a glimpse of the familiar tag was all I needed to go through with my plan. I continued heading to my bike and shoved the box into the basket hanging tightly between the handlebars. I unlocked the bicycle and rode onto the pavement, glancing back at the complex behind me.

I'll be safe, Mom.

Though I couldn't see the car while riding, I vividly remembered following the road last night that led past the airport.

My heart rate seemed to speed as I began to reconsider my decisions. Miles was obviously hiding something, and I wondered if it was really my job to find out what he was hiding. The car was bright red. If Miles *had* wanted to be stealthy, riding with someone who had such a noticeable car wasn't the smartest thing to do.

I pedaled faster and saw a red light up ahead. To my right, I began to pass the car. I slowed to a stop and tried to peer through the tinted windows. Some engines started up, and I looked up again to see the green light. We hadn't passed the airport yet, though I wasn't sure if I really wanted to. The suspect could be anywhere nearby.

I pedaled again, using my memory to make my way toward the airport. The large complex was easy to spot, and it seemed that most drivers veered away from it. People were crowded outside the building, looking at what seemed to be behind me. I steadied myself on the bike and turned my head to see red and blue lights flashing down the road from behind me.

The red car drove quickly past me, and I turned my attention back to it. I'd promised Mom I would be safe, and following a car while on a bike wasn't keeping that promise. Despite my curiosity of the situation at the airport, I turned the corner and followed the car heading toward the city.

Miles had always told me to ride on the pavement, never the road. But the pavement started to end, and a bike lane emerged in the road. Plus, I wasn't too eager to follow his advice. It wasn't as if many people were nearby, so I rode off the curb and emerged onto the bike lane, still following the car as well as I could.

The car went much too fast for me to keep up with. It left skid marks on the road from drifting so much that I knew I might be able to follow it regardless.

We passed a lot of buildings in the next two to three minutes. They were practically identical, which wasn't a good thing. Most buildings were rusting and looked as if they were about to collapse. Some were townhouses that I would've assumed had been built hundreds of years ago. I was on pavement again, following skid marks and praying they'd lead me the right way. If they didn't, I'd be stranded in an unfamiliar place, with no phone, and no idea of how to get home.

The next set of skid marks turned left around the corner of another unseemly townhouse. I followed the turn and felt as if I'd entered a whole new city. Farther down the road and to my right was a small brick building. I would've mistaken it for an old house if the words *Mareschal Science Academy Care* weren't written in bold on a sign in front of the building.

There was a small parking lot in front of it where about five cars were spread out in different spots—well, six if you counted the bright-red car in front of the entryway. The sound of vehicles driving came from down the street. I looked at the vehicles that were on a roundabout, busy with traffic. Nobody had come down this road.

After checking for incoming cars, I rode onto the street and crossed to the other pavement. The building became more interesting as I approached. The front grounds were full of greenery. Some parts of the exterior wall looked old while others looked to be recently built.

I took a brief moment to look around me before riding into the parking lot and toward the main entrance. The red car backed up, and I froze in fear of getting hit. It stayed in front of me and then pulled into a parking spot nearby in one smooth motion. I kept riding to the entrance of the building and hopped off the bike, leaning it against a pole that helped to hold up the large front porch.

The car windows were still dimmed as I raced toward it, starting to regret everything. *What if the person isn't Miles?* my thoughts taunted me. *What if you get kidnapped? What if Mom finds out what you did?* The fears didn't succeed in stopping me.

I slowed down as I reached the car. I pulled on the door handle and wasn't too surprised when it didn't work. Not willing to give up, I cupped my hands above my eyes and leaned toward the window, attempting to look through the dark tint. My eyebrows scrunched in confusion as I leaned in even more. The car was empty.

Startled, I pulled back and looked around me. I caught a glimpse of the academy's front door closing but didn't see who opened it. Of course, I raced toward it.

Going through the door myself, a blast of cold air almost knocked me off my feet. It felt much better than the summer heat and was easier to move around in. I started approaching the front desk, which seemingly sat unattended. There was a bell on the table, which I cautiously rang twice.

"Hi!" I jumped and turned around. "No, over here." I turned, now facing the table again. "Look down a bit." Looking down, I saw a speaker on the lower level of the desk.

I started to raise my head and try to find the security cameras. "Our cameras are too well hidden to be spotted by the naked eye," the voice said matter-of-factly. Embarrassed, I looked back at the speaker.

"Can you, uh, can you hear me?"

"Yes."

"Oh."

"How may I help you today? You don't look to be a student here." The voice sounded like a computer, similar to the voices I'd hear whenever I answered spam calls.

I considered lying and saying I was a student, but lies were difficult to follow through with. They always escalated until you were forced to admit the truth. "I'm not. I'm *looking* for a student here," I admitted. "At least, I think they're a student here."

The robotic female voice waited a couple of seconds prior to responding. "Well, it's Saturday."

"They said they'd be here for a project."

Silence. "It's summer break."

"Then why are you open?"

More silence. "Can you give the student's name?"

"I thought you said they wouldn't be here," I said, wondering if I should leave.

"The name, please."

"Miles," I said to the speaker. "Miles Parker."

I could hear clicking coming from the speaker, almost like fingers quickly gliding across a keyboard, which was odd considering the voice didn't seem to be a human's.

"Absent today," the speaker said.

"Absent? From what? Why would anybody be here today?"

"You ask a lot of questions."

"I have reason to."

More clicking.

"Fine. Access granted."

Well, that was easy. Nothing else came from the speaker, and I waited to see if a door would open.

Loud screeching suddenly came from in front of me. I jumped at the sound and backed up, looking at the brick wall behind the desk. The wall began splitting in half. The concrete separated further, revealing more of the building behind it. Without thinking, I squeezed through the small opening before the wall could conclude its grand reveal.

There was a staircase in the middle of the room, and different doors on either side of me. As I made my way around the desk and into the new area, a loud slam came from behind me. I jumped around, to see that the wall had sealed once again.

I was trapped. Not that it seemed like a totally bad thing.

Loud chatter from the right hallway comforted me, and I went to the right of the staircase down a hallway full of more rooms. Each door had a window and looked as if it had been painted recently. The lights in each room were on, but glancing through each window, nobody was present.

Approaching the conversation, I could hear the voices more distinctly. Teens, maybe a bit older than myself. "Knight…takes rook," said a high-pitched voice. I looked to my right into the room with an open door. There were about four kids crowded near a desk.

One girl was kicking back in a rolling chair that seemed to be the teacher's. The other girl is sitting at one end of the small table, staring intently at the chessboard. One of the boys was sitting at the other end of the table with his back facing me, and the other boy was standing next to him. I pulled my body out farther into the hall, attempting to remain unseen.

"Rook takes king." I assumed the boy playing said it as he reached to move one piece to another spot.

The girl playing crossed her arms. "Dammit."

"You know queen to E5 is checkmate," the girl in the rolling chair stated matter-of-factly. The girl playing turned to her confused.

The one in the chair threw her head back in frustration yet stood and moved the piece. "Check...mate."

The boy playing snatched a piece from the board and stood up to turn around. "Bloody rook," he groaned. The girls laughed.

I was so curious about them that I almost felt invisible. The boy who was playing stopped turning halfway. "Guys," he said, the concern in his voice enough to make them look at what he was facing: me.

The one from the rolling chair approached me. I saw more of her features as she got closer. Her hair was pulled back neatly into a bun, and she's wearing a black body suit that would've made her virtually invisible had it been nighttime.

"Who are you?" she asked.

"I'm, uh, here for my brother."

I internally scolded myself for stuttering, but the girl didn't seem to care.

"Okay. Now can you answer my question?" she asked, the other kids slowly approaching from behind her.

"I'm Jessie," I said, as proud as possible.

She raised an eyebrow before turning to the group.

"Anybody know her?" she asked.

"Yeah," said the other girl. She came toward me, and I was able to see her much better. "Hey, Jess." Before I could see her face well, the high-pitched voice started to make sense. But not the reason.

"Kay?"

"Jessie, why are you here?"

"Why are *you* here?"

"I'm here for camp." She shoved her hands in her pockets and looked down. "I would've told you."

"That doesn't matter right now. I don't think there's time." She looked up, confused.

"What do you mean?"

"I'm worried about Michael. Miles stole his charm, and I'm pretty sure he came here since this place has his school name. It just doesn't look like his school."

I looked down the hall again, still not ready to take in the new surroundings.

"How did you even get in here?" asked one of the boys. "You're not a student."

"Someone at the front desk let me in," I told him. "Well, they weren't really there."

"What?" the girl leaned out the door frame to glance down the hallway.

"It was a speaker. Someone talked through it to let me in. A woman I think. Well, more like a computer voice."

"Since when does Mrs. Kettle do that?" Kaylani asked, but I knew she's not asking me.

"Never," said the other girl. The room practically tensed, and the taller boy moved past me out into the hallway. Kaylani and the girl did too.

"I'm Finniake," said the remaining boy shyly. He had ginger hair, sporting familiar green shoes…too familiar.

"Have I seen you before?" I asked him.

"Do you go to Symson?"

"Yeah."

"Then you probably saw me."

"Does everyone from our school go here for camp but me?"

"Only the best of us," he shrugged, leaving to go after the others.

What's that supposed to mean?

I turned and ran after him, figuring he knew his way back to the group. I followed him up the stairs and ran into him once he suddenly stopped. "Hey!"

"Shhh," he put a finger to his lips. "You hear that?"

A loud pang came from the other side of the wall—the one that had acted as a secret entrance.

Finniake set his hand on my back, gently pushing, urging me to rush up the stairs faster. The pangs got louder and more frequent. We ran down another hall of classes, as glass shattered to our right.

"Get down!" He didn't have to tell me twice.

I dropped to my knees and looked around. One of the windows was shattered, and the wall across from it punctured. That's when I realized that I'd broken my promise to Mom.

36

not yet

It's interesting you don't tire easily when running for your life. Maybe it's the adrenaline rushing through your body, your brain saying your mom will hate you forever, your conscience whisper-shouting at you to hide on the stairs...oh, that was Finniake.

We hid by the stairs, and I looked through the glass banister. The wall was starting to crack, slowly but surely. I heard a collection of heavy breathing behind me and turned around.

"There you are." Kaylani sighed, rushing down from the floor above us. She grabbed my hand, and Finniake and I followed her down the hall where the others were.

"Jessie," she said. "This is Naziah."

She pointed to the girl who looked me up and down, not giving so much as a wave.

"This is River." Kaylani pointed to the other boy.

"Hi," I said. He nodded, and I could hear Naziah scoff.

"We're going to have to break up," River said after glancing at Naziah.

"Finn, you're with me." The boys took off toward the staircase, and I started to ask where they're going.

"You stay with Naziah," Kaylani told me, running toward the same staircase. She moved too quickly for me to protest.

"Where are they going?" I asked Naziah.

"Follow me," she said. I was sure she was aware of her failure to answer the question.

I followed her down the hallway, and we went toward the other side of the building. More glass shattered on the floor beneath us, and I refrained from stopping to look at the damage.

We went through doors that led to another hallway.

"We have to get to the principal's office," she said.

We went down the hall, passing a staircase leading down, and went through an open doorway before she froze, causing me to run into her.

"Why'd you stop?"

"There's no security."

I stepped forward, noticing Naziah's worried expression.

"There's always security," she said, almost to herself. She kept going down the entryway, this time without pulling me along.

I followed her to a room that had a keypad for entry. "This is the office," she said.

"Do you know the code?" I asked her.

"No, but I can hack it." Just as she stepped forward to break in, the sound of metal rhythmically tapping came from outside the doorway. The window behind us crashed, and we fell to the ground.

"Stay here," she said quickly, rushing off. My brain told me to run after her, but I felt glued to the floor.

The window on the other side of me shattered, and I scooted away from it. Crawling, I started to leave the room. Naziah had directed me to stay put, and she probably knew her way around, but whoever was firing would probably come inside, and I wouldn't want to be cornered. More metal clanking came from the hallway, and I went toward the glass banister. It was too late—I was cornered.

From my angle, I could see two people dressed in black slowly making their way up the staircase. Each one had what seemed to be a gun in their hand, and a larger one hanging on their back.

I crawled back toward the principal's office and tested the code. *0000. 1234. 1111.* More clanking. Pressing buttons desperately, I could hear the clanking getting closer from behind me. Sitting still wouldn't do much.

There was no time to think, just to do. I stood up just beneath the view of the windows and went to one of the walls. A mirror hung on the wall to my left. I lowered myself more and reached for it, pulling on it as hard as possible. It came off and threw me on my back.

More clanking, and faster.

My hands fumbled with the large mirror, but I managed to steady it and point it at the window across from me. The sunlight from the window against the mirror made a light shine on the floor. I adjusted the mirror to get the light to reflect toward the door.

Even faster clanking.

I held the bottom of the mirror with one hand and used my other hand to cover my mouth. My breathing was too loud to stay hidden. Balancing the mirror, the light shone onto the keypad by the door.

Just as it did, the keypad blew up. I gasped and started to drop the mirror. I fell on my side and caught the mirror and then brought it to my chest. Sliding back into the nearest corner, the clanking had stopped.

As much as I wanted my eyes to close, they wouldn't. They wandered over to the keypad, which was split in half. Wires were coming off the side, and the front half of the device had fallen to the ground. It worked. Whoever saw the light had fired at it.

I waited for more clanking, but there was none. *Was it the keypad making all that noise?* The clanking started back up again and seemed to grow more distant. I sat still for what seemed to be a whole minute before gaining enough courage to look out the doorway. Someone was standing, dressed in all black, with their back facing me. Their shoes looked heavy and seemed to be metal.

Why would someone break in with loud shoes? I quickly moved to the principal's door and opened it. The door creaked, and I slid between the part I'd opened. A loud pang came again, and I slammed the door shut. The sound of the heavy shoes approached me.

I dropped the mirror and grabbed the chair closest to me. My hands lodged it underneath the door handle so that it'd take a bit longer to get in. I ran around the large table in the middle of the room and toward one of the windows. Above the window was a sign reading EMERGENCY EXIT.

The sign was crooked and obviously misplaced. But there was no time to look for what door it had originally hung over.

The window handle was easy to unloose, and it began to open with a small tug. I heard banging at the door and tried to pull the window up higher to get through. The chair was flung against the table as someone opened the door. The glass of the window shattered, and I dove right. There was no way to hide by now. I slid underneath the table.

There was a purse hanging off the chair beside me, which I quickly grabbed. My ears were ringing from the constant sound of the gun, and things around me started crashing. *Maybe they don't see me yet.* I quickly unhooked the leather strap of the purse and tied one end of it around the leg of the chair. Things on the table flied off, and one of the bullets ricocheted off the walls and hit the shelves.

I waited to hear the gun start to cock so that I could make a run for it. I didn't know much about guns, but I knew that they had to be reloaded eventually. The clanking moved around the edge of the table, and I feared they were getting closer to me. The firing stopped for a second, and I tightened my grip on the end of the strap that wasn't tied to the chair.

There was no time to think of the consequences, only to move. I took off from my hiding spot and raced toward the broken window. My arm shielded my face and I burst out, pieces of broken glass already cutting through my clothes. I heard the gun cock and a quick fire, but a miss, just as I rolled outside the building.

The strap was short, and I made it down the wall barely a floor. I took an abrupt stop that made my ears stop ringing, but the strap slid off the chair leg and I started to fall faster. My hands dropped the strap and reached for the wall I was tumbling beside. I pressed every part of my body that's near it against it to slow the fall, but my whole body burned badly.

Through my watering eyes, I saw sky, wall, grass, sky, wall, grass. I desperately turned my body to start rolling away from the building as I hit the grass. I tumbled over about five times and ended with my face buried in grass. My ears weren't ringing any more. I was attached to the ground and too scared to move my limbs.

My head lifted off the ground so that I could take in air. I turned myself to lay on my back and looked up at the sky. On my way down, I must've been screaming, because everything seemed suddenly silent...except for the stomping approaching me. I closed my eyes, knowing that trying to run would be a waste of time. The field was open and would make a great shooting range for even a beginner.

The stomping soon stopped by my head, and someone picked me up by the back of my shirt. My eyelids felt heavy, and they barely opened. I could see my feet being dragged against the grass, and feet wearing only socks walking alongside me. Eventually I was plopped on grass again, my back against a cold wall. The two people walked from my side to stand in front of me.

The guns on their backs were visible above their shoulders, and their handguns were now settled in the holsters on their belts. I softly took my back off the brick wall and started to stand up. As I did, Kaylani came from around the corner of the building. She didn't look at me yet stood in front of the people in black. *Is she...with them?*

Naziah came from the same corner, standing next to Kaylani. Finniake and River came from the corner as well and stood together next to Naziah. Naziah crossed her arms.

"Duck," she said.

In the peripheral of my vision, I saw the wall start to retract, and I jumped back. One large square area of the wall pushed out by my head and came toward me.

I backed up more and glanced behind myself to see that I'd almost run into River. The square stopped moving, and the front of it lighted up. Almost like a projector. I squinted until the picture became more vivid and clear. There's the back of someone, a woman, with shoulder-length blond hair.

"Hello, Jessie." I heard the voice practically surrounding me but couldn't find the speakers.

"Who are you?" I asked.

The voice laughed. I could tell it wasn't a still photo, because the woman's head moved as she did so.

"You'll find that out tomorrow. For now, I'd like to tell you who *we* are."

"We?"

"This isn't a science academy, Jessie. You've displayed real bravery and wits during your time here today."

"What are you talking about?"

One of the people dressed in black steps toward the wall.

"If I may, ma'am." His deep voice startled me. "You might want to reconsider your decision. The girl showed wits until she fell almost three stories."

"She survived, didn't she?" said the lady.

"Well, yes, but she isn't fully qualified. We don't even know if she's good in physicalities…"

"I believe she can do more than she's shown today."

The man lowered his head and returned to where he stood previously.

"What about my brother?" I asked her.

"He's here."

"Where?"

"Nearby. He'll be taking you home."

"Well, what about those people shooting at us? Where are they? Assuming it's not them…" I motioned toward the group.

"It was them, but they're no threat to you. You've proven yourself worthy of a chance here at IFON during the test."

"IFON?" I echoed.

The woman sighed. "Miles will explain more to you, Jessie. You can wait by the car you followed here for him to arrive."

"How'd you know I followed—" The image faded quickly, and the block of the wall started to move back into place. The squealing of mechanics made me cringe until the loud machine stopped.

I heard footsteps behind me and noticed everyone heading back to the building—everyone except Kaylani. She stepped toward me. "I know you are very confused by everything," she said. "Maybe you're even terrified. But you'll get clarification soon. I'm just not allowed to give it to you."

"What do you mean, you're not allowed?" I asked.

Naziah called Kaylani from around the corner, and Kaylani glanced in her direction. "I'm sorry," Kaylani apologized. She stepped toward me hesitantly but gave in to her thoughts and wrapped me in a tight hug. I winced from the pressure on my arm, but she didn't seem to notice. After hearing Naziah call her again, Kaylani rushed away. She glanced back and gave me a look that seemed to say something, but I couldn't make it out.

I saw Miles standing by his car and motioning me over. While running to him, my arm hurt even more.

"Are you all right?" he asked.

"Where were you?" I asked. "I fell out of a building, and I can't move my arm!" I looked back at the building where I thought I'd encountered a near-death experience, though nobody seemed to think the same thing.

Miles glanced behind me as if to make sure nobody was looking. He reached for my arm hanging lifelessly by my side.

I cringed as he raised my arm. He placed one hand on my shoulder and the other on my wrist.

"Brace yourself," he warned, not allowing much time for me to do so. I shouted at the pressure, hearing my voice echo against the brick building. I snatched my arm back and lifted it to see what he'd done.

"See? You can move it," he said.

"You're welcome."

I moved my shoulder a bit, relieved from the pain.

Miles climbed into the driver seat, and I rushed around to the passenger's.

"What'd you do?" I asked, closing the door as I climbed in.

"Something I learned at school. One of my professors taught it to me. Your arm was just twisted in its socket. Twisted limbs are surprisingly easy to fix."

"What about my bike?" I asked. "I still have to deliv—"

"It'll be taken care of," he said.

Miles hit a button on the dashboard, and the engine audibly started up.

"This is your car?" I asked, though I was pretty sure I already knew the answer. The interior smelled like pumpkin…his favorite scent. The seats were a luxury brown and lined in shiny gold. Even the tinted windows seemed to fit him as he's always been private. I thought to ask something that I didn't already know the answer to.

"How much did this cost?"

"Free," he said, pressing on the gas and taking us forward.

"School gave it to me. Sweet, right?" I nodded and looked at the rest of the parking lot. Kaylani and the kids she introduced me to were nowhere to be found.

We started to get onto the odd-looking road, that still nobody else had come onto. Miles turned right and merged onto the roundabout, which felt surprisingly more comfortable. It felt better to be surrounded by a lot of other people, even if they were in cars.

"Do you know anything about IFON?" I asked, turning to face him.

He glanced at me, before turning his attention back on the road. "Yeah. It's my school."

"Don't lie to me," I told him, and he glanced at me again. "You go to a science academy."

"You sure?"

"I'm sure, Miles. It's just…hidden. Why didn't you tell Mom and Dad the correct address?"

"Mareschal Science Academy," he whispered, almost to himself. The car came to a stop. "Mareschal Science Academy doesn't exist." He noticed my eyebrows furrowed in confusion and adjusted himself in his seat as if about to explain. "I don't go to a science school, Jessie. I hate science. I go to a more…sophisticated school," he said, chuckling at his own sentence. "Definitely more fun."

A car behind us honked, and Miles looked up at the green light. He quickly pressed on the gas and moved down the road.

"You remember those guys who tried to kill you?"

"How could I forget?"

"It wasn't planned, no matter what you were told. The building *was* under attack, and you just happened to be there. Despite my instructions for you *not* to come." He gave me a brief, yet cold stare.

"You took Michael's charm from me and kept leaving with it," I defended. "And now you're telling me that the building was under attack? Was that really your school? Why was Kaylani there? Who were the other kids?"

"You'll learn a lot more tomorrow when we come back to school." I sat back but realized that he wasn't making sense, per usual.

"Why would we go back to school? It's summer break."

"You'll find out tomorrow."

"Tell me now."

Miles sighed again, and I felt the car jerk forward. The car came to a sudden stop, and someone in front of us honked. Two cars came speeding from the right, close enough to us to shake the car.

"These people are crazy, man," he fumed, the same way dad would whenever he witnessed road rage.

The car picked up speed again, and we got onto a familiar road.

"Are you gonna tell me the truth?" I asked, annoyed that he hadn't given me more information. He turned the corner as we got closer to the complex.

"Not yet," he said.

secrets

I didn't even notice my hands fidgeting until they started to make a tedious noise. The elevator dinged loudly and I jumped a bit, but Miles didn't seem to notice. We exited the elevator and walked down the hall toward our apartment. I walked a bit ahead of him, and he grabbed my arm as I reached toward the door.

"Wait," he whispered, pulling me toward him a bit. "When you get in, you're most likely gonna hear some news. Pretend like you're excited."

I was once again confused by his statements, but he knocked on the door before I could ask any questions. I heard shuffling on the other side of the door before Mom pulled it open.

"Hi, kids!" She smiled and looked fairly happy to see us.

"Hey, Mom," Miles greeted her.

Mom wrapped her arms around us and sighs. I assumed she'd been worried for us with what had been on the news earlier.

"Did you two come home together?" she asked, hesitantly pulling away.

"Yes," Miles assured her.

He slightly pushed me forward, and I walked into the living room. Dad was back already and was sitting at the dining table.

"Hey, kids," he said, not looking up from his laptop. I stood awkwardly in the middle of the room, not sure what to do. I felt a

46

hand on my shoulder and looked up to see Miles. He tilted his head to the right and started into the living area. I glanced over to Mom before following him.

Miles took a seat on the couch and reached for the remote on the coffee table. I sat next to him and stared at the television, waiting for him to flip through channels. Miles changed the channel once before nudging my arm with his. He looked at me disapprovingly and slouched against the arm rest a bit. I noticed my tense posture and leaned back on the couch. The look on his face didn't seem too approving. *Sorry*, I told him in my head.

My eyes were watching someone with a shield running on the television, but my mind wasn't paying attention. Thoughts in my head wonder about Kaylani, and about when Miles would tell me more about…whatever he called the school.

"Gen? Come take a look at this." I heard Mom set something down in the kitchen before her slippers loudly scuffled toward the table Dad was at. I faced the television and zoned out as blue and white lights flashed in front of me. Looking over at my brother, I could tell that he was fully immersed in the movie. Unlike him, I had never been a fan of action films.

I heard a slightly concerned "What?" from behind me and turned around. Miles turned as well, facing Mom and Dad.

"Jessie, come here," Mom ordered.

I looked at Miles, whose eyes were on Mom. My curiosity forced me to get up and approach the unknown. As I got closer to the small table, Dad turned his laptop to face me.

I bent down a bit and heard Miles approaching from the couch.

"What?" I said, hearing the confusion in my own voice. My hand reached for the mouse to read the rest of the email.

Greetings,

I am writing to inform you of your daughter's acceptance into Mareschal Science Academy. It is with my understanding that Mr. Miles Parker is already approaching his senior year, and his performance has been exceptional so far—we are blessed to have such a talented attendee. With your permission, we'd like to accept Ms. Jessie Parker to MSA.

Her work in public school has been exceptional, and with our new curriculum could be even more improved. If she chooses and you permit, she would be at the academy for summer school alongside her brother. One scholarship has been granted to Ms. Parker that would cover the expenses of her full first year. Many of our dual-enrolled students are especially eager for more education this summer in not just standard academics but other lessons that aren't taught in the public education system.

Like Mr. Parker, a dual-enrolled student (attendee of systematized and summer school), Ms. Parker would attend Mareschal during this summer with the option to be dual-enrolled in September. She would receive a scholarship for her first year as a student.

You will not have to worry about transportation—due to your son's exceptional work at the academy, he has been one of the fourteen students rewarded with a vehicle in celebration of receiving his license and receiving an outstanding 38.8 on his most recent MSA-AP exam, the highest score being a 39.1. All expenses on the vehicle have been paid along with a six-year warranty.

Please reply if there are any questions, and if not, please allow Miles and Jessie to attend the meeting tomorrow at 10:00 a.m. in the main building. If that is not an option, feel free to reply to this email address. Pamphlets from the meeting would be provided to return home with further information to help you make your decision.

Sincerely,
Principal Emircy Kate, MEd

My head turned abruptly as Miles pinched my arm. He raised an eyebrow, and I started to remember what he'd told me before we came inside. "When you get in, you're most likely gonna hear some news. Pretend like you're excited." I didn't have much time to debate on if I should follow his instructions.

"That's…awesome," I faltered, looking back at the screen. Miles scoffed quietly at my performance, which urged me to prove him wrong.

"I can't believe I got accepted!" I looked up to Mom and Dad. "Can I please go? They even gave Miles a car! They're only bad at recognizing talent, considering they think Miles is exceptional," I joked.

"Jessie!" Mom warned.

I didn't have to turn around to know that the look on Miles's face was hilarious. Mom smiled at Miles, as if proud of him for doing well on his exam. After the amount of lies I'd been told recently, I had a feeling his grade was just another one.

"It sounds good," Dad said, turning the laptop back to him. "Plus, Miles already goes there. Much less transportation for you, Gen." He looked to Mom, who's hovering over him. She twisted her mouth the same way she did when deep in thought.

"I don't know," she said quietly, still looking at the email.

I heard a small bark from down the hall. "Even Temmie agrees, Mom," I told her, but her sharp glance told me not to say much more. Dad said something else, but I was not listening. My mind was wandering through the possibilities of attending Mareschal Science Academy.

"I drove here from there." Miles spoke, but I didn't know when the topic of his car came in. Mom probably asked if he knew his way around. "It's really nice. Not the most expensive thing, but I guess they can only afford so much, especially to pay off the vehicle at one time."

"When did you get it?" Mom asked.

"Last week. I didn't tell you as the principal said she would inform you. I didn't expect the email to come this late, though."

I wonder if anything he just said is true.

Mom shook her head, still looking at the screen. "Summer school…," she said. She looked at me. "Do you really want to go to *summer school*? I thought you were excited about the break."

"I was," I admitted. "But this is a once-in-a-lifetime opportunity! They're a private and pristine academy, even if they did let Miles in."

He stepped on my foot, but Mom didn't seem to care much about the comment. I laughed in my head at the idea that she might agree.

"Kaylani's going too," I thought to say. "She told me at the ice cream parlor on the last day of school. I'd have a friend and would be studying different areas of science. It's bound to be fun."

Dad nodded his head, and I was glad one person agreed. Now for Mom.

"Attending a private academy will be much more impressive than a public school. Plus, I won a scholarship, Mom. A scholarship! For a full year! Maybe I could get another for the next year."

"I just don't understand how you won when you didn't even apply," Mom interrupted.

"The school searches for people based on their performance," Miles told her. I nodded my head in agreement, though I couldn't tell if he's lying or not. "If you excel in math and science, they will offer scholarships based on that. You just have to be at the top of your class. That's why I didn't qualify for one."

Mom twisted her mouth again and looked down. "Jessie has always been great in science," she said, almost to herself.

"Let's at least let them go to the meeting tomorrow," Dad offered. She looked at him, and they did that weird eye-talking thing that I'd never quite figured out. After seemingly having a brief conversation with Dad, Mom let out a soft "Okay."

"But I'm driving you there," she added.

*****

I quickly shoved my phone under my pillow at the sound of the door opening. It's about midnight, but I couldn't sleep. My mind was worrying too much about tomorrow, well, today, and what might happen. "You can stop fake-sleeping now," I heard. I flopped onto my side and saw Miles standing in the doorway.

"Can I come in?" he asked but entered before I got a chance to answer. He closed the door and darted his eyes around the room. I propped myself on my forearms.

"May I help you?" He put his finger to his lips in response, motioning for me to be quiet. Miles then approached and sat at the end of my bed.

"Why are you in here?" I asked quietly.

"You said you had questions earlier," he replied. "Ask away."

"Miles, it's midnight."

"One a.m. actually."

"Exactly. Go to sleep."

"Says the girl on her phone."

"We have school tomorrow, Miles," I told him. "As much as I'd love to ask you a ton of questions, I need to sleep."

"Fair enough." He stood up and approached my door. As he reached to turn the knob, I heard something clatter as if falling to the floor. I looked down by my bed to see what fell, and the door closed when I looked back up.

I reached for my lamp on my nightstand and turned it on. The room grew much brighter, and my eyes felt blinded. In front of my door, I saw what looked like a key. I quickly got out of bed to pick it up, and the "key" got more into view. Bending down, I saw that it's really something that I'd forgotten all about. And for some reason, Miles had gotten his hands to it.

Now, I just had to find out why.

IFON Academy

Azariele Apartments
Apartment 51
Sunday
0940 hours

"*Hurry up! You never take* this long, Jessie!"

"I'm hurrying!" I blocked out Mom's calling and frantically move through my closet. If I was about to go to a school where I was being offered a scholarship, it'd be foolish not to make a show of feeling perfectly fine and well-balanced...even though I was quite the opposite.

The door opened just as I took my jean jacket down from its hanger. I looked to Miles who stood in the doorway.

"Ready?"

"Of course." I caught a glimpse of him rolling his eyes when I went to grab my phone from my desk.

We walked out together and met Mom at the front door. She held it open, giving me a disapproving look as I approached. As soon as Miles and I got into the hallway, he bent down toward my ear.

"You're gonna have to be more prepared if you want Mom to let you go to the school," he whispered.

"I'm not sure I even wanna go," I whispered back. "I'm only doing it to find out why you stole Michael's charm." I stopped myself, causing Miles to run into me. Michael's charm was still in my room.

Before I could return to get the charm, something shiny caught my eye—Miles held it in front of my face. I snatched the charm from his hand and looked at him, wanting to ask why he took it. He quickly walked in front of me, approaching the elevator. I stashed the charm in my pocket as a hand pushed me forward—Mom.

"We're going to be late at this pace," she said, though I couldn't tell if it truly upset her.

The elevator was silent except for Mom's foot tapping impatiently. The bell dinged as we reached the main floor, and I jumped at the loud sound. Mom put her hand on my shoulder and pulled me forward, making sure I kept up with her. She softly pushed me toward Miles while she went over to greet the doorman as she usually did. I speed-walked until I met Miles's side, and we rushed to the parking garage that was beside the building. Miles spotted Mom's car and took my hand as we approached.

We stood by the car for a few seconds as Mom was running toward us. She unlocked the car and we got in, but I didn't try to call shotgun. Mom usually talked the most to whoever was right next to her, and I had too much on my mind to carry a conversation.

"You know your way around the building, right?"

"Yes, Mom," Miles replied, obviously tired of answering questions. I gazed out the window, trying to make sense of where we were going. We'd turned a lot of corners by now, and I was starting to lose track. There wasn't much to keep track of when we suddenly came to a stop.

"This is us," Miles said, opening his door.

We were stopped on the side of the road, squeezed between cars in front of us and behind.

"Hurry, Jessie," Mom told me.

"Bye, Mom," I said, still in shock.

We climbed out of the car, and Miles said something to Mom through the window. He stood there for a few seconds talking with her, probably assuring her that we'll be all right. I stood on the sidewalk and looked at the huge building in front of us. It looked gray and gloomy and majestic, but this couldn't be my brother's school.

Tons of cars sped behind me, and I felt the weight of the wheels shake the ground. I jumped at the touch of a hand on my shoulder and saw Miles hovering over me.

"I've never been here," I said, though I was sure Miles already knew. Looking through the many windows of the building, I could see tons of bookshelves filling each room of the five stories.

"This is a library, Miles!"

"It sure is," he replied.

I struggled to look away from the strange building and look up to him.

"Then where's your school?" Miles laughed at the seemingly stupid question and set his other hand on my right shoulder.

He turned me around to face down the sidewalk, and I saw something even better than what I could've ever imagined. After staring at the sight, Miles took my hand and pulled me toward the huge complex. It's almost like a high school, no, university. I could tell the library from the dining area from the main education building. The complex is pushed far back from the sidewalk, with lots of greenery brightening the front view. At the start of the pathway leading to the main building was a sign that seemed to stand out the most. *Mareschal Science Academy*, it read on both sides, announcing its presence to all who passed by.

Miles pulled me farther down the pavement, and we walked onto the clear path that led us to the building.

"The parking lot is behind the complex," he told me, though I wasn't fully listening. "It's just as huge as what you can see," he continued. "Pretty impressive, eh? I'm sure you're glad you decided to come." Miles squeezed my shoulder with his hand. "Yeah, you'll like it here, Jessie," he said, his voice seeming distant.

I looked up to him and noticed he's gazing off, leaving only enough attention to keep his legs moving.

We got closer to the main school building, and I saw some people standing by one of the many front doors. The glass doors were in between large windows on a wall that stretched for what feels like miles. Against each window was a long bench, yet only two of them were occupied. I noticed the kids I'd met yesterday sitting together on one bench, along with Kaylani. Some other teenagers I didn't recognize were sitting together on another.

Kaylani leaned her ear toward one of the boys and then whipped her head around and rushed up to me.

"Hey, Jess!" she greeted me.

Her voice was softer than usual, and I wonder if she doesn't want the others to know that she's being nice to me. It's a childish assumption, but there wasn't much to go off.

"Hi, Kaylani."

"You're meeting Lady Kate today," she beamed, as if I was supposed to be honored.

"Who's that?" I asked.

"The principal."

I froze, my brain not able to comprehend that the most important person at the school could be behind me. At least, until the person snickered. I turned around in surprise and saw a girl about my age trying not to laugh.

"You're lucky I'm not her," she jested.

Someone farther behind me on a bench shouted, "Good one, Donnay!"

The girl stepped up closer to me and stretched out a hand. "Donnay Sashille."

"Jessie Parker." I shook her hand, which gripped mine tightly.

"Enough, Donnay. She's new here," Kaylani told her.

"I can tell," the girl smiled, but it's not very comforting. Her eyes softened, and she let go of my hand. I struggled not to wince at the sudden relief of pressure.

"Don't worry, I'm not as bad as Naziah," she assured me before walking off. The remark seemed like a warning, but it wasn't in my priorities to decipher it.

"Well, good luck," Miles said suddenly.

"Where are you going?" I asked as he took a step toward the building.

"I have some business to do," he told me. "But more importantly, I don't wanna be seen hanging out with children."

"He's just scared of Lady Kate." Kaylani laughed as Miles rushed off.

"Should I be as well?" I queried.

"You're about to find out," she responded, looking toward the busy road.

I looked back toward the sidewalk and saw some people in black crowded around a vehicle. Over the roaring sound of cars passing by, I could hear the other kids approaching and effusing. My curiosity drew me a bit down the path toward the vehicle, but I warned myself not to get too close. The people in black shuffled out of the way of an open car door, where someone started to step out.

The person stood tall and removed shades that I would've mistaken for reading glasses. Her heels loudly click against the path as she approached. The woman's white gown was lifted with one hand to keep the hem from brushing against the ground. The chatter behind me grows silent, and I stepped back a bit, feeling as if I was meeting royalty. My feet felt buried in the ground, and I stood waiting to finally meet Lady Kate.

She smiled as she grew closer—the type of smile that made you feel safe and warm, but this one was intimidating as well. Her shoulder-length blond hair was recognizable, and she had unblemished pale skin.

"Hello, Jessie," she greeted me, taking a few more steps. "Welcome to IFON Academy." Her voice was just as elegant as her demeanor, and she stretched out a hand to shake mine.

"Hi, Lady Kate," I said, shaking her hand. "Great to meet you. I'm Jessie Par...well, you knew that already, didn't you?"

The woman nodded gently and retracted her hand to lift her gown once again. I expect someone behind me to snicker at my stupidity, but they all seemed to be on their best behavior around this mystery woman.

"Believe it or not, we've already met," Lady Kate said. "Well, virtually. I accepted you here to the academy."

"I never applied." I felt bad for interrupting and could practically feel the others behind me tense up. *It's a first impression if anything—not too admirable, though.*

"You didn't have to," she explained. "We don't have students apply here. We select them based on how they present themselves. You got in by your academics."

I was surprised to hear such a statement. My grades had always been good—straight A's—but nothing better. Why weren't all straight-A students selected for the academy?

"Greetings, children," her voice startlingly livened as she faced the group behind me.

"Hello, Lady Kate," they said in unison.

Like robots, I compared in my head.

"I'll meet with each of you for grades distribution," she informed them. "Once again, I apologize that they couldn't be delivered on time. For now, I'd like to speak with Ms. Parker."

I looked over my shoulder and watched the group disperse, almost all of them glancing at me. I caught a glimpse of Naziah in the group, and I was sure that she's one of the ones who hadn't looked at me since I'd arrived.

"Grades distribution?" I asked Lady Kate, once all the kids were a bit of a distance away. "I thought this was a meeting for new students."

"That was a lie," she told me, as if I should've known. "You'll be told many of them while you're here. Don't find that to be injurious. It's all in the best interests of our students." She turned around and did a weird hand motion toward the people in black surrounding her vehicle. Two of them started down the walkway, holding what seemed to be a briefcase.

"You will be receiving some pamphlets as described in the email," Lady Kate informed me. "A lot of what's in them are lies as well. They're just to ensure your parents don't catch onto the secret. Which I must say, you've done exceptionally well at keeping it so far."

"It's easy to keep a secret that I don't know, ma'am."

Lady Kate stretched out her hand to receive the briefcase that the people dressed in black were carrying. They handed it over to her, and she turned back to face me.

"Has your brother not told you yet?"

"My brother's a bit distant from me."

"Ah, I wouldn't expect much less." She smiled, as if remembering her own childhood. Lady Kate steadied the briefcase with one hand and opened it with another. I wondered if she's aware of the two people hovering over her like security. Then I thought that she probably was important enough to have security.

She pulled out a folder and handed it to me. I took it gently and resisted the urge to look inside. It might not be meant for me to see.

"That's for your parents," she confirmed my thinking. She closed the briefcase and handed it to one of her guards.

"It has everything your parents will need to know about Mareschal Science Academy."

"I thought this was called IFON Academy," I said.

Lady Kate sighed and glanced up.

"Mareschal Science Academy is a cover name," she articulated. "This is IFON Academy of Espionage."

"Espionage? What's that?"

"I see you have a lot to learn, Miss Parker."

I lowered my head, not sure exactly what she meant. "Take that folder home," she instructed. "I trust you to guard it with your life." She squeezed my shoulder with her hand as she passed by, her guards trailing behind. One of them turned their head to face me, yet I couldn't see their face through their mask. They turned back, continuing walking with the other guard and Lady Kate.

I faced the back of Lady Kate and watched her pull a few students aside—none of them I recognized. They all started to walk through one of the glass doors that I'd mistaken for a window. I saw Miles come out the door as the group entered. He gave a quick nod to Lady Kate and said something that I couldn't make out. When he spotted me, he rushed over and glanced behind him.

"You really *are* scared of Lady Kate," I teased.

He rolled his eyes. "Absolutely not," he denied. "I just owe her. She lied in that email—I don't really have good grades. Not in the academic classes, at least."

"I could've told you that. But what other classes are there? Aren't all classes academic?"

He sighed. "You've got a lot to learn."

"I really wish people would stop saying that."

Miles took my hand, and we headed down the path toward the sidewalk. I still hadn't taken in everything around me and couldn't wait to explore the campus tomorrow. As we stepped onto the pavement, someone tapped my back. I turned around and saw Kaylani.

"Can we meet up later?" she asked. She glanced to her right, and I wondered if it's a setup. The kids sitting together didn't seem to be staring, but I was sure they're glancing frequently.

"Sure," I agreed. "We can hang out at the normal spot."

Kaylani and I would normally meet on the rooftop of my apartment complex on weekdays. Ever since Friday, we hadn't had the chance. I spun on my heel and walked away, approaching Miles. He'd waited a few feet away for me.

"What was that about?" he asked.

"Honestly, I don't really know. I'd rather not think about it anyways."

"All right."

"So when will Mom be back?"

"I told her we'd walk home. Not that we're going to."

Before I could ask what he meant, a familiar car approached from down the street in front of us. It neatly slid between two cars on the side of the road. Miles opened the passenger seat door and motioned me inside. I ducked into the bright-red vehicle and took a seat, half expecting to see someone in the driver's seat. Yet there's nobody.

Miles rushed around to the driver side and slid in, closing the door next to him. "This thing can drive itself?" I asked as I opened my door.

"Of course!" He put his seat back. "Hey, Vessa!" His voice was loud in the car, and I wondered who he's shouting at.

The siding of the seats lighted up, and the dashboard illuminated as well. "Take Jessie and I home," he spoke, his voice lowered. The car started moving, and I heard Miles snicker. I assumed he's laughing at the impressed expression on my face.

"What brand is this?" I asked.

"I don't know." He sighed, adjusting himself in his seat. "I just know it's only for certain people at my school."

I looked out the window and got more nervous each corner we turn. Never would I ever have thought I'd be riding in a self-driving car.

We slowed down and sped up every now and then. I continually glanced at the wheel and watched as it turned with Miles's hands on the arm rests. My arms wrapped around the folder Lady Kate had given me. Her elegant voice with unsettling words echoed in my head.

I trust you to guard it with your life.

"You'll enjoy it here," said Miles, interrupting my thoughts.

"At IFON?"

"Yeah, did Lady Kate tell you anything new?"

"Not enough," I said. I assumed he wouldn't give up any information himself. He confirmed my assumption by simply looking out the window.

"So what's with you and Kaylani? I could practically feel the tension between you two."

I had to replay his question in my head since I'd been distracted by the steering wheel the first time he asked it. "She's just been kinda secretive," I answered, only half aware of what I was saying. "She's... *too* calm in a sense. It's like nothing bothers her."

"You'll see why tomorrow."

I looked from the steering wheel over to Miles. "What do you mean?" The car slowed to a stop, and I looked out of his window. We're in the parking lot. Miles unbuckled his seatbelt, not seeming interested in answering the question. I sighed and unbuckled as well.

The folder was pressed against my side using my arm as I climbed out. We started to walk toward the complex, and I was relieved that we made it home without the car crashing. A soft bell sound came from my pocket, and I reached for my phone.

"Don't text and walk," Miles said, though I was sure he's joking. He was never one for safety.

We continued down the pavement as I looked at my new text— it's Kaylani.

> *11:50 a.m.*
> Kay: Sorry, we can't meet up today
>   I'll call you in a bit so we can still talk
> You: Why can't we meet up?

Miles and I were in the hallway of the third floor by now, and I'd been looking at my phone the whole time. The thought that she wouldn't answer anytime soon frustrated me. Miles reached the door to our apartment before I did and knocked repeatedly. The door opened, and I looked to see our father welcoming us in.

"How was it?" he asked.

"Good," Miles lied.

"Here, Dad. From school." I handed him the folder, wondering if he'd let me read through it with him. Instead, he just gave a quick "Thank you" and started to open it on his own. I sat on the couch while Miles went to his room.

After a full minute of staring at the cooking channel with boredom, Dad called me over. He had already closed the folder and set it on the table.

"You'll be going with Miles to school tomorrow," he informed me.

"All right," I muttered, walking toward my room. There wasn't much to say. Tomorrow would be my first day at IFON Academy.

My phone buzzed again, and I half-expected Kaylani to be answering me. Unfortunately, I was wrong.

> *12:15 p.m.*
> Lion: Hey guys!
> You: Hey
> Lion: Y'all wanna get ice cream tomorrow?

Temmie barked from my room, and I lowered my phone to follow the sound.

"Hi, girl," I whispered in a high-pitched voice once I reached my door. She looked down at the floor she's sitting on as I entered. My phone vibrated again, but I took a seat on my bed before checking it.

> *12:15 p.m.*
> Lion: Hey guys!
> You: Hey
> Lion: Y'all wanna get ice cream tomorrow?

Kay: What time?
Lion: Why not for breakfast?

I was in the middle of typing, "Of course!" when Kaylani's answer came up. "Jess and I have summer school tomorrow," she answered.

I deleted my answer and backed her up with a simple "Yeah."

"Dude, that must suck," Lion replied. Kay sent a shrugging emoji.

I laid down on the bed, blocking out Temmie barking again. She jumped onto my bed and laid down. Usually I'd get upset when she walked on my bed, but it didn't bother me now. What *did* bother me was the fact that Michael had promised to text us a lot yet hadn't said anything. Lion and Kaylani were now in another conversation that I didn't bother taking part in. I ignored the vibrations in my hand, sure that none of them would be from my third best friend.

summer school

Somewhere near IFON Academy
Monday
0840 hours

The rapper was speaking too fast for me to pick up any of the words. Miles seemed to enjoy the song, though—he was bopping his head in time to the music. The wind blew into the car and made my eyes water as the car sped up. I closed my eyes.

"Are we almost there?" The music turned off.

"What'd you say?" Miles asked.

I opened my eyes, deciding to answer the question for myself. The car slowed to turn onto a different street. I vaguely remembered it when we were on our way home yesterday and figured that the school wasn't too far from here.

"Vessa. Transfer manual control," Miles instructed.

"Transfer will ensue during manual acceleration," the car replied. Miles set his hands on the wheel and pressed on the gas, letting Vessa speak again. "Control transfer complete."

"This car is awesome," I observed, looking at the illuminated dashboard. The dashboard showed a map with our destination and the car's location highlighted, as well as details about the other surroundings.

"There's more it can do than this," Miles told me, passing the campus. "But a lot of its abilities are only used in emergencies."

"Like, if the car catches on fire?"

Miles chuckled, turning the wheel and going toward the back of the campus. "Something like that."

We turned another corner, and I was able to see a large parking lot. Miles drove to the section for students, which was practically full. On the side of the lot for staff, every spot seemed to be filled, with school buses being the closest to the campus.

"Follow me to the front desk," Miles instructed. "After that, you're on your own."

I started to reply, knowing that I would fail to find my way around the grounds. Miles quickly opened his door before I could say anything.

I hopped out, too, and slammed the door shut.

"We have to hurry," Miles announced.

I walked around the car and then jogged to keep up with him. We practically raced onto the schoolgrounds and took a stone path that led around the campus.

"Why's the parking lot so far from the entrance?" I asked, suddenly wishing I hadn't said anything. Talking and running was hard, but my brother seemed to do it with ease.

"The front door isn't the only entrance," he explained. "But students can't use the other ones during the first week of school."

We stayed close to the walls of the connecting buildings, running toward the front door. I now noticed Miles's backpack hopping with each step he took, and I started to fear that I'd be in trouble for not bringing one. Then again, I had no idea what kinds of material I might need. Maybe they didn't expect new students to bring one. If they had, then I'd be able to confidently say that I was terrible when it came to first impressions.

Miles held the door open for me, and my eyes widened in surprise as we entered. There's a desk seating one lady that all the children seem to avoid. The walls in the entrance were lined with lockers, and a ton of kids were in the lobby.

As we approached the front desk, I noticed that most of the kids seemed to be young. Fifth-graders, maybe.

"Good morning!" greeted the desk lady. Her cheerfulness and her voice reminded me of Patricia, which made me more comfortable around her.

"Welcome to IFON! I'm Cierra, a senior here."

She looked from me to Miles.

"Hey, Miles!" she greeted him. "Is this your sister?"

"Unfortunately." he sighed.

Cierra giggled in response. "Welcome..."

"Jessie Parker," I told her.

"Jessie," she repeated, reaching underneath the desk, and muttering to herself. "First year... Parker...eighth...here!"

She pulled up a book bag and reached over the desk to hand it to me.

"Keep track of it!" she beamed. "Probably best to place some of the books in your locker and leave the bag in your dormitory."

I worked the book bag onto one arm, but I couldn't help from questioning her statement. "I'm sorry, did you say *dormitory?*"

"She'll learn that on her own," Miles cut in, speaking to Cierra as if they shared a secret.

"I see," Cierra caught on. She opened a drawer in the desk and handed me six papers that were stapled together. "You have a map of the school, your class schedule, room number, and locker information in this packet."

She handed me the papers, which I quickly flipped through. *Not much of a packet, if you ask me.* "Thank you," I said.

"Have fun!" she responded as Miles made his way around the desk.

I thought to ask where he's going but remembered that he'd told me I would be on my own. Instead, I looked at the packet to see the map of the school and my locker number.

Floor 2, locker 494. Making my way toward the larger part of the school, I felt more like an outsider now than during my visit the day before.

There was a tall staircase in front of me that I rushed toward. A few other students were on either side of me, gripping onto the glass railing. Deciding to start looking for my locker, I read the one in front of me. *420.* The one to the right of it was *421.* I turned right into a wider hallway with lockers on one side and classroom doors on the other.

Standing in the middle of the hallway reading locker numbers wasn't the smartest thing to do, which I didn't realize until someone ran into me.

"So sorry," they said, holding my arm to help me balance.

"You're all right," I replied and looked up at the person.

The boy was a bit taller than me, with hair that covered his ears. "You seem lost," he half-shouted over the various ongoing discussions.

"I kind of am," I admitted.

No point in lying. Maybe he can help. The boy gently pulled me closer to the wall as some taller kids rush where we had been standing.

"We don't need two collisions in one day," he joked. "What's your name?"

"I'm Jessie."

"Cory. You know your locker number?"

"Um…494," I recalled.

He looked up as if contemplating how to get around the school. "All right. You can follow me." He made his way back into the crowd, and I followed close behind. We walked down the hallway, and Cory glanced over his shoulder to make sure I was still nearby. He slowed down, reading the lockers next to him, and then finally stopped.

"This one," he said, tapping on the locker.

I stepped up and read it for myself, to see that he *had* found it.

"Thank you," I said, and he nodded.

I glanced at the packet in my hand and searched for my combination. *14-40-28.* I folded the stapled papers so that nobody could read the information on them before entering the code.

Just as I opened the door to my empty locker, the bell rang, and the hall got even louder. Witnessing the school so normal and lively compared to my previous visit was really weird, but I knew I could get used to it.

Now that the bell rang, I was probably late for class. Which was more disappointing as I realized that going to my locker was pointless—the locker was empty, and I hadn't thought to bring a backpack. I quickly slammed the locker door and turned to face the crowd of kids, this time my age and older. I fumbled with the papers in my hand to look for my schedule.

A lot of kids were dispersing and making their way to class. Taking this long to transition from class to class would be exhausting—I'd have to make an effort to memorize a lot of things after the school day. But first, I actually had to get through the school day.

"Sorry," I heard, as someone's shoulder brushed against mine. I turned to see who it was, yet instead I faced a group of kids who were making their way to class. A lot of them glanced at me but didn't comment. I faced my locker and looked back at the paper, not actually reading it.

This is going to be a painfully long day.

*****

The sunlight came through the window and shined on my bed, perfectly illuminating the map. Donnay and Olivia were nice enough to let me have the bed closest to the window.

I prepared to put away the map, which was basically engraved in my brain at this point. Folding the map, I recalled the day's events in my brain—the highlights of it, to be specific.

The academy's food was *amazing* for a school. The lunch still had me starstruck. I'd never known a school to serve well-seasoned steak, mashed potatoes, a side of cabbage, with a large variety of sodas and the option of water. According to the packet I'd received from Cierra, the school served breakfast, lunch, *and* dinner, and the menu for the month was nothing less than mouthwatering.

The school grounds were much larger than I would've imagined. I was late by five minutes maximum to every class, but quite a few kids were late too. The teachers warned us to study our maps and be on time to classes starting next week as there'd be less leisure. In my reading class, someone had mentioned Kaylani's name, but I had yet to see her for myself.

Regarding classes, I learned that I had three out of eight of mine with Cory. Though he wasn't exactly a friend, it was comforting to see a familiar face throughout the day.

As for the dormitories, they felt like tiny apartments. There was a small living area with a dining area that had four seats and a small table. There were two coolers for storing food and drinks, which was very surprising. Each dorm apparently had a small bathroom as well, with a sink, toilet, and shower. Miles never told me that the school was *that* rich—it was beyond me how much I would've had to pay *without* the scholarship. Upon entering my own dormitory, I'd met Donnay and Olivia—my roommates.

Olivia's voice grew louder from the other room. My body jumped at the sound of the door, abruptly swinging open and hitting the wall.

"Olivia!" Donnay hissed.

"Sorry!"

I looked behind me and saw Olivia standing in the door frame. Donnay shoved past her to approach me.

"Olivia was gonna try to sneak up on you," she snitched.

"I was not," Olivia lied, approaching me as well. She wasn't good at lying.

"I'm here to answer any questions you have," Donnay said. "But don't expect me to be this nice all of the time. This is a one-time thing that I'm only doing because you're a newcomer."

"Don't worry, I won't," I assured her. Donnay sat beside me on the bed, and Olivia stood by the window. They looked at me, obviously able to tell that I had plenty of questions. Although, I wasn't sure if they were trustworthy as we hadn't talked outside of the dining hall and our dormitory.

"What does IFON stand for?" I asked. I caught a glimpse of what I thought to be Donnay rolling her eyes.

"I think the principal just found it cool," Olivia replied. "But I'm honestly not sure."

"Don't bother, Olivia," Donnay said. She flipped one of her braided pigtails off her shoulder before leaning toward me. "What do you *really* wanna ask?"

Olivia leaned in a bit, obviously curious as well. Donnay looked up as if annoyed. "If you're wondering whether or not you can trust us, you don't really have a choice," she stated.

"Because I live with you guys?" I asked.

"Because this is IFON," she corrected me. "In order to do our job, we have to trust everyone on our side."

"Other than Naziah," Olivia added.

I scrunched my eyebrows and looked at both girls. Donnay smirked. "Nah, she's trustworthy," she said. "Probably the most trustworthy student here." The sentence had an emotion that I couldn't quite make out, but Olivia explained it for me. "Naziah Vazil is a legend here, if you haven't figured that out already. Her whole family is, and they all were exceptional here. She's the first female from her family line to come to the academy, which I'm sure puts a lot of pressure on her. Gotta prove girls are equal to guys, you know?"

"She's just great at the job," Donnay summarized.

"The job?" I echoed.

Donnay leaned back on her elbows and looked at Olivia. "Does she know *anything* about this place?" she asked.

I readjusted myself, not exactly comfortable with the fact that I didn't know much about the school. "I know I almost died at the other school site," I said.

"Ah! So you've been to the refuge!" Olivia smiled.

"And she almost *died*." Donnay laughed. "That's IFON for you."

Olivia leaned on the window. "IFON," she said. "Or as some call it, the Esoteric Academy of Espionage."

"So the school's a secret?" I asked. "Esoteric?"

"IFON is a combination of the institution's founders' names, but nobody has met the founders," Donnay informed me. "No student, at least. And IFON *is* a secret. I bet you went through a lot to get here—doesn't that prove it?"

"An understatement. But why is it a secret?"

"Spying, Parker. People come here to learn how to defend their country."

"Like in the military?"

"Something like that."

"Why can't our parents know?"

"Parents like to brag. But it's not an adult thing. You didn't know Miles went here until this year, I'm sure."

"So my brother has a reputation."

"More like, everyone knows of everyone around here. Did he tell you anything about this place?"

"Not enough, apparently."

"Miles always appeared to be the secretive type," Olivia stated. Her red hair reminded me of Finniake's, and I attempted to remember if I'd seen him or River during the day.

"I'm sure you haven't seen much. We can take you for a formal tour of the school tomorrow," Donnay said to me. "You have weapons and combat for sixth period, right?"

"I'm not sure," I admitted.

Olivia reached for my backpack that's sitting on the floor by my bed. She went through it for a second before pulling out my schedule.

"You do," she told me.

"Why do we need a class about fighting?" I asked.

"We're training to fight," Donnay sighed. "Among other things, we train to help people, infiltrate places, and be aware of our surroundings."

"So...we're like spies in training?"

Olivia laughed at my comment, and Donnay rolled her eyes.

"Sure, Parker."

"Not all of us," Olivia said, a smile still on her face. "Naziah is basically a retired spy."

"That wasn't funny," Donnay shook her head, though she seemed to want to laugh. "Not your best."

"I'm just telling the truth!"

"Which she never does." That was the first rude comment I'd heard Donnay make about Naziah Vazil, though I had a feeling that she had a bit of a rude personality.

Both girls seemed to get a kick out of the joke as they snickered together. I smiled and leaned back on the pillow.

"Let's hope Naziah doesn't rub off on Kaylani," Olivia bantered.

"Oh no." Olivia laughed harder, and Donnay glanced at me. "Let's hope she doesn't rub off on the newcomer here," she said.

"I doubt she'd talk to one."

The girls continued to gossip, and Donnay was the friendliest I'd ever witnessed. She was a lot different than I'd first imagined her when we met the previous day. I commented every now and then, but mostly listened to what they said. They gave me a lot of information about some of the students, which I was sure would help me in my social life at the academy. Even better, they gave me a good relationship. *Maybe Miles was right. Maybe I really will like it here.*

the bad kind of nostalgia

IFON Academy
Dining hall
Tuesday
0830 hours

Donnay returned to the table, holding her tray. Olivia slid closer to me to make room for Donnay.

"What happened to you?" Kaylani asked, seeming to be amused by Donnay's new expression. She had left the table to get her breakfast happily yet was returning with an angry look on her face.

"The boy in front of me took the last of the gravy," she complained, taking her seat next to Olivia.

I thought Naziah had rolled her eyes but couldn't tell if I'd seen it very well.

"It's not a big deal," Olivia disagreed, but her voice was soft as if she didn't fully want Donnay to hear.

"That's because you have yours," Donnay replied. "Mashed potatoes without gravy is disgusting."

"It's also terrible for breakfast," Kaylani added.

"I'll take it then," I suggested, partially nervous about commenting. I wasn't very close with anybody at the academy except for Kaylani, but we hadn't had the chance to talk one-on-one since I'd started yesterday.

"I can deal with it." Donnay rolled her eyes playfully, and I felt a bit more comfortable.

"I love your bracelet," Kaylani said, and we all looked at Olivia.

"This? Oh, thanks."

"The charms look nice," Naziah complimented.

It was the first thing she'd said all morning, and we had been at the table for at least fifteen minutes. Then again, she seemed a bit introverted—Kaylani had to talk to Naziah for about three minutes to get her to sit with us. She had been sitting by herself toward the middle of the room, and only Kaylani dared to approach her. Then again, this was only my first impression of her. First impressions could be deceiving.

Olivia slid the charm bracelet off her wrist and set it on the table. Kaylani gently touched it and verbally complimented it again. I squinted at the bracelet and stared at one charm. From my view, I was pretty sure it was Michael's. But I had kept his charm in my book bag—*How did Olivia get it?* Donnay picked up the bracelet and tried it on.

"That cross charm looks just like Michael's," Kaylani observed. "But his is silver and yours is gold. They're still cool, though."

At least it's not his.

"Who's Michael?" asked Donnay.

"A friend of Jessie and I," Kaylani replied. "Hey, did you ever give him his charm back? Mail it to him or something?"

"I don't think it's the biggest issue," I admitted. "I still don't know where he is. It's like he went missing."

Talking about Michael made me feel like a terrible friend. Four days ago, I had gone to his house and found clues as to where he might be, yet coming to IFON had distracted me.

"Professor Jones could probably help you find him, if he really is missing," Naziah suggested.

I raised an eyebrow as if to ask, *Who's that?*

Naziah sighed in annoyance at my ignorance. "Professor Jones instructs math for juniors and seniors here," she informed me.

"Do you have your phone with you?" Kaylani asked. "We could show the pictures to him."

"Right now?" I asked, and she nodded her head. I wasn't sure if we were allowed to just get up and leave the dining hall, but not all students came to breakfast anyways. "All right."

"Can I have your food?" Donnay asked.

At first, I thought she was talking to Kaylani until she stood up to take my seat. "Um, sure."

Kaylani rushed around the table and took my hand, leading me away from our group. I glanced over my shoulder at them, but none of them seemed to be missing our presence.

"How do you like it here so far?" Kaylani asked. She had to speak loudly over the other kids conversing. "It's all right," I replied as we made our way toward one of the doors.

Kaylani held the door open for me, and we stepped into the hallway. Once the door closed, our surroundings were significantly quieter than the dining hall. It was almost comforting.

"Mr. Jones teaches in the second auditorium," Kaylani told me. "But since classes haven't started, he's probably in his office."

When I studied the map yesterday, seeing two auditoriums was unbelievable. Hopefully we would be back before first period so that Donnay and Olivia could take me on a tour of the school. Thinking of a tour made me start to question my time at the academy.

"So students come here for regular school *and* summer school?" I asked.

"Exactly. So far, I've only gone to summer school. But some students like your brother are dual-enrolled, so they study here during regular school times and over the summer. But those students get the longest winter breaks."

Kaylani sure knew a lot about this place.

"How long have you been here?"

"At the academy? I was chosen in fifth grade and came during sixth. The fall welcome ceremony was really fun."

"Welcome ceremony?"

"For new students."

We were on our second flight of stairs. "Why didn't I get a welcome ceremony?" I queried.

Kaylani looked at me, then back ahead of her. "You don't know? You weren't supposed to attend IFON in the first place. It was a last-minute thing."

"Last minute? But they had the test set up for me. When I fell out of a building, remember?"

Kaylani froze to look at me again. "Nobody told you, Jess?"

"Told me what?"

"That whole incident wasn't a test. Some people really did break into the academy."

"I do think Miles mentioned it…but we saw them outside."

"Those were guards who after the incident tricked you into believing that you were being tested. We all met on the main floor and came up with a plan to cover what happened, since nobody knew Lady Kate would invite you to join us, and outsiders can't know about the academy. Some officers caught the real gunmen and put them in prison.

"Actually, an investigation was held that evening to find out why Mrs. Kettle wasn't attending the front desk. She usually attends the desk at the refuge where we were, and the one on the first floor here."

"Then there's been a girl taking her place here. I think her name's Cierra."

"Yeah, I know. Mrs. Kettle claimed that she was told someone else would be tending to the desk while she took the day off. Cierra is taking her place for the time being." Kaylani scrunched her eyebrows and looked down. "I'm surprised nobody's told you all this. That's no way to treat a new student."

"Hiding secrets is no way to treat a best friend," I noted.

Kaylani looked at me and started walking again. I followed behind. "I really am sorry. When I heard of the academy, I wanted to tell you everything, but if I did, then I wouldn't be able to attend. I couldn't even tell my parents."

"How'd you get permission to come here? I mean, didn't your parents have to approve?"

"Yeah. They received an email then drove me here. Toward the end of the visit, Lady Kate talked to me privately in her office about what this place really is. I was…overwhelmed, to say the least.

"When she said not to tell anyone or I'd lose the chance to attend, I was really torn. But they'd shown us a lot. My parents loved this place and I've grown to love it too." She looked around the empty hallway as if it was her first time seeing it. "There *are* flaws. Secrets too. But you'll grow to love it here just as I have. And honestly, I'm looking forward to this school year a lot more now that you're here."

I couldn't help but smile at her remark. Just as I started to reply, a voice came from behind us. "Good morning, ladies." Kaylani and I turned around to face the man. He had a white lab coat that practically reached the floor, with a fully brown outfit: brown shirt, brown khakis, brown dress shoes.

"Professor!" Kaylani smiled. "We were just looking for you. This is Jessie, my best friend from Symson. She's new here."

"Nice to meet you, Jessie," the professor greeted me. "How can I help you two?"

"We have an issue with a friend," Kaylani told him. "His name is Michael." She glanced over her shoulder. "Would it be all right for us to speak in your office? This is confidential."

"Of course," Professor Jones replied, understanding what she meant. I had an uncomfortable feeling that *I* didn't understand what she meant. Some of Lady Kate's first words to me began to echo in my head. *You have a lot to learn...*

Professor Jones walked past us, and Kaylani gave me a reassuring side hug. We followed him farther down the hall and stopped at a door where he pulled out some keys from his pocket. "You girls can start talking now," he said, opening the door. Kaylani looked at me as we stepped into the office.

Professor Jones's office smelled like cinnamon. His large desk was toward one end of the room decorated with a snow globe and what seemed to be family pictures. There were bookshelves lining two adjacent walls and a linen-colored rug in the center of the room. Professor Jones motioned at the two seats on one end of his desk as he went to the other end.

"Naziah Vazil suggested that Kaylani and I speak to you about this," I said, taking a seat. Professor Jones smiled in amusement at my statement, and Kaylani did the same. *What was it I said?*

"There's only one Naziah here," the professor explained. "And she has a pretty big name for herself."

"I've noticed," I replied, more bitterly than intended.

Thankfully, the professor didn't seem to realize. "Well, if she recommended you to me, then I am sure that I can assist."

I reached for my phone in my pocket. "I believe him to have gone missing on Friday," I said, my own words feeling impossible to be true. I opened my photos. "These most recent ones are pictures that I took at his house." I handed the phone across the desk to the professor, who squinted at the images. "Michael is supposed to be staying in Southern California for the summer. I went by his house to give him a charm that he left behind, but nobody was there. There was a note in his house that I believe to have been written by his mother, but it seemed…kind of like a threat." I'd never recalled the day's events back-to-back aloud, but all the memories came rushing back as I did. It was almost like I was back in the eerie, empty house, fearing for one of my closest friends.

"Do you have this note, Jessie?" Professor Jones asked.

"It's in my room at home," I replied. "Last night, my dad texted me to go back tomorrow and pack more things for my dormitory. I could get the note when I go back."

"And how did you get into Michael's house?" The professor swiped his finger across my phone, observing each photo.

"The door was unlocked, but the windows had locks on them. Kaylani and I have been to Michael's house with another friend tons of times. So it was easy to tell that whoever cleared out the house didn't leave anything behind."

"I assume you ran the license plate?"

At first, I was slightly surprised that the professor would expect me to do so, but he hadn't been speaking to me. "I observed it," Kaylani told him. "That license plate doesn't conform with any state rules. I assumed it was foreign. The phone number didn't comply either."

"Calling the company itself would be useless anyways. But you can still get information from the plate," the professor informed. He set down my phone and brought up a laptop from underneath the desk. Kaylani and I looked at each other in confusion.

The professor opened his laptop and began typing rapidly. "Only computers directly monitored by the government can run plates," he said. "Thankfully, devices running our academy's software fall under that category. So for things like this, you can easily use the desktops in the library." Kaylani looked at me as if to say, *You got that?* It occurred to me that what he was saying was nothing new to Kaylani.

"I appreciate this, Professor," I thanked him.

"Kaylani, do you have your phone?" he asked, giving his fingers a break from typing to scroll through something on his screen.

"Yes, sir."

"Look up *Kasheille's Moving Company*. Go on that secret mode, or whatever it's called."

"*Incognito?*"

"Yeah, that."

Kaylani pulled out her phone. "It seems like your story checks out, Ms. Jessie," the professor said. "The license plate is connected to Southern California."

"I thought it didn't fit any of the states," I disputed.

"It doesn't. The plate is *connected* to that area. Meaning it's registered there. I could send a request for the previously monitored locations on the license plate so we could try to figure out where it's going."

"There's nothing online by the company name," Kaylani reported.

"I didn't expect much." The professor sighed.

"Listen, the best you can do right now is research about California. The entire state. I definitely have books about it on some of these shelves."

Kaylani nodded and stood up, approaching one of the bookshelves. I stood up as well. "Girls, I have to get to auditorium two," he stated, rising from his desk and closing his computer.

"I'll leave my keys on the desk, so lock up the place and bring them to me in the auditorium before you get to class."

I thought to ask if he's really sure that he wanted to trust us with his keys but realized it wouldn't be appropriate to question his authority. He obviously trusted Kaylani, if not me.

"We will," Kaylani promised.

I approached Kaylani as Professor Jones made his way to the door.

"Ms. Jessie?"

I turned around. "Yes, Professor?"

"Make sure you get the note tomorrow, and bring it straight to me as soon as you enter the building. Understood?"

"Yes, sir." He held my gaze for a bit longer, ensuring my realization that I held a large responsibility. I nodded my head, silently promising to retrieve the note. The professor nodded in content prior to exiting the room.

I sighed as soon as he closed the door, hoping that I wouldn't forget to bring the letter from home. "You should check the other wall, Jess," Kaylani suggested.

"All right," I conformed, breaking out of my thoughts to do the task at hand. Kaylani had already taken down a tall stack of books from one of the shelves, and she set them on Professor Jones's desk.

She picked up my phone and handed it to me before returning to the bookshelf.

"Why does he want us to study California?" I asked, grabbing some selections myself. *California Mood, California: Tips for a Successful Trip, Around the Golden Gate Bridge.*

"Maybe he thinks we'll have to go there or something," She shrugged, setting another book on the desk.

I took my books and stacked them next to hers. "That's across the country," I replied. "I highly doubt he'd think that."

Kaylani stood next to me at the desk and spread out the books— her eight next to my three. She opened one of her books and flipped through the pages.

"A little pre-class reading?" she joked, taking a seat in one of the chairs. I half-smiled and grabbed a book myself.

We flipped through different pages, making mental and verbal notes of the newfound things we read—so just about everything we read.

"It's like a whole different world on the west coast," Kaylani pondered. Despite all the new information, I couldn't help but feel that Professor Jones had given us a lousy task. We were reading up on a state across the country rather than figuring out where Michael was. I longed for my phone to buzz in my pocket with a text from him saying that he was all right. Of course, there were no texts from him or anybody else. Just Kaylani and I studying, with my mind vividly recalling the terrible end to a school year that I'd had. Hesitantly, I pondered the idea that Friday had been a frightening ending to Michael and I's friendship and an even more frightening beginning to my summer.

home sweet home

Mom and Dad argued with low voices in the living room. It was about five in the morning, and I was packing most of my things to take to my dormitory. On Monday, someone had stashed some clothes and a pajama set into my book bag. I'd assumed that Miles had stuffed them in there before we left the apartment. I was able to use my clothes that had been in my book bag for yesterday. I had been texted by my dad to return home today before class. Apparently, he hadn't told Mom that I'd be staying at the school. He hadn't even told *me*. Mom was exasperated that she hadn't been told I'd be living on campus, and she felt I wasn't ready for it. I understood her frustration but felt it wasn't as bad as she made it out to be. The campus was barely twenty minutes from our apartment, and I would be with my best friend *and* my brother.

It was obvious that Mom had been very angry, though. She hadn't texted or called me since the first day, despite my initial anticipation that she'd call me repeatedly throughout the school day. I just hoped she wasn't blaming me for attending as Dad was the one who approved me to go. The dorm rooms were something exciting, though, and as much as I enjoyed being home, IFON was a lot more fun to explore.

Two knocks hit on my open door, and Miles was standing in the doorframe. "Ready?"

"Almost." I zipped one suitcase closed and scanned the room for anything else I might need.

Miles chuckled. "You're way overpacking."

"Well, I'm sorry I've never moved out before."

He didn't respond, but the look on his face said enough. I was definitely packing too much. "Which one has your clothes and hygiene stuff?" he asked. I pointed to the suitcase on my bed that wasn't closed.

He approached it and zipped it up and then raised it by the handle. "There. Now let's go."

I followed him toward the door, slightly relieved that I wouldn't have to bring so many things. The other suitcase was filled with framed photos, some board games, and decorations for my locker that I could probably buy at the stores near campus. Plus, the note from Michael's house was in the suitcase Miles had taken, and Michael's charm was in my locker. Nothing important would be left at home.

Miles stood still in the hallway and cupped his hand behind his ear. Assuming he's listening to Mom and Dad, I did the same.

"To read about this in a *letter*," Mom stated. "They sent a letter yet didn't meet us in person? And you wanna give her over to them?"

"You could've talked to the principal at the visit, Gen," Dad replied.

"I had business to take care of. You knew that!" she countered.

"Miles already attends. Her best friend goes there too, and we know Kaylani's parents. This could be a great opportunity for her to grow!"

"Grow? She can grow by enjoying her summer break."

"You heard her. She *wants* to go to summer school. This shows maturity and the fact that maybe she could handle this. Maybe you could as well."

"Right. Because hiding from your mother that a shooter came to your school is *so* mature."

Dad sighed at her argument, and I couldn't help but to do the same. She had a right to be angry, but it wasn't like an actual *shooter* came to Symson.

"And to think *you* would hide this," she continued. "The letter she brought home had all this information about her moving into the school and you didn't say a word. Why would they even wait so long to tell us?"

"I don't know. But I saw how excited she was for the opportunity, and I know how hesitant you are to let her go."

"At this point, I'm hesitant to even let Miles go."

Miles perked at this and started walking into the living area. I shuffled behind him.

"Love you both," Miles said, nodding to Mom and Dad before approaching the door.

"Miles," Mom called, and he turned to face her. Even in the dark room, I could tell that he seemed afraid. He looked worried that Mom would try to keep him from going to school. "If anything makes you feel that you should come home—and I mean *anything*—then you come straight back, okay?"

"Of course."

"Same for you, Jessie."

I kept looking at Miles, surprised by his sudden change in emotion.

"Jessie," Mom repeated. "Do you understand?"

Miles looked at me, the same fearful expression, but now with a hint of desperation.

"Yes, Mom."

Miles opened the door and quickly slipped into the hallway, clearly unsatisfied with my response.

My eyesight was blurry now, but I refused to let myself cry. If I did, Mom could get even more emotional and want me to stay home.

"I won't be far off," I promised, lowering my head to shadow my sorrowful face. Mom walked toward me and wrapped me in her arms. I heard her sniffle, causing me to struggle even more in containing my tears.

"Do your best, and be careful," she told me. She stepped back and looked at Dad.

"Have fun, Jessie," he said. I nodded and made my way toward the door.

"See you later," I told them, trying to smile through the bitter-sweet moment.

Pulling the door closed behind me, I saw Miles standing in the hallway. "Let's hurry," he whispered, before speedwalking down the hall. I quickly followed behind.

There wasn't noise coming from any of the apartments since it was such an early hour. My phone beeped in my jacket pocket, which I ignored until we got onto the elevator. I quickly pulled out my phone and saw a notification: "You were added to 'BFFs For Life' group chat."

The elevator dinged, and the doors opened. Miles was eager to get into the lobby, and I practically had to jog to keep up with him. Since it's so early, most of the lights in the lobby were off. The most light was coming from the sunrise, which I could see through the windows that stretched from the polished floor to the high ceiling.

My phone dinged again as we stepped outside, and I unzipped my jacket. The breeze was something to be cherished, as by noon it would no doubt be very hot. I glanced at my phone repeatedly as we walked toward the parking garage.

> *5:28 a.m.*
> Kay: She's chill guys don't worry
> Finn please get rid of the group chat name
> Unknown: Why? I love it!
> Unknown: Jessie this is River
> You can add me to your contacts if you want
> And the other number is Finniake
> You don't have to add him
> Unknown: Rude :(
> Unknown: Kaylani is right Finn
> This name is stupid
> Unknown: But we're BFFs!
> Unknown: Why don't you tell Naziah that?
> Unknown: Hey Naziah!
> Pick up your phone!

Being added to the group chat was a pleasant surprise, though I couldn't really tell if I was wanted. I glanced up from my phone occasionally as Miles and I entered the parking garage. We reached Miles's car parked in one of the guest spaces just as I finished adding River and Finniake to my contacts. Since the school had given Miles his car, he would have to register for a dedicated residential parking space. Until then, he would have to park in the guest spaces, which were farthest in the garage from the apartment building.

Miles put my suitcase in the trunk, and I made my way to the passenger seat. Just as I closed the car door, my phone beeped again.

Finniake: Rude :(
River: Kaylani is right Finn
This name is stupid
Finniake: But we're BFFs!
River: Why don't you tell Naziah that?
Finniake: Hey Naziah!
Pick up your phone!
River: She rarely ever texts—I wouldn't bother
She'd also probably hurt you if you called her your BFF
Kay: I'd wanna see that
Finniake: :(
Kay: I'm just joking…kinda

Miles entered the car and started the engine. "Vessa, take Jessie and I to school." Various parts of the car lit up—something I had never grown used to. The car pulled out of its parking spot, and the wheel turned itself, taking us out of the parking garage.

I texted the group chat "Hey guys!" to which Finniake responded with "Hi Jessie!"

Kaylani greeted me the same way, then followed up saying, "Did you get it?"

"Yep," I respond.

River chimed in and asked what Kaylani was talking about, to which Kaylani instructed him to mind his own business.

"How's your first week so far?" Miles asked. "If you're not too busy texting."

I quickly set my phone on vibrate before turning it off. "No, I'm not," I told him. "And it's…all right. Weird."

"You learned a lot?"

"Not academically, since it's still the first week. But I know my way around the school. No wonder it's so expensive without a scholarship, since we have a dorm, public laundry room, amazing breakfast, lunch *and* dinner, *elevators*…"

"You know students can't use them during school hours, right?"

"Yeah, sadly."

"Spoken like a true IFON student."

I smiled at his comment, which felt a lot like a compliment. Only then had it occurred to me that fitting in at IFON was possibly something that I really wanted. My priorities had really changed a lot since Friday. At first, I'd wanted to have a fun-filled summer with my friends, but now, I wanted to excel in summer school.

Miles's car slowed to a stop at the red light, making my eyes widen in amazement. "It's a good thing Lady Kate saw potential in you," Miles said in a nonchalant, much less amazed manner than how I felt. He was obviously accustomed to his vehicle.

"What do you mean?"

"I mean, Lady Kate was crucial in getting you into IFON. I guarantee you that the guards had planned to wipe your memory of the last twenty-four hours and send you home."

"What? Why? Wipe my memory? That's not possible."

Miles looked at me as if I must be joking, and his car sped up again. "No, it's possible. Risky, and can have some weird side effects, but possible. And they would've done it because you knew a lot about the academy. I don't know what Lady Kate saw in you, though."

What did *Lady Kate see in me?*

"Just don't make a fool of yourself, Jess," Miles advised. "All of the new students have already had their orientation and moved into their dorms except for you. That makes you different. And as pristine and dreamy as the academy may seem, on the inside, it's just as filled with hormonal adolescents as any school. Everyone is big on drama, always wanting to know secrets and sticking their nose in somebody else's business."

Part of me doubted that his words were true, contradictorily making them appear even more accurate. A school was a school no matter what. I wondered if I'd been too excited about all the changes to realize that IFON may not be as different from Symson as I would've liked it to be. Still, I was hesitant to let go of the possibility that IFON was unique in every way possible.

My phone buzzed on my leg, and my screen lit up. There was a text from someone that I wouldn't have expected but was too busy with my own internal conflicts to feel comforted by their virtual presence.

> *5:40 a.m.*
> Lion: Hey Jess
>   U heard from Michael? He hasn't texted me since Saturday
> You: Nope I'm sorry

It felt like I wasn't getting a chance to take my mind off Michael anytime soon. However, something my friend had said made me curious, and a little hopeful.

> *5:40 a.m.*
> Lion: Hey Jess
>   U heard from Michael? He hasn't texted me since Saturday.
> You: Nope I'm sorry
>   What did he say 2 u on Saturday?
> Lion: I asked him if he was already on the plane, and he said he was still packing but would text me later
> You: Oh ok—just wondering
> Lion: Pls let me know if he texts you
> You: Of course

Michael was never one to lie. Why would he say that he was still packing? Did someone else have his phone at the time? Or was he back at his house?

The car turned onto the street that went past the academy complex. I looked out of my window at the huge campus that felt like a home I'd never had. It felt like a home that I still wasn't sure I wanted.

the fearless five

If applying to IFON was possible, I may have attended simply due to its location. As if the campus wasn't big and mesmerizing enough, it was very close to downtown, which has everything. Tons of stores— expensive *and* cheap ones—with amazing restaurants. Malls were the best of both worlds. Getting to shop and take breaks at a restaurant? The best combination ever. Out of the three of us, Donnay was taking the most advantage.

"Honestly, I'm surprised she paid for everything." Olivia laughed. I smiled and nodded in agreement. Donnay was walking back to our table with a bag of clothes. Donnay slid into her seat at the table and shoved her bag of clothes under her chair.

"'Bout time they brought the food," she said, picking up her burger from her plate.

"They just brought it over," Olivia told her as Donnay took a bite of her burger.

Olivia began eating her salad, and I started to eat my pasta. Both of my roommates commented on each other's food and one another's classes.

"Speaking of math, I still have homework," Donnay recalled, wiping her hands on a napkin. She removed her purse from her shoulder and dug into it.

89

"Did you seriously bring your homework to the mall?" I queried.

"Why would you wait until Saturday to do your homework, Donnay?" Olivia added to the questioning.

Donnay pulled out a crumpled piece of paper from her purse and a pen. "It's just a survey," she told us. "I kept putting it off, but it's due Monday morning." She clicked her pen and wrote what I assumed was her name and then froze.

"Dang, this is actually hard," she observed. "Maybe I shouldn't have waited until today."

I snickered at her comment, to which Donnay gave me a sharp look. "Watch it, newbie," she playfully scolded.

"Did you like your first week?" Olivia asked me.

"It was okay," I admitted. "We haven't started fighting in weapons and combat yet, but we're starting next week. I'm a bit nervous about that."

"Oh, you'll do great," she assured me.

"Maybe you won't," Donnay muttered, to which Olivia poked her shoulder.

"I'm just being realistic!" Donnay defended. She clicked off her pen and looked at me, waving the end of it as she talked. "How well you do in that class—well, all of them—will determine your classes next year. *If* you have the guts to come back."

She leaned back at her own comment, expecting Olivia to charge again. Olivia shook her head and smiled. "You'll be fine, Jessie. Just do your best in all your classes. I'm sure you had great grades at your old school."

"Straight A's," I responded, side-eyeing Donnay. She didn't notice my bragging attempt.

"There you go! You just have to adjust to the new classes," explained Olivia. "You'll find a lot of things at IFON to be new."

"Yeah, like Naziah going to a mall," Donnay stated.

Olivia questioned her statement, but I caught on immediately. Naziah was directly in my view. "Naziah's here," Donnay explained to Olivia and then pointed in the direction of the mall's entrance.

"I'd expect her to be studying or doing whatever Naziahs do." Olivia smiled at Donnay's joke, and I leaned forward.

"Kaylani's behind her," I observed.

Donnay set a hand on Olivia's shoulder and whispered something that sounded like "She really is rubbing off."

Kaylani noticed us at our table and waved, and then said something to Naziah. They both approached us, Kaylani appearing more excited to see us than Naziah. Kaylani jogged over to our table and leaned on it, taking exaggerated breaths.

"Hey guys!" she greeted us.

Donnay waved, and Olivia and I responded with a "Hey." Naziah walked calmly behind Kaylani, obviously in no rush to meet us.

"Are you guys here to hang out?" Olivia asked, to which Donnay rolled her eyes. I knew it wasn't far-fetched for that to be Kaylani's reason for meeting us, but Naziah didn't seem the type to hang out at a mall.

"I'd love to, but we came to give you guys a message from Professor Jones," Kaylani responded.

Naziah finally made her way to our table and didn't give so much as a wave. I couldn't say that I'd expected much more. "Do we get a free meal or something?" Donnay asked, perking up at her own suggestion.

"Pipe down." Kaylani laughed.

"This is actually—" Naziah gently pushed Kaylani and then motioned at the table. Kaylani nodded and knelt down, looking underneath the table. Naziah started to dart her eyes around the area, and I wondered what they were looking for. To my surprise, Olivia and Donnay were looking around also.

"Clear," Kaylani reported, standing up straight. She noticed my confused expression and started to explain.

"Microphone check," she told me, her voice just above a whisper. "We have to make sure no microphones are nearby to overhear this. Thankfully, no other people are sitting close enough to hear if we talk at this level."

"I would hate to sit by such vexatious eating as well," Naziah finally said, looking at Donnay.

"Shut up," Donnay mumbled, her mouth full of the last of her burger.

"What don't you want others to hear?" I asked, while Donnay reached for another napkin.

"You remember Wednesday when we showed the note to the professor at school?" Kaylani asked.

I nodded, eager to know the secret. "He asked us if we recognized the handwriting," she recalled, now speaking to the whole table.

"Jessie recognized it to be written by Michael's mother, and the professor tried to call different members of the family. None of them picked up."

The others seemed to understand her words which surprised me. Naziah, Donnay, and Olivia had never met Michael as far as I knew. I assumed Kaylani had told them about him, or they had just learned not to ask questions that might soon be answered.

"Professor Jones thinks Jessie and I should investigate this," she continued. "But he said that having extra people is always helpful. To put everything in short, the five of us are going to southern California on Saturday!" Her tone perked up, as did Donnay and Olivia's attitudes.

"Today?" I asked.

"The one *following* today." Naziah shook her head.

"California…," Olivia echoed. "That's amazing! It's far though, but still amazing!"

"This will not be a vacation," Naziah informed. "Think of it as a business trip. Our intended goal is to either find Michael or find information about whoever kidnapped him."

"So it's official?" I wondered. "It's confirmed that he was kidnapped?" My own words felt so far from me. *How could one of my best friends be missing?*

"That's the most logical explanation," Kaylani responded, almost like she was trying to convince herself.

"We'll find y'all's friend," Donnay promised. It was the most sympathetic I'd ever witnessed her. She looked at Naziah. "So, when and how are we getting to Cali?"

"By plane," Naziah replied. "I suggested we take an IFON-AV, as the academy has access to aircraft hangars. Lady Kate politely declined the offer, explaining how we may either run into our target or more likely gather useful information in a public environment." I thought to ask what an "IFON-AV" was, but Donnay spoke before I got the chance.

"Lady Kate knows about this?" she questioned.

"Obviously." Naziah sighed. "Most students do not fly across the country on a mission organized by a professor. So Lady Kate had to approve. We will return to the academy at 6:00 a.m. sharp to meet our chaperones."

"Ew, chaperones," Donnay groused.

"I can't believe we're going on a mission!" beamed Olivia. "Especially you, Jessie. Most first years never get to do anything this exciting."

"An understatement," I said. "But how are we allowed to do this? Not all of our parents are IFON legends."

Naziah didn't bother to look at me regarding my comment, but Donnay smirked proudly.

"Lady Kate will meet with them in person, so I'm told," Kaylani said. I highly doubted the plan would work. With my mom on edge after my dad basically sneaking me into school without her approval, it'd take a miracle for her to be open to letting me go across the country.

"I've got it!" Olivia exclaimed. She lowered her voice at Naziah's cold glance. "We can call ourselves the 'Fearless Five.' Isn't that great?" Kaylani smiled at the suggestion, and Donnay rolled her eyes. Naziah sighed, articulating her words to show playful amusement.

"On that note... I will be on my way." Donnay chuckled as Naziah walked from the table.

"As coldhearted as she is, she can be tolerable sometimes," Donnay stated. Kaylani shook her head, smiling herself.

"I thought it was a nice name," Olivia muttered.

"It's perfect," I assured her.

Kaylani looked at me, and her smile had almost fully faded away. I scrunched my eyebrows, trying to silently ask *What's wrong?* She tried to force a small smile and hesitantly looked away to the large crowd that had just entered the mall.

Thinking about travelling to California made me sick. Here I was relying on three associates and one best friend to help me find Michael. But to me, IFON had made itself evident to be an academy full of secrecy. I couldn't help but wonder if Kaylani was keeping secrets too.

socialize

Ten minutes from home
Sunday
1400 hours

Lacy and Kaylani having to study was no surprise to me. Lacy was a bookworm who preferred fiction stories over real life. I couldn't blame her—my life had been very chaotic since the first day of summer. As for Kaylani, she simply loved to learn. I learned a lot for the benefit of it. If I could breeze through classes, school would be less stressful and I'd be more successful. Kaylani learned a lot because she found it entertaining. It still was a bit disappointing not having them with us.

Tori, being the outgoing girl she was, had been super nice to Donnay and Olivia ever since we'd arrived. "Your summer school friends are so nice, Jessie," she said. Donnay wasn't impressed by Tori, but Olivia seemed to love her.

"It kinda makes me wish I went to summer school."

Alexis looked at me and shook her head, both of us knowing that Tori could barely handle regular school.

We were sitting in the grass not too far from the playground, closer to my apartment than to IFON. There were a lot of people selling food and drinks here, with plenty of kids at the playground. It felt good to be with some people whom I hadn't just met in the last two weeks. Naziah had been invited to come hang out with us, but it didn't surprise anyone when she declined. It was probably for the better anyway. Alexis would've talked Naziah's ear off, and Tori would've accidentally insulted her. Or purposefully.

"So this girl is lactose intolerant." Tori pointed to Alexis.

"No! I'm *allergic*," Alexis corrected her.

"Psh. Same diff." Alexis rolled her eyes at Tori's ignorance. "She's *allergic* or whatever. And turned down going to the best end-of-the-year party because the only food that didn't contain milk was the crackers."

"That's not a valid reason?" Donnay asked.

"Maybe," replied Tori. "Had the party not been the best party in the universe. Max's house is so huge that I didn't recognize a lot of the people there. They had to have been his friends, because I know *everyone* at our school."

"More like everyone knows you," Alexis muttered.

"This was an end-of-the-year party?" I asked.

"Yeah! It was yesterday," Tori said.

Olivia looked at me with a hint of sympathy, while Donnay was snickering.

"Well, why didn't you guys text me about it?"

"Because parties aren't your thing, Jessie! Plus, I heard you were in summer school, which, like, *totally* suits you. I didn't want to ruin your time there." Tori's excuse seemed genuine, but knowing her, she probably just didn't want me to come.

"Going to the mall yesterday was fun, though, right, Jessie?" Olivia pressed. I forced a smile and nodded. Going to the mall had been great, but apparently, it hadn't compared to Tori's experience.

"I'm gonna get some sodas," Alexis announced, getting up from the grass. "Y'all want anything?"

Olivia and Tori requested a sprite, and Donnay wanted a cherry coke. I simply asked for water.

"Yeah, summer school totes fits you," Tori said to me, and Donnay laughed. Olivia nudged Donnay, but her laughter didn't bother me as much as Tori's comments.

My phone beeped in my pocket, and Tori looked over to me. "Who ya textin'?" she asked.

"Probably Kaylani," Donnay replied.

I reached for my phone as Tori and Donnay went on talking about who could've texted me. Unfortunately, I couldn't tell them.

2:30 p.m.
Unknown: Let's meet by the hot dog stand.

Clicking on the unknown title, no number was revealed.

That's weird. I swiveled my head, looking for the stand, and saw a long line of people there. Did the person have the wrong number?

"You looking for a friend?" Olivia asked.

It took me a second to realize she'd been talking to me. "Oh, no, I'm just looking for the hot dogs," I replied quickly. "Be right back." I stood up and brushed the dirt from my shorts before walking toward the long line.

Even walking in the blazing heat wasn't ideal, but my curiosity got the best of me. I walked across the grass until I was in the back of the line. There were people my age and older, sweating and talking, eager to get their hot dog and drink.

I looked at my phone again, rereading the text. Another text came from the unknown number, an image, that took a couple of seconds to load in. Part of me wished I had never waited for the text.

There was a picture of me, standing exactly where I was and looking at my phone. Involuntarily, I looked to my left, where the picture had been taken from. By one of the benches close to the street, there was what seemed to be a shoe just barely sticking out from the side. I rushed toward the bench, despite the heat, the shoe getting closer into my view.

At the bench was a single shoe holding down a piece of paper. I looked around again, wondering if I could catch who had left it, but everyone in my sight seemed focused on themselves. I bent down to grab the paper and smoothed it out against my leg. Just reading the note made me nervous, and even scared.

Rushing back to the others was the best option, but this wasn't something I could talk about with Alexis and Tori around. I started back to the others, glancing behind me frequently. The note had made me paranoid.

Yeah, just wait until tomorrow. You can tell Donnay, Olivia, Naziah, and Kaylani altogether. They'll be able to help.

I knew I'd have to hide the letter before my friends saw me. I reread the letter one more time, which made no more sense than when I'd first read it. If anything, it only made me feel worse: "I'm not where you think I am."

look out

The van is surprisingly comfortable. Although, it would've been more enjoyable if we were going to Disneyland.

"Buckle up, y'all," Balson instructed. He helped Kaylani climb in next to me before shutting the door. I buckled my seatbelt along with Kaylani, but Naziah had done so as soon as she entered the van.

School had finished about an hour ago. I'd used forty-five of those minutes finishing homework and the other fifteen minutes finding out that I'd be taking a brief road trip.

"I'm glad Professor Jones wanted us to come with you," Kaylani said.

"Me too," I agreed. "Especially since I have something to show you both."

The girls looked at me while Balson climbed into the driver's seat. Balson was a senior at IFON and one of Professor Jones's favorite and most trusted students. That was why he'd chosen Balson to drive us to the penitentiary. I still wasn't fully sure why we were being sent instead of staff or faculty, but the girls had promised to explain on the way there.

I pulled my purse off my shoulder and reached inside for the note I had saved. "I found this yesterday near the playground by my house," I told them, unfolding it. I held it out for them to read.

"I assume you do not recognize the handwriting?" Naziah inquired. I shook my head in response.

The engine started, which startled me a bit. I'd jumped at the sudden movement, but not enough for the girls to notice. At least, if they had noticed, they didn't mention it.

"I don't recognize it either." Kaylani shrugged. "May just be something to mislead us. I wouldn't think much of it."

Naziah nodded, approving Kaylani's suggestion.

I refolded the note, slightly surprised by their commentary. Part of me had prematurely hoped that the note would lead us directly to Michael. Balson drove forward, taking us out of the academy's parking lot.

"So why exactly are we going to a prison?" I queried.

"To convene with the gunmen who invaded our refuge last Saturday," Naziah informed. "Professor Jones wants you to be present and find out what information you can. The people were most likely either a distraction from focusing on your friend Michael, or simply an attack that needs investigation. The professor wants Kaylani and me to be present to supervise *you*."

The last sentence sounded backhanded, but most of Naziah's comments did. "We're in an IFON-AV, so we'll get to the penitentiary in no time," Balson reported.

"What's that, and how does it help us get there faster?" I asked.

"An IFON-AV is an IFON-authorized vehicle," Kaylani explained. "It'll help us get there quickly because the monitor shows the driver where red lights are, how long they last, and shortcuts to our destination. Like a regular driving app with extra benefits. But the penitentiary is pretty close anyway."

Balson drove on roads I didn't recognize for around three minutes. He eventually pulled into the parking lot of a building that looked like a day care on the outside. We sat parked for a minute, until Balson opened his door and signaled for the rest of us to exit the van. The penitentiary sat on a busy road with lots of noise that I was sure would bother the inmates and even staff.

Kaylani, Naziah, and I climbed out of the van. We walked toward the building, with glass doors that let us see the front desk.

Balson held the door open for the rest of us to enter. As soon as the door closed, the building was very quiet. There was a guard on either side of the door, both of them in uniform as well. Balson went up to the front desk and pulled from his pocket a card that looked like an ID. The guards shifted their hands to their waists as Balson reached in his pocket. I wondered how many visitors were brave enough to pull out a weapon in a prison.

There were some low whispers at the front desk, but I couldn't make out the conversation. I subconsciously reached to adjust my purse on my shoulder but realized I'd left it in the van. Kaylani took my hand while Balson stepped back from the desk. The man who was at the desk stood and motioned for us to follow him. I looked at Kaylani, who appeared just as nervous as I felt. She held my hand tighter, and we followed behind the officer.

The officer led all of us down a hallway with two sets of stairs. We approached the one leading down and could hear some discussions underneath us. At the bottom of the staircase, our footsteps echoed in the dimly lit room. We turned right into what seemed like a lounge. The ongoing discussions became quieter the more we advanced.

What appeared to be cells were on either side of us, but it was too dark to tell if anybody was inside of them. The officer stopped walking at one cell and hit his hand on the bars. He stepped back with his hands behind his back in a waiting position.

Someone emerged from the dark cell and leaned on the bars. The light in the hallway illuminated his face. He appeared about eighteen and gave us a sly grin.

"Who is this?" Naziah asked.

Her voice startled me as we'd been in silence for a while. "This young man is one of the invaders at the refuge," the officer explained.

I assumed that the officer worked for IFON or was connected to it as he spoke as if he held authority regarding the refuge. "So he's one of the people who tried to kill Jessie," added Kaylani.

"Which one of you is that?" the boy asked.

"Me," I announced, stunned by my own intrepidity.

"Come closer, let me see you better," he said. The officer looked at me and raised an eyebrow. *If something goes wrong, you'll be pro-*

tected, I told myself. I stepped past Balson and stood a few inches away from the cell. Now I could see that the boy had dark-brown hair and green eyes. He smiled at me, but it wasn't comforting.

"They don't care for our eyesight as I'm sure you can tell," he said, looking at the ceiling. It *was* odd to me that there weren't lights in the cells.

"What's your name?"

The boy looked at Naziah as if she was out of her mind to ask. "Royal," he told her. "What's yours?"

Naziah laughed derisively at his question, and it was the first time I'd ever heard her laugh. Even her laugh sounded as poised and controlled as she carried herself. Part of me wished I'd been looking at her to see her smile.

Balson stepped back, letting Kaylani come closer to the cell. "How did you get into the building that day?" she asked.

"I walked in the front door," Royal sneered.

"If you would suppress your smarm, this will not be a long process," proposed Naziah.

"Why? It's fun having you all here. Our only interactions are when those aphasic imbeciles bring us food." Royal smiled slyly at the officer.

He looked at the rest of us. "What's *more* fun is how your ill fate brought you to this dungeon where people like me are held until they go deranged. And you're only here for my entertainment since I have nothing valuable to offer. Unless, of course, you allow me to stretch my legs outside of this hellhole so my mind can refresh. Or I could remember as much as possible *first*, and you could grant that temporary freedom for me in return."

"You are in no position to negotiate," Naziah observed. "You partook in an attack on a virtually vacant building, allowed two guards who happened to be on the scene disguise themselves as you and your partner, *and* you failed to escape the premises without leaving enough evidence behind for the authorities to track you down. That sounds quite ill-fated to me. Now you are behind bars, and you best believe that until you utter words that are actually valuable, you will stay in this dismal basement, ploddingly losing your mind.

So again, cooperate and your process of serving time in jail will not have to last over three years, as that is what you will indubitably be sentenced to in a court hearing."

Royal's cunning demeanor seemed to escape him at Naziah's words, but it didn't last for more than a second. "Well, aren't you quite the highbrow?"

Naziah held her posture, unfazed by his repulsive response. He surely knew that everything she said was right, and being uncooperative with us would ultimately make his life more difficult.

"Fine." He pursed his lips and took a deep breath. "I got in by shooting down the barrier. You know, that stone wall you have behind the desk. And the front desk was unattended. *That* was pretty stupid."

"You didn't arrange for Mrs. Kettle to be somewhere else at the time?" Kaylani asked. Naziah shot her a sharp look, as if mentioning Mrs. Kettle's name in front of a stranger was dangerous.

"Yeah, I don't know who that is," shrugged Royal.

I looked at Kaylani and Naziah, Kaylani sharing a worried look with me. Mrs. Kettle had claimed that she was told someone else would attend the desk while she took a day off. Who had told her?

"What else can you reveal?" Naziah questioned.

"I can 'reveal' that your school should have bulletproof windows," he jested. "Juan shot in from the outside, but I think it was really just to test the windows. Then he rushed inside and we started shooting the place up. Honestly, your building is *really* vulnerable."

"Why were you there?" Kaylani asked.

"And why test the windows?" I added.

"One at a time, ladies." He chuckled. "We were ordered to test the windows, but I wasn't told why. Probably so they could know how weak the windows are for a future attack." He paused to look at Naziah. "They're very weak, by the way. And we were there because we were told to be there."

"Who is 'they'? Who told you to go to the building?" Kaylani asked.

"Juan did," Royal replied. "Whoever orders Juan around is who you're looking for. I take all my orders from him."

"And what's in it for you?"

"Money. I do what I'm told and I get cash."

"How much?"

"My previous jobs were simply mailing packages for about five hundred bucks a week." He glared at the officer. "I don't know what they were gonna pay me this time. They don't pay people for getting arrested."

"Where'd you mail the packages?" I asked.

Royal sighed. "I don't remember. This was my first job in *weeks*. Probably my last, considering nobody wants to hire a criminal."

"If you are working for whom I think you are, they are always hiring criminals," Naziah said.

I looked at her, wondering who she thought Royal was working for.

Royal raised an eyebrow and laughed. "Well, this has been fun, ladies. Really."

"One more thing." Naziah held up her hand. "What were you wearing that day?"

"Let's see, what was I...oh! Well, I was wearing underwear, you know, obviously. I had a shirt. Some pants that are *really* tight around the waist. I had socks, shoes..."

"The shoes. What type were they?"

"The expensive type. Which is surprising considering how tight they are."

"Stop playing games, Royal," Kaylani ordered.

"I'm being honest!" he maintained. "I can tell you that they're heavy and announce your presence with every step you take. I've also heard that they stick to walls and ceilings. But I've never tried it before."

"We only have the truck for twelve more minutes," Balson whispered. "Let's move on."

We all nodded in agreement. "Watch out for Juan—he bites!" Royal chuckled before he turned and went further back into the dark cell.

The officer spun on his heel and kept walking down the hall. The rest of us quickly followed him toward another cell. It felt like eyes were watching us from each cell, staring at us from the darkness.

We finally stopped walking. I looked up to see fluorescent lights that looked just as old as they were dim—as if they had never been turned off. After banging his fist on the bars of a cell, the officer stepped back to let us converse.

A boy emerged from the cell and stood close to the bars. He was shorter than Royal, with straight brown hair reaching past his ears and scars on the right side of his face. *This must be Juan.*

"Who are you?" The words spat from his mouth at his inquisition.

"Who are you?" Kaylani deflected the question. Juan simply stared at Kaylani and shook his head. Unfortunately for us, Juan seemed pretty similar to Royal. It'd be hard to get anything out of him.

"We come from the building that you infiltrated last Saturday," informed Naziah. "This will only take a moment with your cooperation. Who instructed you to break in?"

Juan rolled his eyes. "You ain't gettin *nuthin'* outta me. Whatever my idiot of a partner gave up is all you gonna hear."

"How long have you two known each other?" I questioned.

Speaking to Juan made me nervous—despite his small size, there was something about him that made him appear more dangerous than Royal. Almost like a sense of determination, or even insanity.

Juan muttered something under his breath before turning around and going deeper into the cell. "Let's not waste our time," Naziah suggested. I was surprised at her statement as Juan obviously knew more than Royal. Then again, he would have to give up information at some point if he wanted to get out of jail.

The officer walked past us and back the way we came. We followed down the hall in a line, and I felt uncomfortable being in the back. I lowered my head and made an effort not to look directly in any of the cells.

As we got closer to the staircase, a *psst* came from one of the cells. It was loud enough for all of us to stop and look around. The person started snapping, and we approached where the sound was coming from: Royal's cell. He was leaning on the cell bars again and pointed to each of us girls before motioning for us to come over. My stomach turned as we approached, and I felt that he definitely wasn't going to be helpful.

"A piece of advice for you," Royal whispered. "You can't watch your front and back at the same time."

Kaylani and I looked at each other, wondering what he meant. Royal went back into the darkness before we could ask for clarity, but I had doubted he would give it to us anyway.

Naziah started walking back to Balson and the officer. Kaylani gripped my hand and gave a small smile. Even though I wasn't sure what Royal was trying to tell us, I knew that there was no time to get distracted. All of my attention had to be on my main problem—the whole reason I was at IFON: Michael.

déjà vu

The last time something like this happened was at the playground a few days ago. I'd been texted anonymously until I found a note, which two days ago, was dismissed by Kaylani and Naziah. For it to happen a second time was unsettling, even having Naziah with me.

The bus pulled to a stop, and Naziah rose from her seat. I stood up as well and walked down the aisle behind her. We made our way off the bus and onto the sidewalk. Our destination wasn't too far from here.

School had been out for less than an hour, but Naziah insisted that we leave as soon as I received the text. It read, "Meet me alone at the ice cream parlor." Whoever was sending me these things wasn't one to specify.

We walked down the sidewalk, the sun's heat already making me sweat. Naziah had on a black full body suit—the same outfit she'd worn daily since I'd met her. Somehow she seemed perfectly cool.

"You will enter first," Naziah instructed. "Whoever this person is wants to see you alone. Although, they may have seen us through the windows already." Her sentence caught me off guard, and I looked at the windows of the building we were approaching. I couldn't see anyone watching, but then again, I couldn't see *anything*. All the lights were off.

106

I sped up at the observation and jogged toward the front door. Naziah was still walking, making no effort to catch up. There were no cars and no bikes. The sign in the door said closed, but I tried pushing it open anyways.

The door swung open faster than I would've liked, with a blast of cold air hitting me at once. I stumbled back and looked over my shoulder at Naziah. She's standing still on the sidewalk, hands behind her back. I forced myself to enter the building.

Sunlight shone in through the glass door and the windows. My eyes adjusted, and I could see all the chairs unoccupied. *Where would the light switch be?*

"Hello?" I turned right, facing where the sound had come from. "Anyone there?"

"I'm here," I called back.

"Help!" the voice faintly called. *The voice is too familiar.* "Are you there?"

"Yeah, I'm here Pat!" I shouted. I walked down the aisle of booths surrounding empty tables. My stomach turned as I passed the booth where I'd last been with Michael.

"Help!" Patricia cried. "Please, help me!"

I felt the adrenaline throughout my body as my friend called in despair.

"Help!" I looked left at the girls' bathroom door, where the sound was coming from. Pushing open the door, Patricia called for help again. I turned on the bathroom light and saw all the stall doors open. *Where is she?*

"Down here!" I followed the sound and saw the large vent in the floor. "Please help!"

"I'm right here!" I called back. I bent down and reached for the vent, trying to pull it open. I jerked back while gripping the vent, but it wouldn't pry off.

I could hear Patricia sobbing from inside. "I'm gonna get help," I told her, rushing out of the room.

She pled, "Hurry!" as I run back through the parlor.

"Naziah!" I shouted. My voice bounced off the walls. I opened the parlor door and saw Naziah standing just outside of it. She started entering before I could explain anything as the urgency on my face said enough.

Naziah stayed behind me as I led her back to the bathroom. Patricia called for help again, and I picked up speed. My sneakers slid against the floor as I tried to turn the corner.

"We're here, Pat!" I ran into the bathroom and knelt down at the vent. Naziah knelt down and looked inside.

"Pitch-black," she observed aloud.

She raised her black vest and pulled a screwdriver from her utility belt. I stepped back and watched anxiously as she unscrewed every bolt. She moved pretty fast, taking about five seconds to undo each bolt.

Naziah soon set down her screwdriver and gripped onto the vent. I grabbed onto it and helped lift it up. We leaned the heavy piece of metal against the stall next to us.

"Reach up!" I shouted while Naziah reached into the vent. She moved her hand around and dug deeper.

"Is she all right?" I asked, the worst possible result coming to mind.

Naziah pulled back suddenly, a box in her hand. "Please, hurry," Pat's voice begged from the box. Naziah dropped the speaker and snatched what looked like a gun from her belt. She aimed the weapon past me at the door.

"Scream if you need me," she directed quietly. I looked over my own shoulder at the open door. Naziah stood and walked past me, aiming her weapon into the hall. She looked behind her before walking out of my sight.

I sighed and looked back at the speaker. *How did they set this up? Who set this up?*

Being in the bathroom alone made me feel nervous and unprotected. At least Naziah had something to defend herself—I had nothing. I walked out of the bathroom and rushed into the main seating area, looking for Naziah.

I turned to my left where the storage room was, wondering if she went there. Suddenly, a loud crash came from behind me. I turned and raced down the aisle, darting my eyes helplessly, looking for Naziah. After passing the front door, she's still nowhere in sight.

To my right on the floor was broken glass, and I looked at the window that had been shattered.

"What happened?" I wondered aloud, walking toward the window.

Without warning, a force struck me from behind, sending me forward. Two loud sounded come from behind me, and I didn't have to think twice about them being gunshots. I gasped for air, the force having pushed all of it from my lungs. Naziah knelt beside my head and sits me up.

"Better you choke than die," she said.

I breathed heavily and looked at the wall across from the broken window, which was now punctured with two bullet holes.

Naziah stood up and ran toward the back door. I wanted to help her but knew I'd only get in her way. Relief washed over me as I could breathe better, but there's still a job to be done. Calling 911 could easily backfire, considering Naziah was also carrying a gun. Instead, I pulled my phone from my pocket and dial Kaylani's number.

The phone went straight to voice mail. I started scrolling through my contacts, wondering who else I could call.

Quick footsteps rushed from the back door toward me.

"What are you doing?" Naziah asked

"Calling for help."

She huffed and grabbed my shirt, pulling me off the ground.

"Come on," she muttered, letting go of her grip. I stuffed my phone away and followed her, subconsciously crouching. There weren't any windows on this side of the building, but taking chances wouldn't be smart.

"Cops will definitely arrive soon. We have to get this person ourselves," Naziah said. Hearing her speak as if we were working together felt good, but I doubted she would have me do much.

She swung open the back door and stepped outside, looking left and right. "Watch my back," she instructed. I turned the other way, looking around for whoever I could find. There was only grass and a corner store farther down the sidewalk. A lot of cars were driving on the road that was on the other side of the building. One of them had to have seen the person.

"There!" Naziah announced. I turned around and saw a person dressed in black racing down the sidewalk. They had a long black ponytail dangling from their hair as they ran. The sunlight glistened in it, almost like there were crystals in their hair.

I thought to ask if Naziah was sure it's the person, but there was no time to question her. Naziah aimed her gun at the person and stepped forward. My chest pained as she held her finger on the trigger. There was no doubt in my mind that she could make the shot.

Standing out from the cars speeding on the road, a very faint siren came from the distance. Naziah scolded under her breath and lowered her weapon.

"We have to move," she said.

The person had obviously called the cops, if not a bystander. She put her gun back in her belt and pulled her shirt to cover her belt before leading me around the building.

"Where are we going?" I asked.

"The academy," she replied. "I would assume this was an attempt to get us arrested, but it would be a lousy one. We can think about it more when we get back."

I couldn't help but notice Naziah's hand shaking as we ran onto the sidewalk. She seemed off guard to me—not looking behind her at the mystery person (I'd glanced back repeatedly from paranoia, but the person had gotten away) and physically shaking even if only in the slightest way. We were close to another bus stop that wouldn't be too hard to catch. But I wasn't as worried about getting back to IFON.

My mind was on a question that I knew Naziah wouldn't answer. *Was she going to pull the trigger if the cops hadn't been called?*

reunion

In front of Azariele Apartments
Thursday
1845 hours

Whoever owned the apartment complex also owned its parking garage. The garage was public to everyone. However, there were assigned parking spaces filling most of the first level for residents. Since Miles had gotten his car, he never applied for one. Part of me wished he had applied, because Mom and Dad's cars were parked, and there was no way we'd find an empty space.

"What the..." Miles slowed the car down, not that he had much of a choice. There was a lot of traffic, with people honking left and right. I leaned forward and looked out of Miles's window.

"I don't think we're getting a parking space," I said.

Miles looked at the parking garage, a confused expression washing over his face.

The four-story garage was full of cars either parked in a space, or on the ramps. Some were even pulled over next to the sidewalk. The traffic was standstill—we weren't getting any closer to the apartment.

"Text Mom and Dad," Miles told me, pulling out his own phone.

Mom and Dad had texted in the family group chat asking when we would be able to visit back. Miles said that after school today would be fine, and we were supposed to be meeting with them. *There's a lot of traffic so we may be late*, I texted.

"There's nothing online about this," said Miles, turning off his phone. He turned on the radio and set it to the news station.

Many people were still honking, some getting out of their cars to look for the source of the traffic.

"Get out and walk to the apartment," instructed Miles. "Tell them I'll be in soon." I opened my door, the honking of other cars drowning out the sound of Miles's radio.

My hands covered my ears as I walked in front of Miles's car and behind another. Walking to the sidewalk, I felt somewhat exposed. Not that many people chose to leave their car, and it seemed like everyone was watching me. Rushing down the sidewalk and toward the apartment, the standstill traffic seemed to go on for a long ways.

In front of me was a long line of cars that reached from the road to the entrance of the garage. The security officers who usually scanned the garage from time to time were now stationed by the entrance. Some people who had gotten out of the cars were talking to the officers, but I doubted the officers knew much about why there was a lot of traffic.

The windows in the apartment lobby that reached from the high ceiling to the floor allowed me to see how there were quite a lot of people inside the building. Since our apartment was so close to the city, it didn't have any food outlets like some other apartments. The people inside were either very lost, wondering about the traffic, or all the residents who decided to gather in the lobby together.

The honking had died down for a while but quickly picked back up, ten times louder. *What are they doing?* I looked down the street where most of the cars were honking and saw one person dashing down the sidewalk. Someone who looked very familiar.

The apartment entrance was directly to my left, but I wasn't about to go inside. Our parents already knew Miles and I would be late, and I wanted to know what this person was up to.

I raced toward the person, who was now running around the apartment building. They weren't going to slow down, so I called after them.

"Naziah!"

She stopped and turned around to face me. I ran faster, feeling breathless, and was relieved when I finally reached her.

"What are you doing?" I bent over, my hands on my knees, taking in as much air as I could.

"Not hyperventilating," she replied.

I looked up, surprised by her words. She'd never seemed like the sarcastic type.

"If you want to do well at IFON, then you are going to have to expand your physical abilities. That includes running." Her lecture wasn't the most comforting, especially knowing that she was right. Essentially every IFON student was self-assured and confident in having earned their place at the academy. A lot of them appeared as if they were fighting to keep their place. Then there was me, who didn't know much about the academy at all and knew even less as to why I was there.

"What are you *really* doing?" I asked.

"Examining your apartment," Naziah explained, looking up toward the top of the building.

"Why? How do you know I live here?"

"I do not know your room number if that makes you feel any better. Although, I *do* know how to get it, so do with that fact what you will. And I am examining the building for weak spots."

"Is someone planning to attack my building or something?" The words were meant as a joke, but the more they lingered in the air, the more I felt that they were a possibility.

"Maybe," said Naziah. "Someone is always sent to examine the exterior of new students' buildings in case of that scenario. You joined the academy unpredictably, so that process never occurred. Until now."

"It's really that likely for someone to attack a student's building that IFON sends people to examine them?"

Naziah walked forward and didn't reply, which made me sure of the answer.

A lot of cars started honking abruptly, and I turned my head to look at the road. "Do you know why there's so much traffic?" I questioned.

"Why do you assume I would know?" Naziah kept walking, still looking at various parts of the building.

"Well, you came from the other direction."

"Very true. There was an accident. Somehow a truck ended up sideways on the road. Nobody will be moving for a while."

"Oh."

Naziah stopped suddenly, and I almost ran into her. She looked directly through the tall windows to her left. "Are all those people residents?" she asked.

I looked through the window as well at the crowd of people on the other side of the building's interior. The crowd had grown larger now, and a couple of security officers were in the mix.

I squinted to see the faces in the crowd better. "I don't think *any* of them are residents." Naziah kept walking, her eyes looking back at the top of the building. Nobody had seen us, or if they had, they weren't worried about us. Usually, people weren't allowed to wander around behind the building. Everyone was preoccupied about the traffic instead.

"Is there any way that I can help?" I asked. Being on Naziah's good side would be an advantage.

"Actually, I am done. Your windows do not appear to be bulletproof, which is not surprising. The building's exterior does not seem very flammable, considering the brick structure. The building's interior is definitely vulnerable to bullets and fire." It was admirable how much she was able to tell just from looking at the building for no more than five minutes. The fact that she *had* to examine it worried me, as apparently the apartment would be a perfect target for arsonists and shooters.

"As for yesterday, we will have to worry about that incident next week. Your entire focus should be on Saturday's trip," Naziah instructed. With the events of yesterday and today, the trip had been the last thing on my mind.

"You're right. Thanks," I told her.

She nodded. "Enjoy visiting your parents," she replied before heading back the way we'd come.

I thought to ask her how she knew, but it was kind of obvious, considering I no longer lived at the apartment. I turned around and walked that way as well.

Tomorrow would be the last day of school for this week, and I'd be going across the country the next day. I still had no idea when or how my parents would be persuaded to let me attend. Maybe they'd bring it up when I went inside.

Some more cars started honking, and a lot of people were sitting on their car hoods, waiting for the accident to be resolved. Part of me wondered if sitting in Miles's car tediously would be more tolerable than tomorrow's school day.

respite...maybe

IFON Academy
Gymnasium
Friday
1500 hours

Everyone was in their own space, some doing flips, others practicing kicks. If any other school would've required the class, weapons and combat would've been my least favorite. Any other group of kids my age would've made it awkward. At IFON, all the students were trying to be impressive. I'd never noticed anyone refusing to participate.

This class was my favorite as we were in a huge gymnasium with a lot of space, so there was little to no chance of injuring a classmate. During individual practice time, everyone was allowed to practice their fighting forms that we had learned in class. It was amazing as everyone got to be in their own world, fighting a group of people or combating one-on-one.

I imagined a person charging in front of me and dodged out of the way. In my mind, I saw them turning back and kicking toward my head. I ducked down and swung my leg, sweeping the invisible fighter off their feet. Quickly, I backed up and prepared for another potential attack.

Doing these exercises was easy as you were correctly predicting each of your opponent's moves.

My opponent rose up and threw a punch toward my neck. I leaned back, set my hands on the floor, and kicked my legs over my head, practically feeling my feet hit the opponent's hand. I caught a glimpse of Coach Taylor looking at me, which encouraged me to do even more.

Standing back on my feet, I went into offense mode. I threw a punch, hitting the opponent in their stomach. They fell back and rolled over, standing up again. I charged toward them before they could attack.

Charging toward air wasn't realistically the best move, but showing progress to Coach Taylor was my main goal. I wrapped my arms around the air and threw myself in an almost horizontal twist. I landed on my feet and quickly knelt down, imagining that I had the person pinned to the ground.

Our teacher's whistle blew, followed by her saying, "Excellent form, Jessie." I smiled and recalled in my head the move I had done. *Did I do a butterfly twist?* We'd watched Coach Taylor show us how to do the move, but it was supposed to be something we learned on Monday. Doing it after seeing it once would no doubt be an amazing impression.

Some kids looked at me and smiled, others giving an approving nod. The majority of the class kept their eyes on Coach Taylor.

Our instructor furrowed her eyebrows, looking from me to the other side of the room. "Naziah and Jessie, come here." My heart practically stopped as I got called up. Now, almost everyone was looking at me.

I stood up and slowly approached, Naziah already making her way to Coach Taylor. This was the only class I had with Naziah, and Coach Taylor constantly used her as an example for the rest of us. I had a feeling that most of my classmates found it annoying, but nobody would dare say it.

"I know I usually use Naziah as an example, but I'd like to do another brief activity," Coach Taylor explained. Naziah had reached the teacher's side before I did, and she appeared ready for anything. Coach Taylor looked at me. "Before we begin, do you think you're able to do the move again?"

There was no doubt in my mind that all forty-three of my classmates were looking at me.

"Uh… I can try," I told her, immediately regretting my decision. Then again, refusing would have been much worse. Coach Taylor and Naziah stepped back to give me room, the others watching expectantly.

My mind begged for the opponent to return so that I can take them down once again. I imagined the opponent reappearing, standing in a fighting position. With everyone watching me, I'd have to do much better than the first time. This time, I'd have to complete the move fully horizontal.

I leaned back on my right leg and then race forward. Running a couple of steps, I forced myself to wrap my arms around my opponent, incidentally wrapping my arms around myself. My legs pushed me off the ground high enough to twist fully horizontal. *Yes!* Quickly, gravity pulled me back toward the ground. I prepared the landing that I'd done during practice time, focusing on each foot. *Left, right, don't fall…left. Dang it.*

Some kids to the left of me applaud, with a few others on the bleachers to my right doing the same. I felt that tripping on the landing had ruined the whole move, but some seemed to enjoy it.

Part of me had expected Coach Taylor to comment on my performance, but instead, she taught the class.

"This is a move that is typically used in dance, specifically hip hop. With enough momentum and strength…" She ran forward two steps and launched herself into the twist, before landing perfectly. "The move is perfect for taking down opponents in an unexpected way."

Coach Taylor stood up straight. "We will learn how to do this formally on Monday. For those of you who can already do it—"

She looked at me. "You will have no problem acing the assessment."

Some of the kids who were leaning on the bleachers groan. "Yes, this will be an assessment grade. But only because it's very easy to learn!"

She walked back toward Naziah and me. "Before we do the final activity for today, we're going to play a little game of *Baby Mirror*."

Some *ooh*s came from around the gymnasium but ceased as soon as Coach Taylor held up her hand. "Jessie, you're the mirror."

Baby Mirror was a game we played every Friday, where Coach Taylor would choose two students. The mirror is essentially a "baby," who was learning to mirror everything the other player did. It was entertaining to watch as most of my classmates were pretty advanced. To be playing it would be much harder.

Please, go easy on me. Naziah started off with a front walkover. I did the same thing, mirroring her move. She then lowered herself, doing three spins that were similar to the move I had done during practice time. However, I'd never done three successfully. I attempted to spin on my left foot, with my right leg straightened. *One, two, falling...three.* I quickly hit the ground, feeling that Coach Taylor would mark it incorrect.

Naziah looked over her shoulder to the teacher, who didn't call me out. I stood up and looked over my shoulder as well, mimicking Naziah. Expecting it to be a test, a few kids laughed at my move. Naziah and I looked back to each other simultaneously. She turned away and launched herself into three consecutive cartwheels. Each step echoed against the walls, making the move seem a lot more intense than it was. *Easy.* I did three cartwheels in the same direction.

Naziah did a front flip, which had always scared me. Doing the move didn't feel worth the risk of breaking my skull on the hard floor, but the pressure was getting to me. I crouched and then flipped forward, landing on my feet, having to stumble forward.

Naziah turned around to Coach Taylor, probably wanting me to be called out. I turned around too, my back facing Naziah. Some more kids laughed, and it felt nice to be a source of entertainment. I turned around again, Naziah already facing me.

She leaned back for her next move, and I took a mental note of every contact she made with the floor. *Hands, feet, hands, feet, hands, feet...wow...feet.* The gymnasium went silent for a moment. I was not surprised that Naziah could do the move, but my mind couldn't even get myself to attempt it.

Coach Taylor blew her whistle, signaling the game was over. I was somewhat offended by her assumption that I couldn't do the move, but I appreciated her saving my life. Knowing myself, I just might have attempted it and woken up in a hospital.

"Everyone, split up as usual! Cherry, dear, please get the weapons. This will be our final activity for today!" We followed our instructions, and everyone started to get into two lines.

A hand set on my shoulder, and I turned around to see River. "Keep your head up," he said.

I nodded, embarrassed that it was easy to tell how disappointed I was. *If only I could've shown her up.*

"You know, there's a one percent chance that you had Naziah threatened there. She doesn't usually show up on newcomers like that."

"That's a pretty big chance."

River laughed, and I felt a bit more relieved. Donnay, Cory, and a girl whom I don't recognize came rushing over. The girl and Donnay obviously knew each other as they're whispering to each other while they approached.

"That coldhearted witch," Donnay scolded. "How dare she show off like that!" I could tell Donnay's joking, but Cory seemed to find it serious.

"Let's not insult her *that* much."

"She acts like we don't all know how good she is," the other girl said, ignoring Cory's comment.

"Right! If she was so exceptional, she would've skipped this grade," Donnay agreed.

Her comment made me wonder about Naziah, who was easily the most talented student in our grade, if not our school. Why hadn't she skipped?

River lowered his voice and leaned forward. "Let's go before Coach Taylor puts *all* of us up against you-know-who," he suggested. The girl laughed and was the first of us to join the rest of our class. There were two lines of students facing each other, most people standing in the line closest to their side of the gymnasium.

Our classmate Cherry was walking in between the two lines of students, pushing a red cart. She frequently reached in the cart and pulled out weapons, handing them to students from each line. Cherry had brown hair, neatly tied into pigtails that hung over her shoulder. White ribbons tied her hair and complemented her gorgeous white boots and white jumper. Just seeing her, she appeared very gentle and kind, like she'd never even harm a fly. Knowing what I knew about IFON, it was ironic and funny to me how she probably could fight very well and would effortlessly harm a person if it was necessary.

Cherry made her way to me and handed me a weapon. Thinking about how threatening the students at IFON were, I partially felt scared of her.

The weapons that were handed out were shaped like a pistol, but I was sure they were fake. "When you receive your weapon, practice the preeminent basic position," Coach Taylor instructed.

I leaned back on my right leg, holding the weapon straight, refusing to let my arms lock. Coach Taylor walked in between the two lines of students. To some students, she said, "Great job," and she stopped to adjust the form of other students.

After evaluating all of us, she gave her next instructions. "Aim your weapon to someone in the line you're not in." Many kids aimed their weapons at their friends. I aimed my weapon at a random girl in the other line. She scanned my line to see who—if anyone—was aiming at her. When she saw me, I expected her to get upset. To my surprise, she shifted her aim toward me and gave a cocky but playful smirk. I smiled, already excited for the next part of the exercise.

"On three, fire at your opponent. One, two, three!" I pulled the trigger, and water squirted from my weapon across the room. I felt water hit my face, and a lot of the room broke into laughter. My opponent and I fired at each other twice more before having enough water on both of us.

I attempted to dry my eyes with a damp part of my shirt and looked at the others. A few were still firing, with some trying to shake the water off them. Other students held their aim at their opponent, with a focused look on their face. They didn't appear like the type to play around during class. I couldn't see her from here, but I had a feeling that "you-know-who" was one of those students.

overdue

IFON Academy
Main entrance
Saturday
1750 hours

It had been two weeks since Michael had been taken. At this point, part of me wondered if there was even purpose in going on this trip. Michael was owed a lot, but he could've been anywhere by now.

To my right was the front desk, and Mrs. Kettle was seated at it. Olivia had told me that Lady Kate supported Mrs. Kettle returning to her position and believed that Mrs. Kettle wouldn't help people attack the refuge.

"It's almost six," Kaylani told me.

"I wonder where the others are," I responded.

Naziah was sitting on the bench opposite of us, reading a book. Unlike Kaylani and I who had each brought a large suitcase, Naziah had a relatively small suitcase with a black briefcase.

I looked over at Mrs. Kettle and thought to myself how she could potentially be dangerous. *What if Lady Kate misjudged?* Surely everyone at IFON was good at lying and defending themselves. Then again, why would Mrs. Kettle be against IFON? Maybe some people held grudges against the school. Maybe Mrs. Kettle wanted to be the principal but instead was assigned to desk duty. *You're just being paranoid.* Then again...

One of the front doors opened, and I looked to my left. Olivia pulled her rolling suitcase inside the building. To my relief, Olivia didn't appear as paranoid as I felt. She had the same upbeat and positive attitude that I needed this morning.

"Good morning!" she called, her voice loud in the room. Naziah shooshed Olivia, but I was pleased to hear my friend's voice.

"Well, she's cranky today," Olivia observed, coming to sit with Kaylani and me.

As Olivia sat down, I gave her a hug. "Aw, you all right, Jessie?"

"A little nervous," I admitted.

Olivia hugged me tighter and motioned for Kaylani to join in.

"You're with us, Jess," Kaylani said, joining the hug. "No need to be nervous. Everything's gonna go perfect."

Olivia's understanding with Kaylani's assurance felt just like what I needed. All I was missing was Donnay's aggressiveness, telling me how stupid I was acting.

"Did you see Donnay out there?" I asked Olivia. We separated the hug, and Kaylani kept her hand on my shoulder.

"No, but I saw two really big guys who looked important. I think they might be our chaperones."

The doors opened, and two men stepped inside the building. They're both dressed in tuxedos and big like Olivia had described them. With these people as our chaperones, I wouldn't have feared anyone would approach us. Then again, they would draw a lot of attention in an airport. We would appear as famous kids with two bodyguards. It would be funny if people started taking pictures and thought that we were celebrities.

The men approached the front desk, probably to tell Mrs. Kettle why they were here. Other than Mrs. Kettle's sweet "Hello!" I couldn't make out the rest of the conversation.

One of the front doors opened again, with another man entering the building. He had a clipboard under one arm and a pencil above his right ear. His pink hair was a bit lighter than his magenta pants, and it was obvious that he didn't wear sunscreen properly as patches of his pale arms were heavily tanned.

"Are these the children?" he asked, and one of the bigger guys turned around and nodded.

"Great." The skinnier guy sighed. "I'm Brian Smith, but you can call me Brian."

"Hey, Brian!" Olivia smiled.

Brian's voice was high-pitched, and he talked so fast that I had to replay his words in my head to understand them.

The bigger guys approached one side of the room each, picking up our luggage. Naziah sat a hand on hers, signaling that she'd carry her own.

Brian pulled his clipboard from under his arm and reached for his pencil. He muttered to himself, checking things off on his paper.

"Wait, wait!" He scanned the room. "There are supposed to be five girls. Where's the other one?"

"She should be here soon," Kaylani told him.

Everyone turned their head as the front doors opened, and Donnay came inside. She dropped a plastic bag on the floor, swung forward her two rolling suitcases, and snatched her other suitcase that was stuck in the door. She breathed heavily and leaned on one of the rolling suitcases.

"Hey, guys."

"Grab those and let's move," Brian directed to the guards before rushing past Donnay and stepping outside. The guards grabbed some of Donnay's luggage each before following Brian. Donnay took deep breaths while looking outside at the men departing.

"Those are our chaperones?" she asked.

I nodded and then stood up with the other girls. Naziah rushed outside.

Donnay shook her head and took another deep breath and then laughed. "This is gonna be fun."

improvise

We hadn't even been inside the airport for one minute before Donnay fell asleep.

Kaylani had suggested we wait until we boarded the plane before taking naps. Donnay had agreed but obviously failed to maintain her compliance. Brian was still making his way inside, saying that he had something to do. As for me, I was astounded by the fact that I'd made it inside the airport without my parents calling me to tell me that I wasn't allowed to go. Whatever Lady Kate told them had obviously worked.

"I still don't get why we're going on this trip," I whisper to Kaylani. "Michael could be *anywhere* by now."

"It's worth a try, Jess. And we're not just going to find Michael. There's someone else we have to look for."

A gentle "Excuse me" came from behind us, and I saw Brian making his way past a group of people.

"Who's the 'someone else'?" I asked Kaylani.

Brain waved at us and motioned us over.

"I'll tell you later," Kaylani responded.

Olivia shook Donnay awake, and we rose from the benches to approach Brian. Brian started walking, leading us to where we got our bags scanned.

The airport was very loud and crowded. There were a lot of older teens and young adults travelling. Part of this surprised me, as

125

going to IFON had made me forget that most people were on summer break. *How great for them.*

We walked past a lot of people in groups with their family or friends, and as I suspected, we got a lot of stares. The guys dressed in tuxedos didn't exactly blend us in well, and none of us looked related. One person had their phone pointing at us, though I couldn't tell if they were taking pictures or recording.

At the area for baggage checks, we were somehow able to skip the line. Brian had shown an ID to an officer, or *tried* to, at least. He had dropped his ID, and one of his bodyguards had to present it for him. After observing the ID, the officer escorted us past the line and behind those who were already getting their bags checked. This special treatment put more eyes on us, and I felt very conscious of everything I did. We'd probably draw a lot of attention until we actually boarded the plane.

The people in front of us moved forward, and Naziah set her things on the belt to be x-rayed. She walked through what looked like a metal detector while the guards set the rest of our luggage on the belt. The rest of us passed through the detector one by one.

The guards took our luggage after they were x-rayed, and they continued to follow Brian. We continued to walk as a group and eventually approached a long line of people. I assumed this was the line for getting the tickets to board the plane. As we get closer to the line, my phone dinged twice.

We stopped at the back of the line, and I looked at the guard holding my luggage. *I wonder if that was my parents...*

"You kids grab some sodas while we get our boarding passes." Brian pulled out his wallet and handed Kaylani some cash. Donnay was the first to exit the line and start looking for a vending machine. I approached the guard holding my luggage and spotted my phone in one of the side pockets. The guard didn't seem to have an issue with me taking my phone. I slid it in my pocket and then quickly followed Donnay, with Kaylani and Olivia.

"How much do we have to spend?" Donnay asked.

Kaylani looked at the money in her hand, and her eyes widened. "A lot," she said.

We stopped walking and observed the money.

"What soda costs thirty dollars?" puzzled Olivia.

Donnay snatched the money from Kaylani and held it close to her stomach. "I'll keep this safe," she assured us, starting to walk again.

"She's going to spend it, isn't she?" I asked.

Kaylani laughed and started to catch up with Donnay.

The four of us spotted a vending machine and raced toward it. A lot of people got out of our way as we ran to the machine like five-year-olds running in a playground. I didn't notice myself laughing along with my friends until I thought to appreciate how much fun I was having.

We slowed down at the machine, and Donnay quickly punched in the number for a coke. *Don't have too much fun. Remember why you're here.* The thought caught me off guard, and I felt my smile fade away immediately. As much as I wanted to find Michael, it'd be almost impossible to think straight if I was feeling miserable and depressed. With everything that happened in the last couple of weeks, having some fun seemed like a good idea.

Donnay refused to hand over any of the money to us and instead had us tell her what we wanted. She spent the rest of the money on a bag of chips and six chocolate bars. Olivia took the snacks and stuffed them inside her purse.

"Are these chocolates for the guards?" Olivia asked.

"No!" scoffed Donnay. "They're for me."

"I doubt we even need guards with Naziah," I commented.

Donnay rolled her eyes. "We don't need guards with *me*," she corrected. Kaylani snickered and side hugged Donnay.

"Flight AR 301 headed to California is temporarily delayed. Please stand by." The words came startlingly from speakers installed in the high ceiling, and I felt my heart rate speed up immediately.

Kaylani urged us to look for the others, so we ran back to the line. The airport was a lot louder with people discussing the delay, and I wondered how many people would be on our flight.

When we reached the line, the guards, Brian, and Naziah were no longer in their spot, but Olivia pointed them out at the front of the line. I assumed that Brian had been able to get us through this line as he had with the line for baggage checks.

We walked around the line, a few people staring at us as we passed. We stopped at the table where our guards were retrieving our boarding passes. They no longer had our luggage except for Donnay's plastic bag and Naziah's briefcase. I assumed they had already traded our larger luggage for the passes.

"There you are." Brian sighed, seeing the four of us returning. "We have to get to the gate. It's not far from here at all."

"There will be an eight-hour delay for flight AR 301 headed to California. Passengers of flight AR 301, please approach gate 11. Once again, passengers of delayed flight AR 301, please approach gate 11."

The intercom turned off as the airport grew even louder. Brian muttered under his breath and pulled out his phone. The guards now had our tickets in their hands and left the table. The rest of us followed, allowing the next people in line to get their tickets.

I glanced at Naziah and saw that she appeared surprisingly calm. Kaylani, on the other hand, looked annoyed.

"You all right?" I asked. She nodded, furrowing her eyebrows as if to emphasize that she was obviously fine.

Naziah made her way closer to the four of us girls. The guards left our luggage against the wall and stood next to them, standing straight and tall, with their hands gripping tickets by their side.

Donnay sighed. "Man. I wish I could be like one of them. Get paid just for standing and looking pretty."

"You should be our linguistics teacher," Naziah suggested.

Her tone had been so solemn that I didn't realize it was a joke until replaying her comment in my head. Donnay wagged her thumb at Naziah, eyes widened and laughing.

Brian walked closer and towered over us. "You girls go stand by our guards."

Naziah was first to leave, and Donnay scoffed at the suggestion. "I'm tellin' you, y'all only need me."

Brian talked on the phone for about thirty more seconds before coming closer to the rest of us. "All right, let's get to the gate," he instructed. We started walking, and the guards took our luggage once again.

The airport was very busy, with a lot of workers in the airline's uniform rushing through crowds. Some passengers were complaining about the delay, with others bragging to their family about how blessed they were to not have a delayed flight.

Brian had been right about the gate not being far. We passed a couple of escalators that went upstairs. I'd wanted to walk on it, even if just to come back down. Although, we still had to get to our gate.

It was easy to point out gate 11 as it had the most people and the most workers. I could see three staff members with one man, who seemed to be in a heated argument. There were families seated who were complaining and other families gossiping as they walked past the gate.

Everyone except Brian went to take a seat. He went to the front table, but I wasn't sure why. The guards sat across from us, a seat apart from Naziah. Kaylani took a seat next to me as I pulled out my phone from my pocket.

As I looked for my recent texts, I remembered the fear of thinking that my parents had texted me saying I couldn't get on the flight. Relief washed over me when I read what they really *had* texted. In our family group chat, my parents had told me to have a great time at camp, with Miles telling me to stay safe. "Thank you, and I will!" I replied.

It didn't surprise me that Lady Kate had told my parents I was going to camp. However, it made me feel bad that they didn't know the truth. My phone vibrated in my hand at the same time that Kaylani's made a sound.

I checked the text and saw it was from the *BFFs For Life* group chat. "Finniake and River wish us a fun trip," I reported to Kaylani as I read the text.

"I wonder who told them," she said.

Even though I'd only been at the school for two weeks, I knew that students at IFON loved gossip. It didn't surprise me that they found out we were leaving. There was no way they knew *why* we were leaving, and as long as they didn't know that, they didn't know too much.

Brian approached us from the front table. "New plan!" he announced, crouching to be on the same level as the rest of us. He lowered his voice and explained the revised proposal. "We may have to take another flight to Missouri, stay there for about two hours, and then get another flight to California if we want to stay on schedule."

My brain said, "What?" but my mouth kept quiet. I didn't doubt that Brian could pull the strings he needed to get us to California, but waiting until the delay was over seemed much easier. Naziah showed no emotion toward the change, and Donnay seemed mostly excited. I looked at Olivia, who was sympathetically looking at Kaylani. Turning my head to Kaylani, I noticed her face buried in her hands, appearing more distressed than I'd ever seen her.

And I couldn't remember a time I'd seen Kaylani distressed.

it takes two

Washington National Airport
Saturday
1855 hours

Olivia, Kaylani, and I had been playing games on our phones and walking around for the past twenty minutes. Donnay was napping, and Naziah was watching everyone. I would've found it boring to sit still and observe everything going on around you, but she seemed to have a blast doing it. Kaylani even asked Naziah if she wanted to join the three of us in playing hand games, but I wasn't surprised when she declined the offer.

We were in gate 16, which was less than a minute's walk from gate 11. By the time Brian was walking over to us with his guards behind him, the three of us were drained and slumping in our seats.

"Good news, girls!" Brian smiled as he approached us. Donnay, laid out across two and a half seats, turned onto her other side at the sound of Brian's voice. "There have been arrangements despite this unpredictable delay. We will be boarding two flights today, flight LS 553 to Missouri, and flight RS 185 to California. We'll still be on schedule!"

Kaylani's tired expression becomes sorrowful, and she quickly asks to be excused. She rose and walked away, leaving the gate. "Our flight's departure should be soon, but it'll be announced overhead," Brian explained to Olivia, Naziah, and me, motioning at the speakers in the ceiling.

Brian's guards took their seats, and Brian sat down as well. I sighed and heard a large group of people passed our gate. They looked like a family and walked down the large and wide hallway. There were a lot of other people at our gate, and they picked up in conversation.

Olivia moved to the seat next to me where Kaylani had been. "Do you know where they're going?" she asked.

"Probably to board their flight," I responded.

"No, not the family. Kaylani and Naziah."

I looked around and noticed Kaylani leaning on the wall across the wide hallway. Naziah said something to her, and they both walked in the direction that the passing family had been heading. Naziah had moved so quickly and stealthily that even the guards who had been next to her didn't seem to notice her absence.

"I guess we'll have to ask them," I said.

"Oh, I already know why. I was just asking if you knew."

"Well then, why are they leaving?"

"To talk about Damian," Olivia replied and didn't seem to have any intention of explaining.

"Who's Damian?"

"You don't know? He's Kaylani's cousin."

"Why would they be talking about him?"

Olivia glanced over at Brian and the guards before leaning closer to me. Part of me felt excited to hear something that was obviously a secret. I pushed down my excitement and focused on understanding whatever Olivia would be explaining.

"Damian was a student at IFON," she said. "A prized student, actually. He's supposedly in California. He got kidnapped during his senior year while Kaylani was still in her first year. From what I know, she's been researching where she might be and is positive that he's in California. Which would make sense considering Michael got kidnapped and is probably there too."

"How would those connect?" I asked. "Michael never went to IFON."

"How do you know?" I scoffed at the idea, but her question seemed to be genuine.

"What else about Damian?" I asked, not ready to think about the possibility of Michael having attended IFON.

"Well, this isn't the first time he's been kidnapped," she went on. "The first time it happened, he came back with his kidnapper. I heard that the person was tortured in prison and still didn't give up any useful information. So he got executed. Killed."

"Yeah, I know what *executed* means. That's crazy."

"Eh, that part's just a rumor. He may still be at the penitentiary. But Damian was able to defend himself that time. This time, he's been gone for... I think seven months." She scrunched her eyebrows and looked up, trying to recall the number of months. I felt myself grow impatient as there were other things I wanted to know.

"Yeah... I was right. Seven months. Kaylani joined the case and found out more than staff members did. Which is why she really wants to get to California as soon as possible. I don't know why she's so upset, though. We're still gonna be on schedule."

Donnay turned onto her back and yawned. "Good morning," she muttered, almost too soft for me to hear over the other ongoing discussions in the gate.

I replayed some of what Olivia had said in my head. It was a lot to process, but I already had my summary determined. If Kaylani and Naziah were planning to help Damian, I'd be on my own to help Michael.

I took my phone from my pocket and started to text Lion. There was a possibility Michael had told Lion more about the trip to California than he told Kaylani and me. Lion had said that he and Michael last talked on Saturday, and Michael had been packing. Maybe there was something else before that...

My only other option would be to go to Michael's house, which wasn't a very possible option. I sighed in frustration that the only thing I could do was anxiously wait for Lion to reply.

Donnay groggily stood up and went to sit in the seat to my right. She leaned on my shoulder.

"So texting's your plan?" she asked. I looked at her in confusion. "To find Michael..." she went on. I felt slightly embarrassed that it was obvious what I was doing.

"Don't worry. I only noticed it because I'm good." She hesitated about saying her next sentence. "And…because I'm an IFON student. We learn to notice things that normal people don't." *I'll have to do just that.*

I couldn't rely on Lion replying. So I acted on plan B: using the information that I already had. If our flight to California was delayed, then Michael wouldn't have gotten there yet. Unless there was another flight that had already left…

"Brian, when was the last flight that left for California?" I asked. Donnay slightly nodded in approval.

"Uh…" Brian stammered, pulling his phone from his pocket.

"When was the last flight that left for California?" he spoke into his phone and then scrolled on the screen. "Three weeks ago."

"I have to use the bathroom," I quickly said before standing up.

"They'll call our flight soon!" Brian called as I ran into the large hallway.

A few people stared at me, but I was too excited to worry about them.

I looked to the direction where Naziah and Kaylani went. *They're doing their own thing. You do yours.* I hesitantly went the other way, back toward gate 11. If Brian was right, then there was no way Michael had made it to California. Unless he was riding in a car, which would take days, there was a chance he was in this very airport.

Running to the gate, I looked at the large groups of people for Michael. It frustrated me that I couldn't remember what the driver of the moving van looked like. I desperately scanned the crowds who were seated and even examined the staff workers. The intercom had yet to be used for announcing what passengers of flight AR 301 should do. I felt bad for them having to wait eight hours, but there wasn't much time to show sympathy.

Nobody at the gate looked like Michael, and the only faces I recognized were faces I had seen earlier while walking through the terminal. Frustrated, I went back to gate 16. I slowed down, unsure of what my next step would be.

From the wide hallway of the terminal, I could see a person in a wheelchair boarding our flight. I went into the gate and went behind the person who was boarding. Two guards—much skinnier than ours—are posted on either side of the door.

The person in the wheelchair pushed their wheels until they made it onto the airplane. I walked behind the person, foolishly wondering if I'd be able to board the plane as well. Each officer stretched an arm across the doorway, blocking me from entering.

"Handicap only," they said concurrently. *Like robots.*

One officer held their unoccupied hand to their ear, and I noticed that each officer had a black earpiece. The same officer lowered his hand to his side. "Please be seated until further notice," he directed.

I turned around, stunned at my nimble ability to determine my next move. I walked forward, not wanting to get into trouble with the officer, and scanned the gate for Kaylani and Naziah. They had already returned and were standing by the wall across from where the rest of our group was seated. I looked to the group, who didn't seem to notice me.

Walking toward Kaylani and Naziah, they saw me right away. Kaylani appeared less worried, and I assumed Naziah had found a way to calm her down. Either that, or they had a decent plan to find Damian.

"We have to board the plane as handicapped," I told them, still approaching. The rest of the gate was pretty loud, and there were no seats this close to the wall. I wasn't worried about people overhearing.

"Why?" Kaylani asked. "I just have a gut feeling, you know?" I explained, not exactly knowing why I felt the need to act so soon. "I think Michael may be here. I just feel like he is. We're close to him. I don't know how I know, but… I do."

There's no way they'll take this seriously. I really did feel like we were close to Michael, and that every second we stood doing nothing was a second being wasted. The only thing I could think of was to board the plane quickly.

"Emotions are not reliable enough to act on," Naziah retorted. I sighed, upset that I'd expected much more. "Although, the gut of an IFON student generally is. Explain the plan."

It felt childish in the moment, but I was sure we were working together as a team. Just speaking to people like Finniake and River,

I'd learned that Naziah wasn't very social and wasn't fond of team-work unless she was the leader. But we wouldn't be able to work together without a plan.

"We have to get on the plane right now," I said. "But they're only letting handicapped people board."

"That's not a plan. That's a conflict," Kaylani explained.

"A *compulsive* conflict," Naziah corrected her. "Airlines would typically not board anyone without announcing it to the terminal to reduce the chance of passengers missing their flight."

I had to repeat Naziah's words in my head for them to make sense. "I haven't thought out the solution," I admitted, relieved that neither of them seemed annoyed at my incompetence.

"Maybe we could get wheelchairs and board the plane," I wondered aloud. "Well, they've already seen me. Maybe *you* can get wheelchairs."

Naziah gently shook her head, seemingly thinking of a better strategy.

Before she could suggest anything, the intercom turned on. "Flight LS 553 is now boarding passengers. Once again, flight LS 553 is now boarding passengers."

The conversations from passengers in our gate had died down while the announcement was made. I could hear Brian's cheerful "That's us, guys!" from across the room before conversation picked back up.

Kaylani leaned toward me. "We still need those wheelchairs?"

I shook my head, and Naziah started to go back to our group. A lot of people stood up to board the plane, and Kaylani and I rushed behind Naziah.

Our group hadn't been seated far from the door, and Brian had raced to be first to board. He stood, waiting for the rest of us. The guards were after him and gave their boarding passes to one of the officers. The officer bent each pass and tore it into two pieces, giving the smaller piece of each pass back to our guards. After returning parts of the boarding passes, the officers allowed us to board the plane.

We walked down the aisle of the plane, and I looked back and forth for the person who boarded the plane in a wheelchair.

"Notice anything?" Donnay asked.

My heart jumped at her voice as I hadn't noticed how close she was behind me.

"Unfortunately not," I told her.

Brian led us to first class, and I still hadn't seen the person in the wheelchair who had boarded earlier. Considering how rich IFON was, it didn't surprise me that we were in first class.

Brian motioned at the eight seats that we were to sit in. In front of each pair of seats was a table and a television, with a three-foot divisor separating each table from the aisle. The chairs were bright white, and the tables were made of glass.

"I call window seat!" Donnay exclaimed, sliding into the row closest to her.

"Not fair!" complained Olivia, tugging Donnay's shirt.

There was no use—Donnay was already comfortable in her seat, and Olivia hesitantly sat next to her.

Kaylani took my hand and went to the pair of seats across from Olivia and Donnay. She took the window seat, but I didn't mind.

I reached for the remote on my table, but Kaylani smacked it out of my hand.

"Hey!" The remote hit the table and made a clattering sound. Part of me feared the glass would shatter, but I was relieved to see that it wasn't even scratched.

"We have something else to focus on," Kaylani said, raising her eyebrows. I sighed, upset that I'd gotten distracted so easily.

"Do you really think he's on this flight?" she asked.

"I pray so," I admitted. "He's either here or waiting to board our old flight. Or riding in a car." It felt hard to determine which possibility was most likely.

"Either way, we'll meet him when we get there," Kaylani shrugged. I couldn't determine if she truly believed what she was saying, but what meant more was whether or not *I* believed her words.

I tried to recall what I'd learned from my friends that would help me, because each second that passed felt like a waste of time. I wouldn't be able to find Michael alone. Naziah would've been someone to help as she proved herself to be very competent.

To find Michael, starting from the beginning may have been the best option. In the beginning, I had taken pictures of the moving truck. Even though Kaylani and Professor Jones had reviewed the license plate, maybe Naziah would recognize it. I didn't know Naziah very well—nobody did—but I had to trust her. *In order to do our job, we have to trust everyone on our side.*

"Naziah," I called.

Naziah leaned into the aisle from the seat in front of me.

"Can you tell me if you recognize this picture?" I asked. I went to the picture on my phone and handed it to her. She sat properly in her seat again, reviewing the photo.

Kaylani looked at me and gave an approving smile.

"Nothing about it is recognizable," Naziah reported. "I can run the plate if you want."

"You can do that?" I asked, annoyed at my response. "I mean, yeah. Thanks."

Naziah stood up and approached where the guards were seated. She retrieved her suitcase and took her phone from it.

"How can she run a plate on her phone?" I asked Kaylani.

"She has an IFON device," she replied. "The school gave it to her. It's separate from her personal phone and has access to a lot of important files and information for the school."

"The plate is dormant," Naziah said to me.

"What?"

There was a loud laugh from farther back in the plane, and everyone with an aisle seat leaned into the aisle to look as far back as we could. Nobody else had boarded with first class yet, but a lot of people were going to business and economy.

"The plate is inactive," Naziah rephrased. "Unregistered."

"It was registered to California a week ago," Kaylani responded.

"It takes months to register a plate, but only about a week to unregister one," explained Naziah. "That means you cannot track it."

"They'd only unregister it if they didn't want to be tracked," I thought aloud. Kaylani sighed, understanding my point. Maybe Michael would be riding to California.

"Nobody would be able to get from here to California with an unregistered plate," Naziah informed. "It would be virtually impossible. News of plates being unregistered gets across the police system quickly, and it takes almost two days to drive to California from here. They would not be able to stay on the road for that long without getting arrested."

"Maybe they got another car," Kaylani suggested.

"Welcome! We ask that all passengers please take their seats as we will depart shortly."

The speaker audibly turned off, and some other passengers eagerly talked louder.

"Whatever you do to find your friend, you should do it fast," Olivia said to me. "Unless you don't like it at IFON, in which case you'll be fine when you're removed."

Donnay nudged Olivia, and Naziah sighed in frustration. I looked at Kaylani who appeared just as confused as I was.

"What are you talking about?" I asked.

Olivia pursed her lips and looked from me to Donnay. Donnay rolled her eyes and sat back in her seat. "Olivia, what are you talking about?" I repeated, raising my voice. She sadly looked down, and part of me felt bad for snapping at her. Then again, she was obviously keeping secrets from me.

"You're only here because of Michael, you know that, right?"

Kaylani repeated my "What are you talking about?"

"Michael's parents work for an agency that's trying to put IFON out of business. Since you're close to Michael and your brother already attends, Lady Kate thought that bringing you to IFON temporarily would only do some good. You might be able to find Michael!"

"No, that's not why I'm here," I shook my head. "Obviously, I'm not here to find Michael. I'm here to take the risk for IFON and find Michael's parents."

"That's not it, Jessie," argued Donnay.

"No, it's definitely it. So the whole school knows I'm just a pawn?"

Kaylani shook her head, but I was too upset to feel comforted about Kaylani's honesty. "Your brother mentioned it one time, but I didn't think much of it," she told me.

Naziah reached back with my phone in her hand. I snatched it from her and shoved it in my pocket. "Have a great flight," I said. I stood from my seat and started walking down the aisle out of first class. Brian called after me but was interrupted by Kaylani's "I'll do it." I kept walking, hearing Donnay scoff as I entered business class.

There were a lot more passengers than I'd expected, and I hoped that none of them had heard our conversation. Kaylani rushed past me and sat in an aisle seat with an empty window seat next to her. I walked past her, not wanting to stay on the plane.

An officer was standing in front of the closed door that went back to the gate. "It's too late to get off the flight," he called down the aisle before I could even enter the economy class. Some people stopped talking and looked at me. In the terminal, I'd thought we would finally be able to draw less attention when we got on the plane. Yet, here I was, drawing attention to myself. I stopped walking and hesitantly turned around.

Kaylani was watching me from her seat and motioned me to sit next to her. "You knew I wouldn't be able to leave?" I asked.

Kaylani gave a small smile.

I looked out the window and saw a flat terrain that seemed to reach for miles. She sighed and leaned on the table in front of her. The tables in business class held desktops and the same glass tables as ours.

"Did you hear about my cousin?" Kaylani asked.

"Yeah, Olivia told me."

"Well, I found a way to contact him."

"Really? That's amazing… I thought he went missing."

"He did. I talked to him on the phone not too long ago. He told me that he was free from his kidnapper and was stuck in California. So I told him I'd be going there with you."

"So this was recent?"

"Yeah. It happened early Wednesday morning. I'd been doing research on the day he went missing and emailed him. He called me instead of emailing back."

"All it took was an email? You'd think the staff could've done that."

"I think he would only talk to me. I told him what Naziah had told me: we would be riding with Teviree Airlines. But when we get to Missouri, we'll have to take another airline to get to California."

She looked at me and held my hand. "I just wanted to let you know that you're not the only one struggling." She leaned into the aisle and looked toward first class. "Trust me, you weren't the only one betrayed here. Miles had tried to tell me that you weren't a real student, but I'm surprised none of them did. Maybe they knew I would tell you in an instant."

Her words made me feel comforted, and the feeling I had during science class on the last day of school came back to me. Kaylani and I shared intelligence, secrets, and a strong friendship. We were inseparable, and everyone around us knew it. Going to IFON made me question our friendship, but my best friend still hadn't changed.

"In all honesty, you can still earn your spot at IFON," Kaylani said. "I know you may not like it here, and I like it a lot less knowing how you've been treated. But if Lady Kate is good at anything, it's recognizing talent. You just have to prove yourself worthy of your spot. Then we can both go to the same place for high school. You could be a legend at IFON by then."

"I think Naziah already filled that spot," I said. Kaylani and I laughed, but what she was saying was true.

IFON meant a lot less to me knowing that I was only a pawn to be thrown into crossfire. Although, if I were to rescue Michael, help Kaylani find Damian, *and* retrieve Michael's supposedly rival parents, then I'd be more than worthy. The idea was near impossible, but I wouldn't have the others to weigh me down. I was no longer fighting with IFON or against them.

Now, it would just be Kaylani and me against the world.

forging fantasy

Washington National Airport
Flight LS 553
Saturday
1940 hours

The safety rules had been explained over the speakers, which was odd, as I'd expected a flight attendant to demonstrate them in person. Hopefully, we wouldn't have to put them to use anyways.

Kaylani and I were back in our seats in first class. Kaylani let me have the window seat, and I had been staring out of my window ever since we returned. Being with the group again felt embarrassing and uncomfortable. I was angry at myself for storming off but upset with the rest of them for keeping secrets.

The speakers turned back on, and our flight attendant announced that the plane would be taking off in thirty seconds.

The engine was already running, and I felt extremely nervous about leaving for Missouri. Over a week ago, I had promised Mom that I wouldn't be far off. Yet, here I was, planning to fly across the country with my best friend and six other people who I didn't know as well as I had thought. *I really have to stop making promises.*

In the peripheral of my vision, I could see the grass starting to move. No, *we* were moving. Kaylani grabbed my hand and smiled, leaning forward to look out of the window for herself. The other discussions in the plane picked up, and more people were talking about our departure.

I looked across the aisle and saw Donnay and Olivia whispering to one another.

"I'm so excited!" Kaylani whisper-shouted.

"Me too," I lied.

The plane started to move faster and approached the runway.

"Takeoff will be the best part," said Kaylani.

I looked at my best friend who was eagerly watching the things we were passing. "I think that's the landing," I disagreed.

Kaylani sat back in her seat and grabbed her armrests. I couldn't help but smile at her eagerness. I slightly shifted my gaze to Donnay, who was looking at me. I quickly looked back outside, trying to reimagine her expression. She hadn't appeared upset, but not comforting either.

I could gently hear Olivia's voice across the aisle and wondered if she was just as excited about the takeoff as Kaylani.

The plane was going very fast now, and my stomach felt as if it was filled with butterflies. I was full of nervousness, mixed with a bit of excitement. The plane gradually slowed, approaching the end of the runway. The wheels turned, redirecting the plane back in the direction we had come.

Everyone could feel the redirection, and Kaylani looked outside again. "What's going on?"

Eventually, we slowed to a stop, and the passengers grew very loud. I could make out some comments, like "What happened?" but it was obvious that nobody knew why we were stopped.

Two loud sounds came from toward the cockpit and echoed throughout the entire plane. Naziah stood from her seat and started going through her briefcase.

Olivia pressed back into her seat to allow Donnay to stand and step into the aisle. I watched as Donnay went down the aisle, heading for the back of the plane and tapping people while she went.

"What're they doing?" I whispered to Kaylani.

"Trying to help people evacuate," she replied. "I think anybody on this plane could recognize that sound, so it's probably not safe to stay here."

Before I could ask what the sound was, it occurred again, echoing against the interior walls of the airplane. The reverberation made me nervous and worried the other passengers as well. Many people were standing in the aisle, and I assumed Donnay was leading them. By now, I was sure that the sounds were gunshots.

The sound of glass shattering came from the front of the plane. Kaylani leaned into the aisle, looking from the front of the plane to the back.

Brian stepped into the aisle and motioned for his guards to follow him. They started walking to the front of the plane.

"Shouldn't we be leaving too?" I questioned, not liking the idea of being trapped in an airplane with someone who has a gun.

"You should," Kaylani told me. "The rest of us are gonna stay behind."

"Why only me?"

"You don't know how to defend yourself," Olivia explained.

I looked across the aisle to her, and she seemed sad about her own words. The thought of protesting came to mind, but it wouldn't have done much good. They obviously knew what they were doing.

Kaylani made room for me to walk past her and into the aisle. Donnay brushed past me, and most of the people in the plane were already outside. I rushed down the aisle, with the eerie feeling that someone behind me was aiming a gun directly at me. My paranoia caused me to glance over my shoulder, only to see that my associates were all seemingly focused on the same task.

I looked forward again, and all the other passengers had left through one of the emergency exits.

Stepping into the economy class, I could see sunlight shining into the plane from where the exit was. I slowed down to glance over my shoulder. *I should've kept running.*

I noticed a movement to my right, and the force slammed into my side before I could react. My head hit one of the armrests, and the person towered over me. They were dressed with what appeared to be a tuxedo, but the black mask that only revealed their eyes was what threatened me. They made a fist and prepared to throw it down onto me.

There was no way I wanted to be in more pain—I rolled myself onto the floor and heard their fist hit the armrest.

"Jessie!" Olivia called for me from the front of the plane.

The opponent's hands grabbed me by the back of my shirt until I was standing. They kept a grip with one hand and used the other to punch my back.

They loosened their grip, letting me fall to the floor. I desperately kicked my legs, hitting the person in the face. Crawling away, I could see Naziah in the aisle, holding something that looked like a gun. *Give her a clear shot.*

The person grabbed my legs and dragged me across the aisle floor. I quickly sit up and put all of my effort into kicking the person. My foot hits them in their stomach, and the person lets go with one hand to grasp where I'd harmed them. I lean forward and grab their shirt, using both legs to lift them over me and slam them to the floor.

"Now, Naziah!" I shouted. I scrambled to one of the seats and watched as the person got back up. They lunged toward me and froze.

Without the sounds of grunting and head-on impact, it felt like the whole plane went silent. The person collapsed to the floor. Everything felt still, and the loudest thing was my heavy breathing.

I stepped over the person and into the aisle to see Naziah approaching me.

"You have to leave with the others," she said.

I looked down at the person and saw a red dart in their neck. Naziah placed her weapon in her pocket.

"How'd you get that in?" I asked.

"Their security is lousy," she replied. "It was easy to slide my dart gun past the x-ray without anybody noticing."

"Surely, you don't think you're the only one taking advantage of that?"

Naziah stared at me, and I couldn't tell if she was annoyed by my comment.

She took hold of my arm and turned around, pulling me back toward the front of the plane. "The others left through the emergency exit in first class. I told them I would stay behind to help you," she explained. "I have yet to enter the cockpit, but I will leave you here in case something happens to me."

"Why am I staying?"

Naziah stopped walking and sighed. "Your audacity can prove useful." She let go of my arm and kept walking. I followed her, passing two small bathrooms and going through the business and first classes. Naziah motioned for me to stay where I was while she kept walking forward.

Directly to my left was the open exit in first class that I assumed the others had used. Looking out the door and the window to my right, all I could see was grass. The airplane engine had been off for a while, which would make it easier to hear what was happening in the cockpit.

Having stood for about a minute, I started to worry about Naziah. I didn't doubt that she could take care of herself, but it seemed like she would've called me.

I hesitantly walked forward, noticing that the hallway got more narrow. Naziah was standing at a closed door, looking into the lock. "I doubt you can see anything like that."

Naziah abruptly pushed back from the door and gave me a cold stare. "I need to know how to pick the lock. You cannot see anything inside, meaning it can be one of two styles." She pulled a bobby pin from her pocket and inserted it into the lock.

The door appeared to be white plastic, and I was surprised Naziah didn't just kick it down. "How do you like IFON?" The question caught me off guard as I didn't think Naziah would want to converse while she was trying to pick the lock.

"I think that's more of a question for a student," I deflected.

Naziah shifted her focus from the lock to me, giving me a cold stare. "You *are* an IFON student. Nobody here has promised you friendship or consistent honesty. You cannot blame anybody else for the fantasy that you convinced yourself was real."

Naziah seemed to recognize my frustration. "Lady Kate *is* one of the smartest people in existence," she continued. "She can recognize talent. You were brought in as bait. Although, you can prove you deserve your place at the academy. If that is something you want."

Knowing that Kaylani had said something similar, I started to believe it even more.

"Ultimately, it is better to make a reality than to pretend it already exists," she added. She looked back at the lock and twisted the bobby pin.

Naziah was able to slide the door open in under ten seconds and held out a hand as if to say, "Stay put." I watched her disappear into what I assumed was the cockpit.

"Uh, Jessie?"

I stepped forward and looked into the room.

The cockpit had lots of lights and controls lining the walls and on the ceiling. There were even more controls and switches in front of each seat for the pilot and copilot—neither one was here. The floors were covered in broken glass as the three windows of the cockpit had been shattered.

"Jessie." Naziah stepped back so that I could see what her focus had been on. "Any chance this is your friend?"

I leaned forward and looked at the boy in the corner. His eyes were closed, and he was obviously unconscious…at the least. Seeing him made me realize that IFON's lies weren't only affecting me, but they were affecting everyone who knew me.

not yet: reprise

Ever since I discovered my true purpose at IFON, I no longer wanted to trust students other than Kaylani. Including Miles. However, one thing he had said weeks ago had proved to be true: memory wiping was real.

I was completely against wiping Lion's memory as he could've provided useful information, and the side effects were close to impossible to predict. Of course, the decision wasn't up to me. At least Cierra had been kind enough to tell me what was going to happen as she knew that Lion and I were very close.

As for how he managed to get on the airplane, I had yet to figure out. My best idea was that he was forced onto the plane before other passengers got to board. Although, that wasn't my main focus.

Yesterday I spent my breakfast, lunch, and dinner trying to look for Michael. Sunday afternoon, I had bought a lot of pre-made sandwiches and snacks from the corner store less than a minute's walk from the academy. While most students were in the dining hall eating and socializing, I would be using the desktops in the library to attempt to find Michael.

Being in the library felt nostalgic, as I could look out of one of the many windows and practically see myself looking at the building for the first time. I'd been astonished by the modern setup and the massive size of the academy.

148

Remembering what it felt like to step on the school grounds for the first time only encouraged me to work enough so that this mystery of an academy would find me worthy of being a student.

I'd spent hours of yesterday and today studying in the library and was proud that I had managed to decide my next step for finding Michael. Getting information from Lion wouldn't be an option, as he was in IFON's care, and had probably already undergone his memory expunging. That felt like a secondary issue, so I'd be focusing on my *first* step with Professor Jones.

"Good afternoon, Jessie!"

"Good afternoon, Professor."

He had a backpack in one hand and his keys in the other. "You're lucky I forgot my briefcase, or I would be going home. I don't usually stick around during after-school hours."

He continued walking down the hall and toward me. I'd been standing by his office door for about three minutes, and there had been plenty of students roaming the halls. Now, they were either on the main floor or in their dormitories. Students weren't allowed off campus on Mondays and Tuesdays without staff permission, so unless they wanted to be reprimanded, no pupils would be off visiting family or shopping.

"If you have a free period, study hall, even during eating hours, I'll be available. You can also schedule a time to talk if you'd like." Professor Jones fumbled with his keys and inserted one inside the lock to his office door.

"Well, this won't take long. I just wanted to get the letter back."

"What letter?"

He motioned me to come inside, and I closed the door behind me. "The letter from Michael's house. I gave it to you the other day and need it to do some research."

He sat down at his desk and grabbed the briefcase lying on top of it. "What are you researching?"

I didn't want to explain too much as I didn't know the professor very well. And after realizing my purpose at the academy on Saturday, I wasn't willing to trust him. But the thought felt worth mentioning.

"I'm just researching his disappearance. Also, I want to ask you something."

"Sure, Jessie. Let me just get this for you." He used a different key to unlock a drawer in his desk. After shuffling through what sounded like a lot of papers, he finally set the note on his desk. The note had been buried in the drawer, which made me wonder if he hadn't reviewed it since I gave it to him.

"Actually, I have two questions." I take the note from the desk and fold it according to its preexisting creases. "Have you reviewed this since Kaylani and I talked about it with you?"

"Yes, of course! I couldn't make much sense of it, though, as I don't know much about the situation. Oh!" The professor quickly reached into his briefcase and pulled out his laptop. "My sincerest apologies—I received this on Friday and forgot to contact you before school let out."

I walked forward and sat down in one of the two chairs on my side of the desk. Professor Jones's office felt like a guidance counselor's office. Part of me wondered what our guidance counselor's office looked like as I'd seen it on the school map but never been inside.

"When you first mentioned this, I emailed Lady Kate requesting the recorded locations of that license plate you took pictures of."

"That's great, but the plate has been unregistered."

"In that case, the locations will be in the government system's archive, but I don't have access to that. Thankfully, Lady Kate emailed the information to me."

Subconsciously leaning forward, I tapped my foot anxiously.

"Here it is. I only requested the last recorded location of the plate, but Lady Kate gave me all of its history. Based on this email, the vehicle was first registered in California. Within two days, it was detected here."

"That's *all* of the history? How did it get here?"

"That's what I was wondering. It was never tracked passing through any other states."

I sighed and leaned back in the chair. "Are you sure Lady Kate gave you everything?"

"I never said it was a lot."

Something had to be missing—cars couldn't teleport from one place to another.

"I really am sorry, Jessie. Especially for wasting your time. I thought that having you and Kaylani research California would help you for your trip there."

"You knew we might go?"

"I suspected. Though I guess learning is never a waste of time."

I nodded my head out of respect, not really sure I agreed with him.

Professor Jones closed his laptop, and I rose from my seat. "Thank you, Professor."

"Anytime."

As I opened the door, the professor called for me. "You said you had two questions."

"Oh, right."

Part of me felt that asking my question wouldn't give me the best relationship with Professor Jones. He slid his laptop into his briefcase and then looked up at me. "Um, I just wanted to ask if you...you know why I'm really here, right? At the academy, I mean."

"You're here to be an exceptional student, just like all of your other schoolmates." His tone seemed assuring, almost as if he was trying to convince me that what he said was true. I nodded and started to approach the front door.

"If you're asking why you were *accepted* here, I would think you know that already," he added.

"I was just curious if *you* knew why," I told him, stopping with my hand on the doorknob.

"Of course, I know why," Professor Jones concurred. "You were an advantage, as you knew Michael Brown's parents who are with an important agency, and could possibly know more than your friend, Kaylani. Your bravery did influence your acceptance, as most staff were skeptical to do something like this last minute. Honestly, your acceptance was a surprise to us all, Jessie. 'Us' meaning staff. Although, I wouldn't be surprised if many students knew about your unforeseen acceptance."

"Yeah, that's exactly what I'm worried about."

"Why?"

I was hesitant to answer truthfully but didn't see much of a downside. "I don't think having the school know me as the one student who didn't earn their spot here is a good reputation." Professor Jones nodded his head in understanding and leaned back in his chair.

"Your being here is a rare exception, but you definitely earned your place. Lady Kate would not pick someone who she found to be completely incompetent for enrollment. Even if they did have potential links to other agencies like you do, no idiot would be accepted here."

"Comforting...at least I'm not an idiot, right?"

The professor seemed to look disapprovingly. Still, there didn't seem much of a point in attempting to fix my reputation.

"Or maybe I'm *Lady Kate's* first exception of bringing an idiot to the academy." I mocked her name, now slightly annoyed by my own childish demeanor.

Professor Jones softly sighed, looking as if he were waiting for me to make another relatively immature remark. After realizing I was finished, he spoke up. "Whether or not you've earned your place here isn't paramount. What matters is whether or not you *deserve* your place. Do you?"

"Do I deserve my place?"

He nodded and folded his hands. I was caught off guard by the question and wasn't sure which answer would be correct.

"I'm not sure, Professor."

He rose from his seat and zipped his briefcase. "Well, Jessie, I'll give you a few seconds to figure that out."

I felt as if a timer had started in my head, forcing me to answer the question. I couldn't even understand why it mattered. If I deserved to be at IFON, then I most likely would've been treated better. If I didn't deserve to be at IFON, then I'd already have a veracious reputation.

I opened the door and stepped outside, the hallway empty. There were no students, but I could hear a lot of voices on the main floor. I started slowly walking back toward the staircase and heard Professor Jones's door closed while the sound of his keys echoed in the hallway.

I hesitantly looked over my shoulder, partially hoping he had put off asking the question. Unfortunately, he was already facing me.

"Do you?" he asked again.

Sunlight from the large window to my right shone onto me, and I squinted from the luminosity. My eyes adjusted, and the voices downstairs grew louder. I subconsciously gripped the note tighter, not wanting to risk losing it.

I stepped forward to get out of the sun, and Professor Jones was still waiting patiently. My grip on the note hadn't lessened, and I looked at my hand which held it. The answer to the question made itself known in my head. Part of me felt as if I had known the correct response all along. I looked back at Professor Jones, confident in my answer.

"Not yet," I said.

jailbreak

IFON Academy
Elevator
Wednesday
0715 hours

Police officers used to be posted on the outside of the school during after-school hours. This had been in place since the first day of summer school. Ever since last Wednesday, they have been monitoring the outside *and* inside of the school 24-7.

When police officers arrived at Symson, I was confused and worried. After Kaylani had informed me about why the cops were at our school, the building's vicinity appeared to be deadly. Even though police officers were only at IFON to protect us, I couldn't help but remember that terrible Friday at Symson every time I saw one.

The elevator door closed behind us. "Good morning!" Olivia greeted the officer stationed by the elevator, who nodded in response. He was dressed in admiral blue and black. I looked at the gold badge on the right side of his uniform, which read *IFON*.

"Jessie! Hurry up."

Olivia was already down the hall, and I quickly rushed to follow.

"So what'd you want to talk about?" she asked.

I'd seen Olivia already awake and dressed in the living area, and I asked her if we could talk outside of the dormitory. Students weren't allowed outside of the building before school began, so we had to talk in the building. I still didn't want to discuss this in an area where others might overhear.

154

"Do you know a more private place we can talk?" I asked, my voice almost at a whisper.

"The dorm was fairly private," she replied. "But that's all right. I think I know somewhere."

I was relieved that Olivia complied as I wasn't ready to explain to her how I didn't want Donnay to know this yet.

We passed the first ever classroom I'd entered at IFON, and I slowed down to look inside. The door was open and the lights on.

"Good morning, Ms. Reyes!" Olivia called.

"Good morning, Olivia!"

I couldn't see Ms. Reyes from here but could imagine her usual smile as she spoke.

"We can't talk in a classroom?" I asked.

"Students can't be in classrooms without permission before school starts," explained Olivia.

I heard some laughter from up ahead and squinted to see who was at the end of the hall. It appeared that a group of kids—maybe five or six—were sitting in a circle together.

"I didn't think anyone would be up this early," I told Olivia.

She smiled and shook her head. "People wake up all kinds of early. You just can't leave your dorm until 7:00 a.m. Without permission, of course."

I looked around the walls for a clock and turned around to see that we had passed one. "It's seven fifteen right now," I reported, turning back around to face Olivia. She was farther ahead of me now, and some of the students at the end of the hall were staring at us.

"This is safe," Olivia reported, approaching one of the walls. The closest classroom door was at least six feet away. Olivia carefully sat on the floor and put her back to the wall. "Careful. The floor is really cold." She quickly lifted her hands from the floor and rubbed them on her pants. I nodded, carefully sitting down next to her.

"So what do you wanna talk about? Is it a secret? Why tell me?"

"Slow down!" I laughed, unable to contain my amusement. "It's not a secret, just something I only want a few people to know right now. And I'm telling you because I need another opinion and I believe you could help."

The kids at the end of the hall started laughing again, and two of them stood up to look out of the window. "Don't worry about them," Olivia assured. "They're sixth graders. Totally harmless."

I nodded, subconsciously smiling.

Olivia leaned forward. "So...what is it?"

"Remember Saturday? We found out that the license plate for the car I thought might've taken Michael was unregistered?"

"Yeah. Why?"

"Yesterday, Professor Jones showed me all the history of the plate. It was registered in California and then tracked here within two days."

"How did it get here?"

"That's the thing."

I leaned forward, looking left and right. My excitement could raise my voice, and I didn't want anybody else to overhear. I turned back to face Olivia.

"The plate couldn't be tracked moving from California to here. There was no information on the states it passed through."

Olivia furrowed her eyebrows. "That's impossible, Jessie."

"I know! That's what makes it crazy!"

"No, Jessie, that's literally impossible. A car needs a license plate to drive, and the plate would get run by cops or recognized on cameras in almost every state it passes through."

"Yeah, which is why this is so interesting."

Olivia sighed and looked down.

"What? You don't believe me?"

"I do, Jessie. Well, I believe that's what you were told." She looked up at the wall across the hallway. "Who told Professor Jones all of this?"

"Well, Lady Kate sent him the email," I replied, already putting the pieces together in my head. "Maybe Lady Kate *did* lie."

"I don't know that she would," Olivia replied.

"She lies to adults all year round about the school that their children are going to. Why would this be any different?"

"Because we're all on the same side."

I shook my head. "Maybe not."

Olivia set her hand on my shoulder. "I have some good news for you. Maybe it'll help ease your nerves."

"I guess," I faltered.

Olivia smiled, already seeming happy about her news. "So, yesterday Lion went through the memory wiping process. I heard that he is already back home and his parents are being talked to. You know, so they don't find out about IFON."

I nodded, disappointed by how my life was affecting Lion's.

"Well, he told one of the people getting ready to do the process that he had been knocked out while passing a friend's house."

"He remembered that?"

"Yeah! And I think it was Michael's house he passed by."

"It had to be. Who told you this?"

"Cierra. She was one of the people doing the process, and I asked her if Lion had said anything."

"Do you know how he's doing now?" I asked. The information was nice to know, but my friend's health was more important.

"Other than being at home, not much. Cierra told me his stomach was hurting afterward, but that's very common. He won't remember anything that happened that day."

"IFON does memory wiping often?"

"Not really, but they've done it enough times to know the most common side effects. It's weird that they chose to do it, though, since Cierra told me that Lion was asleep from when he was knocked out until we brought him here."

"That has to be more than getting knocked out, right? Losing consciousness by force can't last hours, can it?"

Olivia considered my comment, leaning her face onto her right hand. "I think you're right. Maybe he was drugged."

"Hopefully not..."

Olivia mouthed "Sorry." "Wait, what about the guy who attacked you on the flight?"

"They got away," I admitted. "We found Lion in the cockpit, and the person was gone by the time we were bringing him out. I think they're the least of our worries, though."

"Yeah. We still have to find out why Lion was on the plane in the first place."

"Maybe that's exactly what Michael's kidnapper wants us to do."

The kids at the end of the hall stood up and greeted a teacher who was inside of her classroom. Part of me wanted to be them—enjoying my childhood and not feeling that the lives of other people were dependent on me.

"We have to stay focused," I said, speaking more to myself than Olivia.

*****

Science was by far the easiest class and one of the most amusing. Science and math were combined in auditorium 2, which was on the second floor of the academy. It was pretty big, but auditorium 1 was even larger and used for productions.

Half of the auditorium was filled with seats of students who were studying math. The other half—where I sat—was filled with students studying science. There was a sound barrier that appeared as a piece of plastic, which split the seating side of the room in half. This made it easier for students to only hear what their instructor was saying.

The auditorium was always cold, and everyone wore bulky clothing. This was unfortunate, as a lot of people were close together, and it was hard to move around with people's clothes blocking the way.

Kaylani sat two rows in front of me, and Donnay was one row behind me. Our instructor, Mr. Wang, was pulling up the lesson on his monitor. The teachers' side of the room had two monitors and two spaces where each teacher would work. Considering how many students there were and how difficult it'd be to shout answers across the room, we answered most questions online using our laptops. For explanations and presentations, we would have to approach the front of the room and use the microphone.

Every student at IFON had a laptop—if they didn't have one of their own, they were granted one with restrictions by the school.

I looked at Ms. Akachi's monitor, our math teacher. The screen read, "Answer in complete sentences," and all the students on her side of the room were looking down at their computers. The bell in the hallway rang, signaling that any students outside of class were late. After the bell, the loudest thing I could hear was the distant sound of a helicopter. Everyone in the auditorium was either working or waiting.

Mr. Wang turned on his monitor, which revealed a laptop background. He clicked on his browser, which opened a video of a cat. The video was on repeat, and the white cat repeatedly ran into the wall in front of it. Most kids on our side of the auditorium began laughing, and I couldn't help but smile. Mr. Wang loved to start off classes in a fun way.

"All right, shush. Shush, I said!" He spoke into his microphone, quickly closing the tab. The laughter died down, and I noticed some students on the other side of the room looking over at our side. "Now I have to make a lesson out of this," Mr. Wang muttered, fueling some more scattered laughter in our group.

An alarm abruptly sounded, echoing in the auditorium. "Lockdown drill. Stay quiet," Mr. Wang and Ms. Akachi instructed their classes through their microphones. The alarm sounded a lot like a siren, as if an ambulance was in the room. My heartbeat sped up, and my leg bounced nervously. I'd never experienced a lockdown drill at IFON and was sure it would be different from Symson.

I noticed Ms. Akachi leading some students away from their seats, row by row. Although I couldn't see him from here, I assumed that Mr. Wang was doing the same thing.

I was on the sixth row, and Mr. Wang reached us very quickly. He instructed the boy sitting in the aisle seat to rush down the aisle. I was next to the boy and hurried behind him.

Ms. Akachi's class was going to the wall where the doors to the auditorium were. They sat down on the floor and moved as close to the wall as possible. I was nervous being the second person in line, because if the boy in front of me didn't know what he was doing, I wouldn't be able to help him. Thankfully, he followed with the rest of the crowd, looking for a space on the floor to sit.

The alarm was still going, and I could hear it from the hallway as well. Having such loud alarms appeared as if it would draw attention to us and not hide us from a potential threat.

I was standing up, still following the boy. He suddenly stopped walking, and I stepped out of line to see in front of him. Mr. Wang hadn't pulled down the shades to cover the glass in the door yet. Through the glass, I could see a boy at the wall across the hallway, seeming to be waiting for someone. Above him, something was falling from the ceiling, and I had a bad idea as to what could be happening.

I ran toward the door and opened it and then quickly closed it once I entered the hallway. Looking up at the ceiling, I had been right—it was caving in. Plaster was falling to the floor. The boy seemed to be a sixth grader as he looked very young. He noticed me, and I quickly grabbed his arm and then pulled him down the hall.

"Hey!" he cried.

Before I could explain my actions, part of the ceiling came crashing down where the boy had been. There were large chunks of plaster falling to the floor. The boy's eyes widened, and he wrapped his arms around me, burying his face into my side. I wrapped an arm around him, while Mr. Wang and Ms. Akachi stepped into the hallway. Mr. Wang coughed from the plaster and dust but kept his eyes on the boy and me.

Mr. Wang nodded, and I could only interpret it as being proud. The alarm suddenly stopped, and Ms. Akachi looked up at the ceiling.

"Who did this?" she asked.

The boy looked over to my teachers, sniffling. I knelt down and held his hands. "Did you do that?"

The boy shook his head. "My friends were throwing a football and kept hitting there. I told them to stop," he explained.

"That's nothing serious, young man," Mr. Wang assured him. "But they will have that confiscated." He looked up at the ceiling and chuckled. "I knew I heard something out here."

The whole building suddenly shook, with a distant crash. The boy started to fall down, and I cradled him until the shaking stopped.

"What in the world?" Ms. Akachi said, perplexed. Mr. Wang motioned me and the boy to enter the auditorium. I'd felt proud for helping the boy at first, but now, reality made itself known—we were still under lockdown.

Mr. Wang closed the door behind us, and I led the boy to sit on the floor. He looked around the auditorium and pulled closer to me. A lot of the students were staring at us.

Another crash came, much louder than the first. The building shook again, and I wrapped my arms around the boy. Some loud sounds came from outside without shaking. I covered the boy's ears, sure that there were gunshots.

Some students were now talking, wondering what was happening. Another crash occurred, this time, in our auditorium. The loudest scream was close to me, though I wasn't sure if it was mine or the boy's. The wall in the back of the auditorium came crashing down, hitting a lot of seats and throwing some of them toward the front of the room where we sat. As the sounds of the crashing in our room died down, another distant crash came, followed by the ground shaking.

"Everybody out!" Ms. Akachi's voice shouted as many people started to stand up.

"Go find your class," I said to the boy, leading him into the hallway. What I was planning to do would possibly endanger anybody who was with me. The boy raced down the hallway, and he approached the staircase.

Mr. Wang was instructing students to follow him, and the groups of students started to go toward the staircase that led to the first floor.

I pushed through the group of students, rushing to the end of the hallway. Quickly, I made it through the crowd and had a balcony-like view of the staircase. Approaching the window at the end of the hallway, some more gunshots were fired in front of the school followed by another crash. This one was close to us, and I fell to the floor. There were some screams from the staircase, and a lot of students behind me fell down. Some of them fell from the impact, and others were being pushed down.

Other classrooms opened their doors, and classes started to approach the staircase. Their classes were significantly small compared to ours, and it would take them a while to get to the staircase. The loud lockdown alarm turned off as another crash came from upstairs. Just after the crash, with the alarm off, I could hear a much louder sound of a helicopter nearby. I stood up and ran to the window, trying to see what was happening outside.

"Jessie!"

I turned around to see Kaylani racing toward me. "What are you doing?"

"Trying to see what's going on!" I shouted, turning back toward the window. Outside, most of the cars were speeding past the academy. I could see two guards on the curb, aiming their guns at the sky. *Who are they shooting at?*

There was another crash that sounded like it was a couple of stories above us. Kaylani held on to me and looked out of the window.

"Guys!" We turned around to see Naziah approaching us. She looked more angry than fazed by what was going on.

"What's happening?" Kaylani asked, though I didn't think Naziah would know.

"I can tell you what just *happened*," she said. "I just passed by one of our officers. He said that Royal and Juan broke out of jail."

Kaylani looked concerned and turned to face me. "What is it, Jessie?"

I didn't realize she could tell that I was pondering something, and Naziah seemed to realize too. "It's just… I think Royal warned us about this," I said. "At the prison. He said, 'You can't watch your front and back at the same time.'"

Kaylani's eyes widened. "I remember! Do you think he really meant this?"

"I wouldn't be surprised if this was a distraction."

A loud crash appeared downstairs, and people were still working their way toward the staircase.

"Where are they going?" I asked.

"To the underground refuge," Naziah said. "For attacks like this. It has a tunnel that leads to the off-site refuge in case we need to leave this area altogether."

"If this is just a distraction, then it should be over soon," Kaylani suggested. Some cars honked outside, and I turned to look out of the window.

I squinted at one red pickup truck, which was moving very slow compared to the other vehicles. A lot of people honked their horn, while others went around the truck. Someone pushed a sign out of the car window and unfolded it and then held it up. Looking at the sign, I was surprised by what I read. *Watch your side too.*

"Guys," I called, motioning for them to look outside. Before they could see, another crash came from the right. The floor shook violently, and Kaylani and I lost our balance. Naziah leaned forward, gently setting herself on the ground during the shaking.

"The library!" Kaylani cried. Naziah's eyes widened, and I was sure mine did the same.

Despite the chaos around me, I'd managed to completely zone out. While Kaylani and Naziah were realizing the damage done to the library, I was realizing the meaning of this new warning.

There was no more time to wait. We had to save Michael.

nascent

IFON Academy
Dormitory 356
Thursday
1700 hours

It feels pretty surreal to read about yourself in the paper. Not that the article was directly about me, but knowing that I went to the school it mentioned left me with a mixture of emotions.

"The attack lasted no more than five minutes, but the damage could take up to a month to repair," Kaylani read. "Wednesday, July twelfth was a dreadful day for students of the academy. Name currently undisclosed, the campus took at least $500,000 worth of damage. Bystanders say the attack was led by helicopter. With the suspects still unknown, no students of the academy were harmed during the attack."

"The paper should be happier," Olivia shook her head. "They included all these terrible things that happened and they don't even mention the name or location of the school. Why even bring it up?"

"The paper's full of terrible things," Kaylani observed, now reading a different page. "I guess that's why people don't really read them anymore."

"Do you think it'll be on the news?" I asked.

Kaylani shrugged. "Maybe. Well, probably. I doubt Lady Kate would want this broadcasted, but it was a pretty big thing. She might not have control over the publicity."

I leaned back on the couch, and Olivia went to turn on the television. Naziah and Kaylani had visited our dorm, but I hadn't seen Donnay all morning.

"So are we gonna talk about the important things?" Kaylani asked, standing from the floor to sit next to me.

"Our school getting attacked wasn't important?" I asked.

"*Equally* important compared to you believing that you were sent a sign that Michael is in danger."

I sighed as Kaylani didn't seem to believe what I had proclaimed.

"He is," I assured her.

"He has been for a while now," Naziah corrected.

I nodded. "Outside the window I saw a truck hold up a sign. It said…"

"*Watch your side too*. We know, Jess. We've heard," Kaylani said.

"I doubt it was anything more than taunting," Naziah stated. "Would it be a coincidence that as soon as you saw the sign, the side of the library was blown off?"

Kaylani nodded in agreement.

"I don't think it's coincidental. I think it's a cover-up," I explained. "Think about it. Royal said we couldn't watch our back and front at the same time, and two terrible things happened at once. Whoever led the attack was trying to cause a diversion, not murder anyone."

"Though they may have been pleased if someone *was* murdered in the process," Olivia added. She sat on the floor and changed the channel to the news.

"Probably," I agreed. "But if they wanted to really hurt someone, I guarantee you that they would've blown this place to the ground. They had the upper hand. Since they said to watch our side too, Michael is the only thing I can think of."

Kaylani started to say something, but Naziah cut her off.

"Whether you are right or not is unimportant. Michael has to be found. He has been missing for a while and a lot could have happened by now."

"Jessie, why don't you tell them what you told me? Maybe they can help," Olivia suggested. Naziah and Kaylani looked at me expectantly. I hadn't wanted anybody else to know the information, but I was desperate. I trusted Kay, and Naziah seemed reliable, though I still didn't know much about her.

"It's about the license plate I found," I admitted. "Professor Jones got all of its history from Lady Kate. Apparently, it was registered in California and then tracked here within two days. It wasn't tracked passing through any other states."

Naziah sighed before standing up and heading for the door. "I have something to do." She stopped, facing the door. "Good luck, Jessie," she said.

Kaylani was staring at the floor while Naziah left the room. "What's wrong, Kay?" I asked. She looked up as if unaware that Olivia and I could see her.

"I just... I think I know how that happened."

Olivia shifted to face the couch and leaned forward.

"Remember when Professor Jones had us read about California?" Kaylani asked.

I nodded.

"I read something about tunnels. I pointed it out to you, remember? There were old underground tunnels used for transporting and storing goods, but they closed years later."

"I remember. 'Most states closed them because they became either vacant or hazardous.'" I quoted the part of the book that I could recall. "But they haven't been used in centuries."

"Yeah, most states. But maybe they have been used by some," she said. Kaylani stood up and began to slowly pace around the living area. "The book said that the tunnels reopened in central California for renovation and were worked on until the late nineteenth century. That's around fifty years since it joined the union, and that number of years would be a long time to work on tunnels. The book said that they made a lot of progress and frequently used the tunnels but did eventually close them. I doubt they felt the need to do so..."

"Unless they had a different reason from the other states." I caught on.

"Yes! That would explain why the tunnels obviously aren't well known, or they'd be used by tons of people. Maybe people wanted to keep the tunnels a secret or only make them available to locals. But the reason isn't what matters. Using the tunnels is the only logical way a car could get from California to here without being seen," Kaylani declared.

"But what about Lion?" Olivia asked. "Someone drugged him while he passed Michael's house. That means someone is still there."

"They might be gone by now," Kaylani said.

"Why would they drug him?" I queried. "I'm sure tons of people walk by that house. Why would they choose Lion?"

"Maybe he wasn't just passing by," Kaylani suggested. "Maybe he was trying to see if Michael was home. But whoever drugged him probably took him onto the plane too."

"Why?"

We all thought about an answer as to why someone would take Lion onto the plane to California. "Maybe it was the same person you fought, Jessie," Olivia said.

"They had a mask on the whole time," I told her. "It's possible, but we don't know anything about them."

"Lion will be safe, I'm sure," assured Kaylani. "He won't even remember that day."

I nodded, still disappointed that I couldn't have helped Lion. Although, he had been sent home and was said to be fine. At least whoever performed the memory wiping process was very careful and seemingly treated him well.

"I think we all know what's next," Kaylani said.

Olivia looked at me and then to my best friend. "Wait, what's next?"

"We have to tell someone who can do more than we can," Kaylani explained. "Professor Jones would be a start. He usually goes home right after school, though."

"Let's go check now, then," I suggested.

We all stood up and approached the door. Olivia held the door open, and my stomach felt like it was turning as soon as we entered the hallway.

Only weeks after Michael's disappearance was I finally making progress, and not knowing where Michael could be was heartbreaking. I could vividly recall seeing Lion slumped in the corner of the airplane cockpit, and not even knowing if one of my best friends was alive. There would be no way for me to deal with seeing Michael in the same position. I had to save him, even if it meant trusting those whom I wouldn't normally trust.

unforeseen team

IFON Academy
Gymnasium
Friday
1510 hours

Stealth class was a lot like weapons and combat. It took place in the gymnasium, but instead of working with other students in our grade, we were combined with the freshmen. We had a different teacher too: Mr. Kohli. He was very serious when it came to education and constantly proclaimed his belief that "education requires collaboration." This belief led us to be working in a different group at the end of each class, like we were currently. Although I wasn't a fan of working in groups, I was sure the collaboration was harder for students with social anxiety than it was for me.

Each group was huddled in a different portion of the room, whispering to one another. Our goal was to retrieve the water bottle that Mr. Kohli had sitting next to him. The one rule was that we were only allowed to talk with people in our group.

"We have to move at some point," Percy proclaimed. She was a freshman and was easy to spot in the hallways—she typically wore a neon yellow dress with pink leggings.

"Gotta make a plan first, glowstick," Ricardo mocked. He was a freshman too.

Percy rolled her eyes. "And what do you suggest?"

All of us turned to face Mr. Kohli. He was sitting on the fifth row of the bleachers, and his water bottle was less than a foot away from him.

"It would be impossible to get it without him knowing," I observed. Speaking up made me nervous, as three out of five of us were freshmen. Phillip was the other freshmen, but I was blessed to have Cory as the other group member.

"Maybe we can—" Phillip froze midsentence, and we all watched a classmate run across the gymnasium. She was a girl I had recognized from my computer class, though I couldn't recall her name.

She started climbing the bleachers, with the entire class now watching her. After reaching Mr. Kohli, she reached for the bottle. An astonished "No way" came from the group closest to us. Mr. Kohli swiftly snatched the bottle, and the girl had to catch herself from falling off the bleachers.

"This is *stealth* class, Ria," Mr. Kohli scolded, causing most of the room to burst into laughter. Ria visibly sighed and began making her way back down the bleachers. Some people called out to her, but Mr. Kohli held up his hand.

"Hush! Talk within your group!"

The laughter died down, though a lot of people were still watching Ria, amused by her lousy attempt to steal the bottle. "There might be some weapons in the equipment room," Philip suggested.

"Really?" Percy asked.

"Yeah. Weapons and combat goes on in here," said Philip, amused by Percy's ignorance. "So…we gonna do it or not?"

"I think they beat us to it," Cory reported.

We turned to face a group running into the equipment room, and another group started to follow. "I say we let them do it," Ricardo proposed. "We're a class, so if they get the bottle, then we all win."

"I say we do something more stealthy than run across the gym and loudly enter the equipment room," I suggested.

Percy laughed at my proposal. "I agree. Let's climb the side of the bleachers to sneak up behind Mr. Kohli."

"You have to be pretty light to do that successfully," Philip said. "Strong and fast too. But I don't fit the first one."

"Then let's send the young ones," proposed Ricardo. The three freshmen looked at Cory and me.

"Sure," I said, looking for Cory's approval. He nodded his head but didn't look at any of us.

"Nah, only send one. Less weight makes less noise. I say the girl," Phillip reasoned.

I didn't like the feeling that I didn't have a say, especially since I wasn't sure if I'd be able to climb the bleachers without falling.

"If you're gonna do it, you better hurry," suggested Cory.

I looked at the door to the equipment room and saw that one of the groups had exited with pool noodles. They'd probably be useful for knocking the bottle away from Mr. Kohli, but they looked funny being held.

"All right," I said, walking to the wall of the gym. A lot of groups had dispersed, and each member was in a different place in the gym. I noticed my group huddling together and assumed it was to make Mr. Kohli think we were all still together. When I reached the wall, I started walking along it until I was close to the bleachers.

The teacher didn't seem to notice when I'd reached the bleachers. Now all I had to do was climb. Each row on the bleachers got a bit shorter, but not enough for me to grip onto the ledge. The only option was to climb using the railing, and I would have to pray that Mr. Kohli wouldn't notice my hands.

I jumped up and held on to the railing of the third row with my right hand. I swung onto the higher railing with my left hand and then joined with my right. From memory, I could imagine the bleachers being twelve rows high. Thankfully, I only had to reach the sixth. Climbing up twice more, I pushed my feet onto the side of the bleachers. My sneakers squeaked against the plastic, and I was sure Mr. Kohli has spotted me.

Looking to my right, a few people were watching my attempt. I couldn't tell anything from their expressions and decided to keep going. I inched my hands farther up the railing and lifted one leg onto the sixth row. Now, I was able to throw an arm over the railing and pull myself up. I gently lifted one leg over the railing and saw

Mr. Kohli on the row below me. After carefully lifting over the other leg, I crouched as low as possible.

Ahead of me, Cory had climbed the railing too. He crouched down and then motioned for me to get the bottle. I softly walked forward and then froze when Mr. Kohli turned his head.

"Nice try, Ms. Parker," he said. Cory quickly walked closer, careful not to make any noise.

"Remember your mistakes when retrying," he instructed.

"I didn't make any," I replied.

Cory punched the bottle, just as Mr. Kohli turned his head. It tumbled down the bleachers, the crunching plastic seeming to echo in the room. Mr. Kohli quickly stood, stepping down the bleachers. I stood up straight and saw Phillip succeed in catching the bottle with Percy and Ricardo behind him. Mr. Kohli stopped and then slowly clapped his hands.

"Congratulations, class. We have a winner! Spectacular catch, Phillip."

Phillip beamed and raised the bottle in victory. "Seeing as Phillip retrieved the bottle, he wins," Mr. Kohli clarified. Percy sighed, seeming to be frustrated and amused simultaneously.

"All in all, this wouldn't have happened without collaboration," Mr. Kohli said. "There will be a group activity throughout all of tomorrow's class."

Our teacher snapped his fingers twice, the way that he did at the end of every class. That signaled us to grab our book bags, which were all on the other set of bleachers across the gym. The bell rang while I was going down the bleachers, and conversation picked up. Finally, another school day was completed.

"Jessie!" I heard a loud voice call and looked around.

Cory ran up to me. "Great job," he praised.

"You too," I replied, before looking around again.

Whoever had called me sounded like Donnay, but she wasn't in my class. I looked toward the door where most kids were leaving yet saw my roommate racing toward me.

"Jessie, we have to go," she said, reaching me at the bleachers. I noticed my book bag in her hand, which she eagerly shoved in my arms.

"What? Why?"

"I'll explain later!" She grabbed my wrist and started racing to the door, pulling me along with her. I had no idea of how strong she was.

She adjusted the book bag on her own back with the hand she wasn't using to hold me. To get through the crowd at the door, Donnay pushed past people, sending some of them stumbling to their side. We emerged into the hallway, which was a lot louder than I would've expected. I assumed that people were excited for tomorrow as it would be the last day of school for the week.

Donnay pulled me down the hall, and then we turned and started up the crowded staircase. I was relieved that she had enough sense not to push people on a staircase. Having her pulling me around the school felt like a rush of fun and excitement. Nobody else knew what we were doing—technically, neither did I—and nobody else knew what kind of bond we had. We knew a lot about each other, though I hadn't spoken to her in what felt like a long time.

She finally let go of me, and I swung my book bag onto my back. She led me into the hall with all the lockers. She seemed to be going toward the next staircase leading up, which confused me. I'd expected her to be taking me to our dormitory. At the bottom of the staircase, Donnay suddenly froze, causing me to run into her. I stumbled forward but caught myself. As for Donnay, she didn't seem to be moved much at all by the impact.

"We should've taken the elevator." Donnay sighed.

"Where are we going?" I asked, shouting over the other students.

Donnay sighed again and then started up the staircase. I hesitantly followed, worried that she wouldn't answer my question. She walked forward to the elevator, which had five other kids waiting. One rule at IFON was to only use the elevator if you were going long distances, as using it to move less than three floors could cause a temporary ban of elevator access. It was only accessible to students before the first bell rang and after the last one rang. Misconduct on elevators could be followed with a permanent ban for the year or entire course of time at the academy.

"We have to get to the top floor," Donnay finally said, taking deep breaths. She attempted to fan herself with her hand. "Man, it's hot."

"Why are we going there?" I asked.

Donnay raised her eyebrows as if the answer was obvious. I looked around and then realized why she wasn't telling me. This was obviously important, and we were surrounded by tons of people. Some of them were bound to overhear, though I couldn't help but wonder what was so important.

The elevator door finally opened, and everyone outside of it made room for other students to get off. When we entered, someone else pressed the button for the top floor. The ride was silent except for two girls whispering to one another. The first stop was on the floor beneath our destination. To my surprise, everyone except Donnay and I stepped off. Donnay had obviously been right as someone must've overheard our conversation to click the button for the top floor when they weren't going there.

We waited until the doors closed so we could be sure nobody else was going to enter.

"So why are we going to the top floor?" I asked.

"To talk some sense into Naziah," Donnay responded. "I'm getting you for it because she and I aren't on good terms currently. Not that anybody's on good terms with her."

"Why not ask Kaylani? She's known Naziah longer."

"She had linguistics class. That's all the way across the building." Part of me wanted to call my roommate lazy, but I refrained.

The doors opened again, and a teacher stepped on. I didn't recognize her, but she seemed like she had been teaching for a long time.

When we stepped out of the elevator, I had to stop walking. Everything around me looked so different. Being able to take in my surroundings, I realized how beautiful everything was. The entire area was open, and there was a glass banister that allowed you to look on the lower floors.

I slowly walked up to it and leaned over it, noticing that there was a glass cage stretching from the floor to the ceiling. It allowed you to see what was beneath you but kept you from falling off. The banister was a square, and on the other side of the square, there were two meeting areas. Despite the attack yesterday, this floor appeared as if it had just been renovated. The whole area appeared very modern, and I wondered if students were even allowed to be present.

"I know it's pretty. But we're not supposed to be here without permission, so let's go," Donnay said. I sighed, frustrated that we could potentially get in trouble. At least if we did, we could enjoy our surroundings on the way back to the elevator.

"Where exactly are we going?" I asked. Some adults were seated along the wall, talking to one another.

"Wherever Naziah went," she replied.

"Wait." She stopped walking. "What if she's already there?"

"I don't know what you're talking about," I admitted.

Donnay looked up, thinking about where Naziah could be. She seemed to become frustrated at her own thought and then started walking the other way. I trailed behind, still looking around as I went. We passed the elevator, which had a seating area behind it. There were windows stretching from the floor to the ceiling, and the sunlight reflected on the hardwood flooring.

As I followed Donnay into a hallway, I noticed a door at the far end of the hall.

"We can't go in there, can we?" I whisper-asked.

"Just follow my lead," Donnay replied. We walked toward two security officers who were guarding the principal's office.

"Lady Kate instructed us to retrieve something from her office," Donnay said to the guards. I did my best to hide my nervousness.

"What must you retrieve?" one guard asked, holding his gaze away from us.

"Classified. We know what to look for," responded Donnay.

"Pass?" the same guard requested. I now looked at Donnay, nervous *and* confused.

Donnay nodded. "It's in the front pocket of my backpack," she said.

At first, I thought she was talking to the guards until she nodded at me.

"Oh," I whispered, going behind her. I unzipped the front pocket and reached inside. The pass was the only thing in there, though I had no idea how she got it. I handed it to the officer, who briefly examined it. He and his partner opened the doors to the office, and the officer returned the pass to Donnay.

We were in a room that looked like a foyer. In front of us was a door with an electric lock. The doors behind us closed, and Donnay stepped up to the door in front of us.

"How'd you get a pass?" I asked.

"It's from last year," Donnay explained. "One of my teachers gave it to me to deliver something to Lady Kate. I just never returned the pass." She chuckled at her own scheme before she scanned the pass on the electronic lock, and the door slightly opened.

It wasn't until then that I realized Lady Kate could possibly be in her office. Donnay stepped inside the room, still just as calm as before, and I was relieved that we hadn't run into the principal.

"I was worried you would be here already." Donnay sighed.

Naziah was behind Lady Kate's desk, staring at the desktop screen.

"How did you get in?" my roommate asked.

"Vent," Naziah replied.

The office was much smaller than I would've expected. It had three windows on each wall, but they were all covered with curtains. The desk was small too, with only enough space for the one desktop monitor and a stack of notebooks.

"Why did you come here?" I asked.

"Naziah thought that Lady Kate didn't send Professor Jones all the information," Donnay explained. "So she snuck in and tried to view the information for herself." Donnay had a mocking tone, as if she found Naziah's actions to be idiotic.

"We already figured out that the car was moved underground using tunnels," I told Naziah. "We told Professor Jones this morning, and he said he would arrange an investigation by noon." Michael's parents were obviously enough of an issue to IFON for the professor to arrange an investigation so soon. I didn't dare to think much of it as their quick actions could help Michael be saved as soon as possible.

"That does not matter," Naziah replied. She seemed sad if anything, and I quickly worked my way around the desk to see the monitor. On a white screen were a bunch of percentages and letter grades. On the top left I saw Naziah's name.

"They lied to me," she whispered. I scanned the screen until I found what Naziah was referring to: a 98 percentage on the bottom row.

"What was that for?" I questioned.

"Our last math assessment," she replied.

Donnay came around the desk and found the percentage much faster than I did. It was a 98 in a sea of 100s.

"You're upset about a 98?" Donnay asked.

"It will bring my whole average down for the semester, making it impossible to reach 100 percent," Naziah explained. "Lady Kate told me that I aced it, and other staff members praised me."

"You *did* get the highest score in our grade," Donnay pointed out.

Naziah shook her head and closed out the tab. She clicked around on different icons until reaching a warning screen: "Warning! History clear of 'Past 1 hour[s]' is irreversible! Continue?" After clicking CONTINUE, Naziah shut down the desktop.

"All right, Jessie," she finally said, turning to face me. "You need me. I will provide what you need considering you are a newcomer, though I suggest you do not abuse that privilege. Understand?"

"Um, sure."

"Currently, saving Michael is the biggest issue on our hands. I will talk to Professor Jones later."

"Hey, how are we getting outta here?" Donnay asked.

"The vent," Naziah replied.

"Why would Lady Kate's office be so easy to break into?" I asked.

"It was not," Naziah said, almost laughing at my question. "It took patience and strength to enter the vents and navigate them without being noticed. Though there is enough space for each of us to fit behind one another."

She started walking to the corner of the room, and I noticed for the first time since I'd entered that the vent cover was out of place. Naziah entered first, and Donnay motioned me to jump down next. Entering the vent was no more than a five-foot drop, and I started to crawl as soon as I reached the bottom. Naziah had already stopped crawling, and I wondered if she was trying to remember her way back.

Being in the small space made me think about Naziah's sudden cooperation. Lady Kate lying to her about her grade seemed to be fueling her will to help. Although getting the highest score in my class on an assessment at IFON would've been amazing to me, I was selfishly pleased that it had been hurtful enough for Naziah to help in finding Michael. She had proved herself to be competent since the first day I met her, and I was sure she would help in the long run.

As for grades, I now had to worry about my upcoming math test. If Naziah couldn't ace it, I would possibly fail. I hesitantly applied the same logic to my current situation.

Naziah had said that it wasn't easy breaking into the office undetected. I couldn't help but fear that it'd be harder to break out, especially for a newcomer.

redirected

From the rush of adrenaline and the excitement of being in Lady Kate's office, neither Donnay nor I had thought to exit the office through the doors. I wouldn't have even remembered it if a warning wasn't left in each student's locker.

> Two female students entered my office yesterday afternoon. No physical description of the students has been reported. Although nothing has been stolen, security cameras will now be installed on the top floor of the academy. Students also will not have access to the top floor of the academy without an adult accompanying them. This rule will be heavily enforced and remain for the entirety of summer school. Please feel free to contact me by email or request to have a meeting with me before trespassing in unauthorized areas.
>
> Yours truly,
> Principal Emircy Kate, MEd

I placed the letter back in its fancy envelope and slid it in my book bag. For the officers not to remember what Donnay and I looked like was nothing less than a miracle.

I pulled my book bag from my locker and closed the door. The hallway had grown a bit quieter while everyone was reading the letter, and by now, almost everyone was discussing it. Swinging my book bag over my shoulder, I started to head to where the dormitories were.

The dormitories were on the opposite side of the building from the lockers. A lot of students were heading back to their rooms and starting splitting up at the hallway's intersection. I turned left, where the dormitories for girls were. All the boys went the other way. My dorm was number 356 and was very easy to recognize. A lot of girls had decorated their front doors. Olivia had decorated ours even under protest from Donnay. It was splattered with yellow and pink paint and had *The Terrific Three* written in a sky blue. I'd grown to like the decor, but Donnay always expressed that she couldn't wait until the end of the year when students have to wash off their doors.

"Hey, Jess." Kaylani came up behind me and set her hands on my shoulders. "We gotta talk."

"I was gonna take a shower before dinner," I told her, stopping at my room.

"This is more important than showering, Jess."

I shook my head and pulled my key from my pocket. "Nothing's more important than showering," I joked.

I opened the dorm, which appeared to be empty. After entering, Kaylani closed the door behind her. The loud sound of students talking and laughing had significantly lessened, and my ears felt relieved.

"All right, what's up?" I asked.

"I think I found something," she announced, rushing to sit on the couch. I watched in confusion as my best friend pulled her book bag off and set it on the floor. "You know how Professor Jones said he would arrange for people to go to California?"

"Yeah, he didn't want to risk *us* getting in trouble again," I recalled.

"Well, he arranged for a squad to take a flight to California," she informed me. "The professor told me that the squad left for the flight last night. They're going to research the tunnels and investigate them."

"That's great!" I removed my book bag and let it fall to the ground.

"No, it's the opposite," she objected. "The squad doesn't know what Michael looks like, and they don't know to look for Damian too."

The door opened, and Donnay stepped inside. "Can y'all lock it next time?"

"Sorry," Kaylani apologized.

Donnay slammed the door and locked it and then dropped her book bag on the floor. "Imma take a shower," she said, walking toward the bedroom.

I sighed and went to sit next to Kaylani. "Why don't you just tell Professor Jones?"

"Because I don't think he's doing the right thing, Jess. I don't think *anyone* needs to be sent to California. Not right now, at least. Someone was at Michael's house, and they hurt Lion. I think going to his house needs to be the first step."

Lion had been taken six days ago, so I wasn't sure if it was worth going back to Michael's house. Then again, it was a Friday, meaning there was no curfew.

"We can go," I said. "But we have to take people with us. Some guards, maybe. For all we know, a serial killer could be in the house."

Kaylani nodded as if she had already planned to do so. "Of course. I think all five of us should go with some guards."

"I've got homework and Olivia is studying!" Donnay called.

"All right, then three of us." Kaylani chuckled. "I'll see what I can do," she said, standing up. I leaned back and watched her exit the room. Going to Michael's house would be emotionally hard, but I reasoned with myself that Michael could be going through a lot worse than emotional struggle.

*****

The sun was scorching hot. We hadn't even been walking for a minute, and I already felt like I was melting. Officer Cole had insisted that we park down the street from Michael's house as we couldn't park in the garage. It was a smart plan, but it would've been smarter if we could've brought miniature fans.

Everyone was subconsciously keeping their distance from one another while walking as being close together would make us hotter. Kaylani, Naziah, and I walked in a line with two officers behind us and two more in front of us, including Officer Cole. He was the one who Lady Kate assigned to lead the investigation. Professor Jones told Lady Kate about how we wanted to go to Michael's house, but she was hesitant to send any students. I assumed that the professor had explained to her how I would recognize if anything was out of place, though I wasn't sure how he convinced her to let Kaylani and Naziah come as well.

"Stay behind us no matter what," Officer Cole said as we grew closer to the house. All the windows were closed. There were a lot of kids at other houses playing together, and many of them were staring at us.

"Notice anything out of place?" Officer Cole asked.

"No, sir," I responded.

We finally were able to walk up to the house, and Officer Cole and the officer next to him pulled out their guns. Officer Cole was the first to reach the door, and he lunged forward, kicking the door down. The sound was very loud, and I was worried that the entire neighborhood would have noticed us. The sound from the impact even echoed throughout the foyer, which we quickly walked through.

I could hear the officers behind us pull out their weapons. There was a blast of cold air upon entering the living area. Knowing that the air-conditioning was on made my body relieved but my brain timorous. At least we would be comfortable while entering the unknown.

The officer next to Officer Cole went straight toward the dining area, waving his gun into the room before he entered. "Anything different?" Officer Cole asked. I stepped out of the line, with one of the other officers trailing behind me.

"Nothing but the air being on," I observed.

Being in Michael's house encouraged me to do everything in my power to help him. Typically, I would've been afraid and nervous that someone else was in the house with us. Having Michael on my conscience was like a superpower—now, I felt more brave knowing that Michael's suffering could be far worse than my own.

"If anything looks different, let us know," said Officer Cole. Kaylani walked close to me, and Naziah followed Officer Cole into the dining area.

"The windows have locks on them." Kaylani pointed to the right.

"Yeah, they had those last time," I said. "But the door was unlocked last time too."

"Was it unlocked this time?" she asked. Since Officer Cole had kicked it down, we had no idea.

"I'll go check it out," she said, heading back toward the foyer. One of the officers with us followed her, and the other stayed behind me.

"There *was* plastic wrap in the doorway," I recalled aloud, looking at the doorway that led to the dining area. The officer behind me cocked his gun and aimed it toward the doorway.

Kaylani returned to the living area, with the other guard behind her. "The door was locked this time," she reported.

"The plastic wrap is gone too," I told her. "Someone has definitely been here."

"They're definitely *still* here," Kaylani corrected. "Considering the air conditioner is on."

The officer who had followed Kaylani cocked his weapon. Officer Cole returned and tilted his head toward the dining area. That signaled us to follow him, though I couldn't imagine what he had found. At the best, it would be Michael.

"You recognize her?" Officer Cole asked before I could even see the girl. She was sitting at the glass dining table, hands folded in her lap. "Yeah, I do," I said. Naziah stood on one side of the girl, with a guard standing on the other side of her. The guard held his gun to her head with one hand and had his other hand gripping her shoulder.

"You don't recognize me," the girl shook her head. "My name's Riele."

"I recognize your hair, Riele," I told her.

Riele had shoulder-length hair, terribly cut, with tons of glitter coating it. The light from the chandelier hanging over the table caused her hair to shimmer, almost like it was filled with crystals.

"I recognized the hair too," Naziah agreed. "Who are you?"

"I already told you my name," Riele said. "But if you must know, I'm looking for Chris."

"Who's Chris?" Kaylani asked.

All of our officers aimed their weapon at Riele, except for Officer Cole, who was aiming his weapon toward the living area. It was relieving to know that someone was watching our backs in case Riele had other people coming.

"He owes me money," Riele responded, shaking her head as if Kaylani should've known. "He said he would leave a letter in this house explaining where he is, but I've been waiting for a while. Now can you put your guns down?"

"That's not happening," the guard to her right said. "Not until you tell us everything about why you're here."

"I just did," Riele shot. "Why? This private property?"

"Belonging to someone who went missing," Naziah informed. "You know anything about that?"

"Woah, I didn't take anybody." Riele gently lifted her hands. "I'm just visiting every day waiting for the letter."

"And sending anonymous messages?" I asked.

Riele looked at me as if she had no idea what I was talking about. Her dark-brown eyes seemed to shimmer just like her hair did. Her expression softened. "That was for fun. I do it to people all the time."

"You shoot at people all the time too?" Naziah asked.

Now the girl seemed more confused. "What are you talking about?"

"At the parlor. You fired at us," Naziah said.

"No, I didn't," Riele denied. "I heard the gunshots, though. That's why I ran."

"What about the speaker in the bathroom?" I asked.

"I set that up too," Riele said. She smiled a bit, as if proud of her scheme. "Patricia is super nice. She recorded that for my drama class among other things, and I thought it would scare the pants off you if you came."

"And the letter? *I'm not where you think I am?*" Quoting the letter I found sent chills down my spine. They had scared me upon reading them and would scare me more if Riele claimed she didn't write them.

"That was to scare you too." She laughed. "I can tell it worked. You look petrified!" By her words, I practically felt my expression change from scared to embarrassed. "I'll send them to other numbers, then," Riele promised. "I've never met one of my victims. And some of them get a lot worse than you have." I wondered if the officers would try to arrest her as her pranks didn't seem legal. Instead, Kaylani moved on.

"When did that guy say he would send the letter?" she queried.

"Chris? He said it would be here about a month ago."

"A month? And you're still coming back?"

"Maybe he got the date wrong. What can I say? This house is really nice, and he owes me a lot."

"How much?"

"I can't tell you that."

The guard next to her cocked her gun, but Riele didn't flinch. "Calm down, tough guy," she said, turning to face the officer. "It wouldn't be good on your conscience to kill an innocent sixteen-year-old."

"I doubt you are as innocent as you make yourself appear," Naziah claimed. "Lucky for you, that does not interest us. Not yet, at least. Have you been able to talk to Chris?"

"He got a new number," Riele said. "Now, I'm just waiting helplessly for the letter. I'll stop coming in a month if this place is that important to you guys."

"I might have the letter," I said. All of the room looked at me.

"Seriously?" Riele cried. "Give it to me!"

"I don't have it *on* me. Did Chris tell you what the letter would be about?"

"Just that it would show me where he is."

On Tuesday, when Professor Jones returned Michael's note to me, I spent my whole evening memorizing the note. I was bound to lose it at some point, and as much as the letter worried me, it would be much safer to keep the note hidden in my dormitory than bring it with me everywhere I went.

"If I say what the note said to you, do you think you could figure out where Chris is?" I asked.

"Jessie," Kaylani said. "We don't even know her."

"I'm desperate, Kay," I admitted. "Maybe Chris knows where Michael is."

"Or maybe she will take the information and run," Naziah suggested. Riele shrugged, as if it was a possibility.

"She has three people aiming guns at her head," I pointed out. "She can't run anywhere." Riele nodded eagerly, but my friends were obviously adamant in their protests.

"All right." I sighed. I pictured the image of the note in my mind—the bent piece of paper that I'd gripped tight in my hands, reciting it over and over. I said the words slowly, praying that Riele would make sense of them.

"It is with our greatest apologies that we leave on such short notice and will not return until the summer is over. Do not take much from this adjustment, rather, focus on staying cool during this season—that's a reminder for you *and* me. Despite the dreadful hot weather, continue to be active, especially in swimming. Continue in your studies as well, especially science and math. Overall, make the best of your summer even with our absence, so this summer may be a time we will never forget." The words felt like a speech that was either undeserving of applause, confusing to the audience, or so life changing that nobody could comment immediately. Based on the expressions of the people around me, the second option was the most likely.

"I think it has something to do with the fridge," Riele said.

"Why the fridge?"

"Well, he wrote a lot about how the heat was terrible. Actually, 'dreadful.' And Chris has always loved being hot. I never understood it."

"The letter was written in the handwriting of someone I know," I said. "It was also signed, 'the Brown household.' Are you sure Chris wrote it?"

"It's the only letter you got." She shrugged. "And he told me he wouldn't sign it as himself just in case someone else got their hands on it. I'm not sure about the handwriting, though."

Naziah was looking at me, and I wondered if she was trying to make a silent suggestion. "I think your guess is far-fetched," Kaylani said to Riele. "But show us what you mean."

Riele stood from her seat, and the guard closest to her cocked his gun. She looked at him and smiled, seemingly unfazed. "I'll watch the front door," Officer Cole assured us. The other guards followed Riele around the dining table.

She started walking toward the kitchen, and we all followed behind. As we walked through the doorway leading to the kitchen, I noticed how much warmer the house felt. Leaving the front door open would surely take a toll on the air conditioner, as well as on our comfort.

The refrigerator was directly to the right when you enter the kitchen, and it was just as modern as everything else in the house. It had a touch screen that took up at least a fourth of the fridge, with two freezer doors and two doors for the main part of the fridge. Riele opened the fridge, and when it appeared to be empty, she opened the freezer. There was nothing inside.

Riele started to pull the fridge from the wall. I went to the other side and helped her pull it away from the wall, unsure if she really knew what she was doing. Riele was able to reach her hand between the fridge and the wall, and I walked over to Kaylani.

"There's a switch back here," Riele announced.

Before anyone could understand her comment, a loud crash came from the dining area. One of the guards brushed past Naziah, Kaylani, and me, while the other quickly grabbed Riele by her shirt. I walked into the dining area with Kaylani and Naziah behind me. The glass from the dining table was shattered, the chandelier had fallen, and there was a large hole in the floor underneath the broken table.

Officer Cole was startled by the sight as well. "It practically jumped!" he exclaimed. "Just fired to the ceiling!"

The officer from the dining room joined us, pulling Riele with him. Her eyes widened at the sight. "I think that's where he is," she said. She attempted to walk forward, but the officer pulled her back.

"I'll check it out." Officer Cole approached the broken table, trying to avoid stepping on glass, though the floor was practically coated in it.

The hole in the floor had a diameter of at least six feet and looked as if it had been blown up. "The drop is far," Officer Cole discerned, hovering over the hole. "Smells like chemicals. I think there was a bomb."

"Do we go in?" Kaylani asked. She appeared excited to investigate, though I felt more confused.

"We will have to report this before we investigate any further," Naziah said.

Officer Cole stepped back from the broken floor. "That's right. As for her"—he pointed to Riele—"she's coming with us."

working weekend

Somewhere underground
Saturday
1100 hours

Our backs were pinned to the wall, and Kaylani took the risk of turning her flashlight around the corner. "Clear. Path 2," she announced into her microphone. I heard her in person from my left ear and through the device in my right.

"Still on path 1," Officer Cole said, his words buzzing in my ear. Kaylani turned the corner, and I followed behind.

We had used a retractable ladder to enter the dark tunnel and quickly reached a two-way intersection. Now, our group of four was split into two, with Kaylani and me as partners and Officer Cole with Naziah. The other officers from yesterday had the easy way out—they were to watch Riele at IFON and made sure she didn't escape.

Kaylani marked her chalk on the wall before continuing on. Each new path we came on, we were to use glow-in-the-dark chalk for us to find each other easily.

For the eighth time since we entered the tunnels, I turned around, waving my flashlight behind us. "Nobody's following us," Kay assured me.

"You don't know that," I said, hesitantly turning back around. "How are you so calm, anyways? We're in this dark, hot tunnel with no idea of where we're going. How are you *always* calm in things like this?"

"Stressing out only makes things worse," she replied. "If I hadn't stressed out when Damian went missing, I might've been able to help find him before he got too far."

"You can't blame yourself for what happened."

"I guess."

After walking for another minute, I followed where the floor and the wall met with my flashlight. The wall appeared to be made of stone and rocks, while the floor simply appeared to be dirt. Putting the light toward the ceiling, the walls curved to cover our heads. It was like we were standing in an upside-down U that was sealed off.

Finally reaching another two-way intersection, Kaylani and I went right destitute of discussion. "Path 3," my friend announced into the microphone. Going left would take us toward Officer Cole and Naziah, and we needed to stay as far from each other as possible to cover the most ground. Though I was following the floor with my light, I could hear Kaylani drag the chalk against the wall as we walked.

"Jessie," Kaylani whispered. Her whisper startled me as we had been talking at a normal volume at first. I looked to her and then up ahead. My body froze in fear at the sight—what appeared to be green eyes staring directly at us. Kaylani pointed her light ahead, revealing that the "eyes" were much smaller than we'd thought. She started walking closer, and I quickly trailed behind.

There were two green LED lights sticking out of the wall. "We found something," Kaylani said, gripping the microphone on her shirt. My earpiece buzzed as Officer Cole responded.

"What is it?"

"These two green lights sticking out of the wall."

"LEDs?"

"Yeah. This is the shortest path we've come on."

"Path 3, right?"

"Yeah."

"All right. Don't do anything. We'll be right there."

Part of me had expected Kaylani to listen and wait, but instead she set her hands on the wall. She felt around, and I assumed she was wondering if the wall would open.

"Do you think this is the tunnel? The one that goes across the country?" I asked.

"It has to be," she replied. "Either that, or Michael's family has a lot to hide."

Footsteps were running through a path farther away, but there was only one pair. Kaylani and I turned our flashlights behind us, waiting until the sound grew closer.

Naziah appeared around the corner.

"Where's Officer Cole?" Kaylani asked.

"His flashlight battery busted," she replied. "He is changing it right now." She took a few more steps forward and tossed each of us a weapon. I was impressed by how easily I caught it. "Those are dart guns. Officer Cole and I have real ones."

"Naziah's the only student out of the three of us who's taken a firearm course. It's not available for first-years," Kaylani explained, though I could already piece together the mystery.

"Those lights?" Naziah pointed her flashlight at the green LEDs in the wall. She came closer and took off the duffel bag that was on her shoulder.

"Step back," she ordered. Kaylani and I turned around, walking to the front of the short path. Naziah dug through her bag and pulled out a large cylinder. She set her flashlight on the floor and kicked her bag toward us.

Kaylani's and I's flashlights were pointing at Naziah, helping her see what she was doing and helping *us* see what she was doing. She pressed a button on the cylinder, and it started to glow green. There was a soft hum coming from the device.

Naziah lunged back, holding the front of the device with her left hand, and her right arm was over it, pulling it close to her side. Slamming the device to the wall, the green lights immediately went out, and there was a sound like the wall was being electrocuted. After three seconds, Naziah pulled the device back and turned it off.

"We have to hurry," she said.

"Only now?" I asked, slowly approaching her.

"Get my bag. And yes. Someone might have heard the impact."

What we thought were footsteps were echoing from another path, but we all froze just to listen and make sure. Naziah snatched her gun from her utility belt and aimed it past Kaylani and me.

"Just me," Officer Cole called, holding his hands up as he found us. Naziah put away her weapon and Kaylani gave her the duffel bag.

"Are we gonna break down the wall?" Kaylani asked.

"Just part of it." Naziah shoved the cylinder into her bag and picked up her flashlight.

She suddenly kicked the wall, and a large hole formed. The wall seemed to be inches thick, but the electrocution may have made it easier to break. Naziah knelt down and started expanding the hole and then crawled through it. The other side seemed to be just as dark as what we'd explored so far.

We all went through, first me, then Kaylani, and then Officer Cole. Naziah was moving her flashlight around the area, which seemed to just be another tunnel.

"Do you think there was another way to get here?" Kaylani asked.

Naziah pointed her flashlight ahead and started walking. "Perhaps."

All of us were staying together as the tunnel didn't seem to split for a long ways. Instead of sharp turns, the walls curved left or right.

It had been about five minutes of dreadful walking until we reached another wall. Naziah pulled something from her pocket that looked like a snow globe. She put it up against the wall and put her ear to the device.

"Dead end," she finally said.

"Where'd you get all of those things?" I asked. Naziah seemed surprised by my question, though I was curious as to if I could get listening and electrocuting devices too.

"The weapons room at the academy," she said. "First-years do not have access."

"Of course not." I sighed.

Officer Cole and Kaylani turned around and began walking the other way. Naziah turned too, but I stretched out an arm to stop her.

"Can I see your listening thing?"

"What?"

"The thing that looks like a snow globe...that you held to the wall?"

"Ah. This is an *auditory augmenter*." She pulled out the device and held it up. "Why do you need it?"

"Just trust me."

Naziah handed the device without protest, which stunned me. I'd expected her to be hesitant to trust me, though silently reasoned that she could've been trying to prove that *I* should trust *her*. Since I partially relied on her to help find Michael, I didn't have a choice but to trust her for the time being.

I walked closer to the wall and tried the same thing Naziah did. There was just a soft buzzing sound. I then went right to the stone wall lining the tunnel and tried it. There was still a buzzing sound, but louder.

I dragged the device against the wall—when I went higher, it was quieter, and when I went lower, it was louder. I pulled the device down until I was kneeling, pressing it against the dirt floor. The buzzing sound was very loud, almost like a generator.

"Hear something?" Kaylani asked.

"Sounds like some kind of generator. Maybe an air conditioner."

Naziah knelt down and I stood up so she could press her ear to the device.

"Definitely a generator," she confirmed.

Kaylani pulled the cylinder device from Naziah's duffel bag and pointed it to the floor. Naziah quickly put away the auditory augmenter and took the cylinder device from Kaylani, turning it on. "You guys will want to back up." Kaylani took Naziah's flashlight before backing down the path like the rest of us.

The device made a soft humming sound and worked much better than the first time—as soon as the device started to weaken the floor, the floor started to give in. It cracked beneath Naziah's feet, and she snatched a small tube-like gadget from her utility belt. She launched it to the ceiling just as a hole in the ground fell, forcing the rest of us to step back farther. As soon as the floor gave in, the humming of the generator became a lot louder.

Naziah was hanging in the air, gripping onto the device with one hand. "Shine the flashlight into the hole," she ordered.

All of us immediately pointed our lights down, carefully approaching. "It is a short fall," she reported. "About six, maybe seven feet. You guys can make it." She lowered herself with the gadget until she was close enough to the floor to retract the device. The hook attached to the ceiling retracted into her gadget, which she concealed in her utility belt. "Throw down my flashlight!"

Kaylani tossed one of the flashlights she held to Naziah and was first to jump down. Officer Cole insisted I go next. I slowly approached the broken floor and could see Naziah and Kaylani standing by the generator. I jumped down, losing my balance as I hit the ground.

My flashlight clattered against the floor, but Kaylani retrieved it for me. I took back the flashlight and shone my light at the generator. It was about the size of an RV.

Officer Cole leapt down, stumbling forward. After balancing himself, he waved the flashlight around.

"What's the generator for?" I asked, shining my flashlight onto it.

"Maybe it powers the house," Kaylani suggested.

A sound like electrocution came from behind me, and I jumped at the noise. Naziah had used her device again and started to kick down the wall.

"I heard something over here," she explained. Kaylani, Officer Cole, and I approached Naziah carefully. She tore down a huge part of the wall so that we didn't have to crouch to get through.

Going through the wall took us to another tunnel, and I wondered if we were about to enter another maze. This tunnel seemed to be made of the same materials as the others, but it was narrow enough for us to have to walk in a line. "A door," Naziah reported. All of us pointed our flashlights down the pathway, and saw a metal door at the end. It had no locks on it, which didn't surprise me. There wouldn't be much of a need for locks when the door was so difficult to find.

Naziah traded her flashlight for her gun, securing the light in her utility belt. She aimed her gun at the door and carefully opened it. Once we all walked through the door, I pointed my flashlight to the walls and noticed a light switch. There was enough room for us to walk freely, and I went to turn on the light.

"Close your eyes," I said before turning on the switch. The brightness was noticeable even through my eyelids, and I had to blink repeatedly after opening my eyes.

The walls of the room were metal, and so were the floors. It felt like we were in a large interrogation room. Kaylani walked toward two other doors with me—they were directly next to each other and looked to be the same as the door we had entered to get into the room.

Behind us, a door slammed shut. We all jumped and turned around, where Naziah was standing at the door. "I just closed it. Relax." I was slightly irritated by her telling us to relax, considering she had a gun to defend herself. Kaylani and I only had dart guns, and I was clueless on how to use mine properly.

"Let's go right," Kaylani said, reaching for the handle of the door on the right.

"I'll go first," Officer Cole said, setting a hand on Kaylani's shoulder.

Kaylani and I stepped back, while Officer Cole approached the door. He aimed his gun at the door while opening it, and a lot of loud noise started to fill the room.

"Is that music?" Kaylani asked.

"Stay behind me," Officer Cole ordered, going through the door.

We went through another narrow hall, but this one had fluorescent lights on the ceiling. At the end of the hall, light shone from around the corner. I pulled my dart gun from my pocket and held it against my side, careful that I wasn't close to pulling the trigger.

As we turned the corner, the talking and music grew louder until we'd entered what seemed to be a different world.

home sweet home: reprise

Despite our unpredicted arrival, nobody appeared to notice us. Some people with silk sashes and metal rings swung from the ceiling, which felt as if it was twenty feet high. There were tons of people sitting around, with music playing from farther back in the room, but loud enough to coat most of the discussions. Even the room seemed to be the size of a football field—the only wall in sight was the one behind us.

If anything, I would've thought we were in a club. There were disco lights flashing among the plain fluorescent ones. Some kids ran past us, with conspicuous neon necklaces that stood out from their raggedy clothing. Many of the adults had fancier clothing, mostly purple and blue silk attire. They all wore the necklaces as well, some with neon bracelets. There were even neon lights lining the brick wall behind us.

"What is this, a circus?" I heard Officer Cole say.

A lady came up to us with a half-filled glass bottle in her hand and an arm full of necklaces. Her hair was in a very messy bun, and she wore a lot of makeup. "*Harma-sil*, visitors," she greeted, stretching out her arm toward Kaylani.

Officer Cole gently aimed his gun toward her, but Naziah had hers concealed. I put away my weapon, and Kaylani accepted a necklace from the woman. She came over to me, and I slid the illuminated necklace off her arm and pulled it over my head. She then moved

196

to Officer Cole and Naziah who each put one on. "Have fun!" she beamed, turning away and moving into the crowds.

"*Harma-sil?*" Kaylani repeated.

I shrugged and looked at Officer Cole. He started walking forward, and the rest of us followed closely behind.

"If Michael is here, it'll take forever to find him," I said to Kaylani. We walked around groups of people dancing and talking. There were a lot more young children the farther in we went, and only some of them wore silk clothing. All the others had tan clothes that looked dirty and worn-out. Some kids had the same glass bottles that most adults had.

Walking under the disco ball, I looked at the high ceiling again. The people dangling with props looked like acrobats. Some talked to one another, while others performed tricks.

Kaylani nudged me and pointed down, where I noticed was a dance floor. It lit up in different squares of the platform and gave me the urge to join in with the other groups of people dancing. There were a lot of teenagers sitting on chairs and drinking from their own glass bottles, with many of them looking at us.

"Look for Michael," Naziah instructed, shouting over the music and other people.

I looked around me, trying to avoid making awkward eye contact with the many teenagers in this area. Unfortunately, none of them looked like Michael.

After arriving in a less crowded area, there were four doors in our sight. Each one was metal, and two of them were splattered in paint. "The one on the far right?" I queried.

Officer Cole shook his head. "Let's go through here first," he suggested.

We walked against the wall, passing all the doors. From the periphery of my vision, I saw more teenagers staring at us. They were obviously more observant than most of the adults present, though I assumed they were simply more sober.

Toward the far brick wall, there were tent-like areas. Some metal poles reached a few feet high, with cloth draped over them to form the tents.

We approached the tents, and there were at least ten of them lining the wall. Kaylani held my hand and quickly walked toward one of them. I was nervous about entering as the cloth was draped closed.

"The cloth is thin enough to see through," Kaylani whispered in my ear.

We went close enough until we could see clearly into the tent. There were two people with ponytails talking to each other. I looked over my shoulder for Naziah and Officer Cole but didn't see them anywhere.

Kaylani led me to the next tent, but Naziah's voice spoke into our earpieces before we could look inside. "I just talked to a young man who said he saw a guy named Michael in the light green tent. Meet me there."

We both stopped walking, and my eyes widened. I didn't want to get my hopes up as we still hadn't seen Michael, but the possibility of him being near was nothing less than amazing. We started walking again, keeping an eye out for the green tent.

"It's four down." Kaylani pointed ahead, where the tent was. The cloth was draped open so that we would've been able to easily spot Michael if he was inside.

Naziah was coming from the crowd dancing and entered the tent.

"We see you," Kaylani spoke into her microphone, and I could hear her more clearly from my earpiece than in person. I sped up to a run, dodging people dancing and talking until I was in front of the tent. Naziah sat with her back to me, and I saw two people sitting in front of her. One boy had long black hair but an unrecognizable face. The other was directly in front of Naziah, and I wasn't going to wait any longer to see if it was Michael.

I stepped into the tent, and the boy with long hair noticed me first. Naziah turned around, with the other boy standing up. He walked around Naziah and wrapped his arms around me. Not knowing what to say, I started saying what came to mind, and the words came out much faster than I'd intended.

"I was gonna give you your charm but I didn't know where you were and the letter scared me and so did the truck, but I have your charm and I can gi—"

"It's okay, Jess!" he laughed, and I couldn't help but laugh along, hugging him tighter. Someone else came behind me and then joined in on the hug, and I was sure who it was without seeing them.

The embracing lasted without any talking, but relieved sniffles said it all.

"I'm guessing this is Michael," Officer Cole said from behind us. He looked at our group as the three of us separated, still holding back tears.

"Who are they?" Michael asked, sniffling, and looked from Officer Cole to Naziah. Hearing that his voice hadn't changed put a smile on my face, and Kaylani smiled in response as well. One thing that had changed was his appearance—I felt angry that he'd obviously been dismissed as his hair looked dirty and he wore the same raggedy clothes that most of the kids around here wore.

"We're gonna take you home, young man," Officer Cole said.

The other boy stood and approached Michael.

"I'll tell Ozi the good news." The boy had an odd accent and sparked my curiosity.

"Tell Mariah as well," Michael instructed. "Make sure they know that I'll visit when I can."

The boy nodded and stared at Michael for a second, as if contemplating what he should do. He made his decision and abruptly stepped forward to briefly hug Michael.

"See you around, mate," the boy said, a bittersweet look on his face before exiting the tent.

"Who was that?" I asked.

"That was Harry. Mariah and Oziril are my two other friends from here."

"I hate to interrupt the sentimentality, but we need to talk somewhere less crowded," Naziah suggested.

Officer Cole nodded in agreement. "And less loud." He turned to face Michael. "Do you know your way out of here?"

"No, sir."

Naziah sighed. "We'll have to go back the way we came, then," she proposed.

Officer Cole gently extended a hand for Michael to take. "We'll hold hands until we're out of the crowd."

I took Michael's other hand, and Kaylani held mine. Michael looked at the both of us, and exhaled through another smile. Officer Cole started walking and Michael had to look forward, though Kaylani and I kept our eyes on him the entire time.

*****

"Are there sweets in this van?"

"No, Michael. It's not a limousine."

"Sure feels like one."

We were in an IFON-AV, where Michael, Kaylani, and I sat in the back. This one was smaller than the one we'd used yesterday when finding Riele, but just as comfortable.

"How did you even find me?" Michael asked.

"Too long a story to say," Kay responded, shaking her head.

"What was that place? Where we found you?" I asked.

"Even I don't know," he answered. "I don't think many kids do, actually. One day I went to sleep at home, the next, I woke up in what I now know to be an underground facility." He chuckled at his own words and turned around to look out of the rear window.

"The place you were in had a hedonistic ambience," Naziah recalled from the passenger seat in front of me.

"I agree. Almost everyone there was impulsive," Michael added. "I think I was the newest arrival."

"Did you ever hear of a guy named Chris?" Naziah queried.

"No, I didn't.

"I only knew Oziril, who we call Ozi. He's really funny. Then there was Harry who you all got to see. He's laidback for the most part. Also Mariah, who's very outgoing. She came to every party there was. The one you brought me from was my second time going to one, but this time Harry accompanied me instead of Mariah."

"That was a party?" I asked. "How many times would you have one?"

"There were two a week," he said.

"Where did everyone stay?" Kay asked. "Sleep, eat, etcetera."

"We ate in the mess hall," he explained. "And there were bedrooms, but none available for the newer people. I slept in the halls with some other kids who couldn't get a room. Harry would invite me to his room whenever nobody else was present, and we would hang out there."

"Can we put the interrogation on hold? There will be an inquisition and a debriefing when we return to MSA. For now, we have another issue," said Naziah.

"What's MSA?" Michael whisper-asked.

Kaylani and I looked at one another, and I couldn't help but smile. I was sure that she was relieved of being able to share the secret with her best friend, and I was happy to be a part of it.

"Mareschal Science Academy," I told him. "It's where Kaylani and I go to summer school."

"That truck has followed us for five turns," Naziah observed.

"I've noticed. That's why I'm not going straight to the academy," Officer Cole said.

All three of us looked behind us at the red pickup truck.

"I think that's the one that I saw on Wednesday," I said. "The one with the sign."

"There are tons of red pickup trucks," Naziah dismissed.

"I'll still be cautious," promised Officer Cole.

He made another turn on a yellow light, where the light turned red while he was in the intersection. The van kept following us, even running the red light.

"Naziah—"

"Already on it, Officer." I heard Naziah's weapon hit the seatbelt as she pulled it out. A loud sound came from behind us, and I didn't have to think twice to know what it was.

"Lean over," Kaylani said, and the three of us leaned below the windows.

I looked to my left at Kaylani who appeared calm despite our van being shot at. After thinking how she may have endured similar experiences often, I realized why she hadn't been worried on the day someone brought a firearm to our school. It would take me a long time to become as tranquil during life-threatening moments as my best friend was.

"That was a clear shot. They're not trying to hit us," Naziah said.

"Not *yet*," Officer Cole corrected her. "When there are no cars around, you respond."

"Yes, sir. Cover your ears."

The three of us covered our ears, attempting to block out the sound of the next bullet piercing through the air. I could hear Naziah securing her weapon and carefully sat up to look behind us. The car had stopped, and their windshield was shattered.

"When we get to the academy, you will be staying there for the weekend," Naziah told Michael, as if she hadn't done anything out of the ordinary. "I infer that you will stay in the underground safety facility until Monday afternoon."

"Great, more time underground," Michael joked, sitting up as well. He glanced behind us at the truck, appearing more con-fused than scared by the ephemeral attack. I wondered if his memory would be wiped at the academy.

Kaylani held our friend's hand and gave me a concerned look.

"Do you have your phone, Michael?" I asked.

"No, I haven't had it since I arrived," he said. "It was awful, not being able to contact you or Lion. My friends there were what kept my hopes up."

"I'm glad they treated you well," I said, holding his other hand.

He nodded. "Funny, isn't it? There was a whole new world underneath my own house, but the new world felt the most like home."

inchoate

The maps that we received at the beginning of the year had an accurate layout for each floor of the academy, including the library. Although the library was sometimes treated like a second building, it was still displayed on the map. That was why I was surprised by there not being a student-issued map for navigating the basement level of the school.

Professor Jones had arranged for me to be able to listen to Michael's inquisition prior to the debriefing I would go through with Kaylani and Naziah. We had taken the elevator to the basement floor, which was the only way to get there (other than the emergency exit for things like attacks on the building, but those weren't used gratuitously).

The basement level was much colder than the other floors, probably due to the absence of sunlight and the minimal amount of people present. As far as I knew, the level could stretch across the entire campus, even to the parking lot. Today wouldn't be my day of exploration as the interrogation room with Michael was less than thirty seconds from the elevator.

Plenty of staff workers had seen me by now, but none of them questioned my presence.

"Who sanctioned you to come here?" one woman asked. She was tall, with dark skin and blond hair. Her short neon yellow dress and brown high heels would've made me wonder if she was even a staff worker. Although the other workers who passed me seemed benign, this woman appeared to be the opposite.

"Professor Jones, ma'am. He said to wait outside of room 13," I answered.

She looked to her right at the one-way glass revealing Michael sitting at a table. "Why are you here?"

"To listen in on the inquisition of Michael Brown until my own debriefing." Part of me worried that I'd given the lady too much information, but she seemed vaguely impressed by my demeanor. I had no doubt that this woman was difficult to impress.

"I am going to bring you wireless headphones. Leave them on the door handle before you leave," she instructed. I contemplated verbally responding but could only give a nod before she was inside of the interrogation room. She said something to Michael and then took a pair of headphones from the unoccupied chair.

I waited patiently for her to return with the headphones and eagerly put them on. "All right, let's start, Mr. Brown," she said after reentering the room. Her voice was much more cheerful than when she'd talked to me, and I wondered if it was an interrogation tactic.

She took a seat at the opposite side of the small table from Michael. "How did you enjoy your stay at the academy?" she asked.

"It was...odd."

"Why's that?" She picked up the one notepad centered on the table and pulled out a pen from her pocket.

"I just wasn't used to it, that's all," Michael said. "But I liked it much more than this place."

Someone had obviously tricked Michael into believing that he was no longer at the school. I wondered if it was the woman herself or if she was only aware of the deception.

"I'm really sorry about that, but you might have to stay here a little longer," the woman said. "Your house isn't believed to be the safest place right now. Especially since your parents are out of town."

"They're in California," Michael nodded.

The woman wrote something in the notepad. "Why do you say that?"

"Just a guess. They said we would be going to southern California for the summer, but the night before we were supposed to leave, I woke up in some underground place."

"Police are being sent to investigate where you were."

"They're not gonna hurt the people there, are they?"

"Of course not. Is there anyone in particular who you would want to keep safe?"

"Just my friends," Michael told her. "Oziril, Harry, and Mariah. They were the only people whom I met."

"How many people did you see on a daily basis?" The woman wrote in her notebook.

"Maybe about a hundred... I'm not too sure."

"Did you learn anything about the place you were in?"

"I learned a good amount. I mean, I was there for weeks."

The woman chuckled after she noticed Michael smiling at his comment.

"Harry taught me the most," Michael informed. "Mariah was more a source of fun and entertainment. She helped me smile through my homesickness. Oziril was very nice too. I don't know much about him, except for the fact that he's the richest out of all the kids."

"What did Harry teach you?"

"He taught me how in the tunnels there was only rich and poor—no in-between. Not that different from everywhere else, if you ask me. He said that people lived in the tunnels when they didn't have anywhere else to go. Some kids just woke up there one day, like I did. Everyone gets there through the organization."

"Talk to me about the organization."

"Even he didn't know much. Just that they helped homeless people get off the streets. I don't know why I was there, considering I have a house. They've been doing it on the east coast for a while and just started on the west. That might be why my parents went to California: to help get people off the streets."

"Might be." The woman's answer felt halfhearted, as if she knew something about Michael's parents that she didn't want to tell him. "How are people treated there?"

"Terrible clothes, but great food. Nice bathrooms too. Everyone shares with one another, like one huge community."

"Do you know anything about the trip to California? What did your parents tell you about it?"

"They said we were going for the summer. Never told me exactly where. As to *why*, I think they said it would be a great vacation spot and allow them to do business more easily."

The woman wrote eagerly on her notepad. "What kind of business did your parents tell you that they do?"

"They didn't."

I leaned gently against the window and looked down the hall, still listening to the inquisition. "But I always thought that my parents were real estate agents. They probably mentioned it once when I was younger. I don't know anything else about their job, though."

My headphones were pulled off my head, and I turned around. "We have to go," Kaylani said, handing me the headphones. I felt that I'd much rather watch Michael's inquisition than go through my own debriefing. I placed the headphones on the door handle and followed my friend.

"Most first-years don't have debriefings. Not serious ones, anyway," she said. "They're normally for organized missions. I guess this *was* kind of a mission, but I wouldn't call it 'organized.'"

We stopped at a door with *20* on a panel above the door frame. This was the room where Professor Jones said my debriefing would take place. "Isn't Naziah supposed to be here?" I asked.

"Yeah. She's inside," Kaylani said, reaching for the door handle. She sighed and gave a reassuring smile before opening the door.

"Good afternoon, ladies!" A man was seated at a table where Naziah was on the other side. He appeared to be in his late teens or early twenties. "Close the door and take a seat."

Kaylani shut the door as directed, and I sat in the chair next to Naziah.

"I'm sure you girls have a lot of homework, considering it's a Monday, so let's try to keep this brief." Kaylani sat in the chair to my left. "We're going to start with the goal of entering the tunnels. What was most important for you to accomplish?"

Naziah looked from Kaylani to me, making it clear that this wasn't her question to answer. "Don't all talk at once," the man said.

"We wanted to locate Michael Brown," I reported. "He'd been missing for close to a month."

"How important is he to you, Jessie?"

"One of my best friends."

"And you, Kaylani? What's your relationship with Mr. Brown?"

"Same for me, sir. Michael, Jessie, and I have been best friends since kindergarten."

I wondered why Kaylani hadn't mentioned Lion as being a part of our friend group but assumed she didn't feel the man needed to know that much.

"What were the tunnels like, Naziah?"

"There was a sybaritic atmosphere. Where we entered was full of... I'd say at least three hundred people. It appeared almost like a party. There were LED lights on every wall, and each wall was made of brick. We passed a generator on the way, but the name of the company who made it was scraped off." I wasn't surprised that she'd been so observant.

"Did Michael mention anything about his parents?"

"Not to us," Kaylani answered. "He didn't really have time to. Someone shot at us on our way to the academy."

"Yes, I've heard. What about Michael's view on the place he was in? Did he hate it? Enjoy it? Embrace it?"

"I'm pretty sure he...*enjoyed* it," I faltered. "He made three friends there. While we rode here, he also made a bold statement. He said that the place he was in felt more like home than his real home."

"Do any of you know anything about his relationship with his parents?"

"Jessie and I have met them," Kaylani said. "They seem like nice people, but very private."

"I figured that," the man said. "And you, Jessie?"

I didn't want to repeat anything I'd heard Michael say during his inquisition, but the most I knew about his parents came from him during that time. "They're private," I agreed. "Private with strangers, obviously, but I think even more secretive around Michael himself."

Michael hadn't directly stated that his parents were keeping secrets from him, but that was what I'd fathomed.

"All right, that'll be all," the man said, rising from his seat. "You girls did fabulous. Especially you, Jessie. Not many newcomers do anything this important for the academy. This could build you a great reputation and commence opportunities for your future."

"Thank you," I said, wondering if it'd be better to take the words as praise or admonition.

The three of us stood as well and made our way to the door. I'd noticed that the man hadn't written anything down during the session and wondered if he had memorized everything we said.

"Can I talk to you two for a moment?" Naziah asked as we stepped into the hall. Kaylani and I nodded, following Naziah a few steps down the hall.

"I was listening to Riele's inquisition," she reported. "She will be released from the academy's custody as she proved herself not to be involved in the issues we are facing. However, I do not think she is fully innocent."

"Why's that?" I asked.

"Because of how she helped us find the tunnels," Naziah said. "The way she interpreted the note and somehow found a switch behind the fridge that blew up the floor. It was just too simple to me. Plus, there is no way that Michael's house is the only way to enter the tunnels. If they really go to the west coast, then there have to be many other entrances."

"What do you think we should do?" Kaylani asked.

Naziah shook her head. "I just think she is hiding important things and wanted to let you know."

She walked past us, heading toward the elevator. I leaned my back on the wall, still surprised that Naziah had shared that information with me. *Does this mean she trusts me?*

"I talked to Damian," Kaylani told me. "He's in hiding. I told Professor Jones, and he's arranged for the group sent to California to prioritize finding him."

"That's great! At least we won't have to worry about him."

"Yeah. It's still a miracle he's alive. I hope they find him soon."

Down the hall, the door to room 13 opened, and the woman who questioned Michael stepped into the hall. "I'll text you later," I told Kaylani before rushing toward the woman. As much as I wanted to assure Kaylani that Damian would be safe, I had to assure myself that Michael would be safe.

The woman recognized me and stopped walking. "Where is he going to be kept?" I asked.

The woman sighed as if annoyed by my question. "He'll be at one of the academy's refuges. Don't worry about him."

"And what about his friends? From the tunnels?"

She started to say something and paused, like she was trying to figure out how to answer. "Officers were sent to investigate yesterday," she finally said. "They're not going to stop and look for three kids. All they're doing is finding out why people live there and what Michael's parents have to do with it."

"You mean what the organization that his parents work for has to do with it?"

"He will be fine." She turned away, signaling that our conversation was over. I sighed and stepped forward to look through the window.

Michael was still seated at the table. He rested his hands on the table and started talking to himself. I noticed his eyes were closed and assumed he was saying a prayer. Knowing how selfless he was, I assumed he was praying for his friends' safety more than his own.

branching troubles

IFON Academy
Dormitory 356
Tuesday
1620 hours

"*It started with Michael but* turned into a million other issues."

"Like?"

"Well, Naziah doesn't trust Riele, and she was set free from custody yesterday. Then Royal and Juan broke out of jail. Then there's Michael's friends from the tunnels, who he doesn't want to get hurt. Actually, *everyone* in the tunnels. There were a lot of people."

"None of those are your problems. You can't burden yourself with everything that the academy deals with."

"Isn't that our job?"

"Our job is to learn, Parker. You started off going on a mission to find your friend, but that's *extremely* rare. If anything, you need a break. Enjoy yourself."

"I have a ton of science homework—the opposite of enjoyable."

"You know what I mean."

Donnay hadn't been my closest friend at the academy, or exactly someone I wanted to trust. Although, she did give good advice. Being at IFON had made me feel that I was supposed to fix all of the issues I heard of, but not many of them truly involved me.

"The real issue is that they're serving fried chicken for dinner," Olivia groaned.

"That's amazing," Donnay disagreed.

Olivia shook her head. "It's disgusting."

Donnay grabbed her pillow and threw it at Olivia, who was sitting on the edge of her bed.

"Hey!" She threw the pillow back, which Donnay caught effortlessly.

"I've never actually gone to dinner," I thought aloud, lying down on my bed. "Just lunch and sometimes breakfast."

"We're definitely taking you," Donnay promised. "It's in a couple of hours."

"I'll do my homework until then," I told her, reaching for my book bag on the floor.

"Mr. Wang gave us a whole binder," Olivia recalled. "I did some of it while he was talking about neuroscience."

"That unit will be easy." After unzipping my bag, I reached for the yellow binder that was wedged between two textbooks.

"Sounds easy. Probably just memorizing facts, like what part of the brain controls what part of your body," Donnay commented.

"I think every class is just memorizing facts." Olivia laughed.

I set the binder on my bed and opened it. Flipping through pages, I stopped at the neuroscience section. The page had three pictures of the brain from different perspectives, with certain parts and their functions labeled.

"You were right, Donnay," I reported.

"The cerebrum holds your memories, right?" Olivia asked.

I looked for the section of the brain she referred to and read its description. "Yeah, that's one of its functions."

"I'm gonna ace this unit." She smiled, leaning back on her pillow.

"Maybe that's it," I said, looking at my roommates. "Maybe I need to talk to someone who would remember more. Someone who's observant."

"I thought you were finally gonna relax." Donnay sighed.

"I wanna deserve my place here," I admitted. "Even if it's just to prove others wrong. Lady Kate had a mission in mind when she brought me here, and it hasn't been completed. If I can solve it before everyone else, I'll deserve my place."

Donnay and Olivia looked from me to each other. "I think you should rest, Jessie," Olivia said. "But since it means that much to you, I'll be willing to help you solve your mission."

"Me too," Donnay agreed. "It sounds fun."

I took my phone from my nightstand and went to my contacts. The person I needed to talk to was Naziah, though I wasn't sure if she would answer my calls. I scrolled through names until I found Naziah's and then hesitantly pressed the button to call her. Putting my phone on speaker, it started to ring. Olivia seemed curious about whom I was calling, but I had a feeling that Donnay could tell.

After about four rings, she picked up the phone.

"Hello?"

Olivia's eyes widened after hearing her voice.

"This is Jessie," I said.

"I know," Naziah replied. "What do you need?"

"I was just wondering if you noticed anything from Michael's house."

"What do you mean?"

Talking to Naziah over the phone weirdly made me feel more nervous than when I'd talk to her in person. "I was wondering if there was anything you noticed that you didn't mention out loud. Specifically regarding Michael's parents."

"If you know the first and last name of each parent, then I could tell you how to find them." Naziah had quickly caught on to my goal, and I was impressed by her cooperation, but I didn't have the information she would need.

"I don't think they ever told me their first names," I said. "Not recent enough for me to remember, at least."

"Fine. Meet me in the library as soon as dinner is over," Naziah instructed, before ending the call.

"Isn't the library being renovated?" asked Donnay. "From the attack last week?"

"The bottom floor is the only part accessible for students," Olivia informed. She turned to face me. "If you ever need our help, just ask."

"Of course," I complied, aware that I was still hesitant to completely trust them. Alternately, if there was no chance of me finding

Michael's parents alone, then I'd be willing to ask my roommates for help. I was only worried that there was no chance of me succeeding alone, in which case, the potential reward for finding Michael's parents wouldn't be entirely mine.

*****

"Look away while I enter my password." I turned around and closed my eyes, tempted to look back before she finishes typing. "You can turn around."

Looking back at the desktop, Naziah had logged onto a database for airline information. "After you called me, I looked at all the airlines on the east coast and used my laptop to search them for any flights booked under the name Brown for two different airports."

"Thank you so much. You didn't have to do all that."

"It only took three hours."

"Then you *really* didn't have to do that. But…thank you. What did you find?"

"Hundreds of names. But none of them were headed to California. I thought it was a mistake at first but realized there were two other possibilities. Either Michael's parents booked a flight that has not left yet, or they are driving to California. Remember when I told you that the plate for the moving van was dormant?"

"Yeah. I thought they'd be using it to keep from being tracked, but you said it'd be impossible to drive that far without cops arresting them."

"It would be, but only if there were cops around."

I considered Naziah's words and finally caught on. "You think they're using the tunnels?"

"If they bring petroleum with them, yes, I think it would make sense. Although, there is another possibility that we can assess right now. I never got to look at the flights for the closest airport to us."

Naziah typed *Brown* into the search bar and opened a drop-down menu. She checked the box reading *Prospective Flights* and then the one reading *This Month*. The screen showed a list of various names that included "Brown."

"Do you recognize any of them?" Naziah asked.

She slowly scrolled through the results but quickly reached the bottom of the page. There were less than a hundred names.

"No, I don't."

"In that case, let's see how many are going to California."

She clicked a button that took her to another page where each name was beside the person's destination. Naziah scrolled through the entire list and then returned to the two names that were destined to California: Xavier L. Brown and Lucy T. G. Brown.

"What airline are they using?" I asked.

Naziah clicked on *Xavier L. Brown*, which opened another page. *Travelling by "Teviree Airlines"* was in bold at the top of the page filled with information.

"That's gotta be him," I said.

"The flight leaves in ten minutes," she reported, leaning back in her chair.

"We have to catch them, right?"

"That is not our job, Jessie. If I could do this in a few hours, Lady Kate has probably learned this *and* more."

"Can you at least look up if Riele is taking any flights to California?" I asked. Naziah looked at me curiously but started typing before I could explain.

I anxiously tapped my foot until Naziah leaned back, signaling that she had finished. There was one name on the screen: *Riele T. Mana-Kahananui*. I reached for the mouse and clicked the name, opening another page that was both exciting and anxiety-inducing to read.

"Travelling with Teviree Airlines," I read. "Why would they book a flight under their real name?"

"They have to," Naziah explained, pulling her phone from her pocket. "You have to use the name on your ID to travel. They would not be able to use an alias when dealing with IFON either, because IFON would check their physical IDs *and* the ones in the system. The real question is: Why would they wait until now to leave?"

"Do you think Royal and Juan are getting on the flight too?" I asked.

"I doubt it matters," she replied.

"Well, how far is the airport from here?"

"Too far to reach in ten minutes. Which is why the flight needs to be delayed."

Naziah pulled her phone from her pocket and appeared to be dialing a number. She set her phone on the desk and put it on speakerphone.

"Do you have authority over Teviree Airlines?" she asked after the ringing stopped.

"Yeah, especially since the incident. They want all the help they can get, so I'm basically promoted. Why?"

I didn't recognize the voice, but they obviously were close with Naziah.

"I need you to get flight..." Naziah scrolled down through the page. "AR 400 delayed."

"They're gonna start boarding in, like, two minutes."

"The sooner the better."

The person on the other end sighed.

"How long do you need it for?"

"As long as possible," Naziah said. The other end was silent, and then the person sighed again.

"I'll do what I can," they eventually said before ending the call.

I looked at Naziah and noticed how engaged she was.

"If the flight wasn't delayed already, then Lady Kate might not have figured it out," I thought aloud.

Naziah stood from her seat and walked into the aisle. "Not yet, at least. Shut down the desktop."

Sliding into her seat, I closed each tab before turning off the device. Naziah was already close to the door going from the library to the school, and I quickly followed. Through the tall windows, I could see a lot of cars on the road. Naziah's friend would have to pull extra strings for us to get to the airport in time.

"Call Kaylani. Tell her to meet us in the parking lot," Naziah called over her shoulder. I quickly took my phone from my pocket, while the whole library seemed to dim. Looking out the window, everything appeared a lot darker.

While calling my best friend, the entire mission felt as if it would be easier. If I were to succeed, I'd be happy to share the prestige with Kaylani.

aviation academy

Although our surroundings were pretty much the same as our first visit, the atmosphere seemed to carry an entirely different feeling. Part of the new feeling came from my expectation that we were in the center of imminent danger.

Naziah rushed toward us from the front table, with two of our ten guards behind her. "Two people checked in as the Browns," she reported.

"And Riele?" I asked.

"Nobody checked in under that name," she said. "Either she is still on her way or not coming. I doubt the latter—she booked a first-class ticket across the country."

"Yeah, she's not missing that flight," Kaylani agreed. "We have to move toward the gate if we don't wanna scare her off."

"I will stay here and wait for her. You all find the Browns. The flight is at gate 20," Naziah directed.

Kaylani took my hand and started walking. "I can't believe this." She sighed. "What if they're really here?"

"Then IFON gets what they want." I shrugged.

Kaylani shook her head. "But what if this was too easy? I mean, there's no way they're giving up without a fight."

"I wouldn't say this was easy."

We got a lot of stares from other people, and some of them took pictures. "I'm just worried they could be expecting us," Kaylani said.

Before I could comment, a group of airport security turned the corner ahead and crossed our path. Some of them nodded at us while the intercom turned on. "All passengers of delayed flight AR 400 please report to gate 12. Again, all passengers of delayed flight AR 400 please report to gate 12. Thank you." The voice belonged to the same woman who Naziah called from the library.

"We don't know what Michael's parents look like," Kaylani said.

"What do you mean? We've seen them before."

"Yeah, months ago. What if they disguised themselves?"

"Airport staff were covertly directed to report if they saw either Browns," one of the guards said, lowering his voice. "They were shown images from their IDs. If they didn't look similar to their headshots, then they wouldn't have been able to check in." Kaylani nodded with a sigh—she was still incredulous.

We walked a good distance through the terminal and drew a lot of attention to ourselves. The airport was just as crowded as it was during our first visit, making it even harder to find Michael's parents. "I see gate 12." Kaylani pointed past a group of adults and toward the gate down the hall. Every seat appeared taken, and I assumed that the people from gate 20 had already moved to gate 12.

Two female staff workers left the gate, and once they saw us, they immediately came our way. "The people you're looking for haven't come to the gate yet," one of them said.

"So they're still in gate 20?" a guard asked.

"Most likely. Security footage is being reviewed to find out where they went," the other worker replied.

"They're not in gate 20," I observed. Down the hall, a man and a woman were racing toward the escalators.

"That's them?" Kaylani asked as our guards started racing down the hall.

"One of them has a gun," I observed as the man pulled his weapon from his pocket.

"Yeah, that's them."

I pulled my phone from my pocket and quickly dialed Naziah. The guards were on the escalators by the time she picked up, and Michael's parents were already on the second floor.

"We found them, and Mr. Brown has a gun," I reported.

"I know," Naziah said. "I just watched the security footage."

"What? Where are you?"

"In the surveillance room, obviously."

"Riele isn't coming?"

Kaylani looked at me curiously as she was only hearing one side of the conversation. I placed the call on speakerphone so that she would hear better. The crowds in the gates were loud, but we could still hear Naziah.

"Riele is with me tied to a chair."

"Oh..."

"She put up a fight trying to get away. Expect the Browns to do the same. But do not follow them."

"The guards already left to go after them."

Naziah sighed on the other end. "The last thing you would want to do is lead a chase in the middle of a crowded airport. Either they have backup to drive them away or they are going to try to get on another flight. The former is more likely."

"What do we do?"

"Just keep them in the airport's vicinity. I will see if I can get the airport on lockdown."

The call ended abruptly, leaving Kaylani and me just as frustrated as before.

"How are we supposed to do that?" Kaylani huffed.

I thought about where Michael's parents were headed. They immediately went to the second floor. A possibility of their plan came to mind.

"Where's the surveillance room?" I asked.

"I think upstairs," Kaylani replied.

"Is there a rooftop exit?"

"Probably. Why?"

"I think I might know what they're doing."

"You're gonna need my help," Kaylani said. I nodded and turned to head back the way we'd come.

"You have no idea."

We ran through the terminal, dodging groups of people on our way. "Flight GI 531 is now boarding," came from overhead. I picked up speed, and Kaylani noticed my urgency. Being more accustomed to running than I was, she reached the exit before me.

"Where are we going?" she asked as I met her at the door.

"To the plane that's taking off," I said.

"You think they're boarding it?"

"And trying to get Riele on the way. That gives us some time."

We made it to the sidewalk outside of the terminal, which was underneath a glass structure reaching across the road. I took Kaylani's hand and raced down the pathway.

"Terminal C is closest to us," Kaylani reported, shouting over the sound of engines running. "Let's go there first!"

Finally reaching the side of the airport, terminal C stood out from the rest. What made it noticeable was the person standing on the rooftop, aiming a recognizable device toward the sky.

"That's one of them!" I said, pointing at the person.

"You were right." Kaylani sighed. I let go of her hand so that she could move faster.

Arriving outside of the terminal just seconds after her, Kaylani had already spotted the plane. She merely pointed toward it, signaling for me to keep running until I reached it. The airplane seemed to grow larger the closer we got to it.

I covered my ears while racing toward the plane and hoped that nobody would see us.

"Both of them aren't boarding?" Kaylani called.

"I think the other one is trying to get Riele!" I shouted. "Get on the plane!"

Kaylani sped up, though I couldn't push myself to run any faster. As she reached the plane, my phone vibrated against my leg. I reached in my pocket while trying not to slow down.

"C'mon, Jess!" Looking up, I saw that Kaylani had already reached the airplane. I put off checking my phone, despite my fear that it was Naziah calling me.

Approaching my friend, we saw that the doors were closed and far too high to reach. Unless the driver were to lower the staircase for us to enter the plane, we couldn't get inside.

"This thing is huge!" Kaylani said. She leaned forward, taking in vast amounts of air each breath. My lungs felt as if they were on fire, and my legs felt weak.

Kaylani turned around and looked up at the rooftop of terminal C.

"I see Naziah!" she exclaimed. I turned as well, seeing a familiar figure aim a weapon toward the airplane. The weapon fired, releasing a long rope toward our way, with a hook on the end of the rope. It quickly flew over our heads and stuck to the top of the airplane.

Naziah tugged on the gadget before abruptly being pulled with it. Kaylani and I watched the device quickly pull her toward the plane. She stopped on the side of the plane, her feet pressing against it. She carefully approached one of the doors, still holding on to the device. After retrieving something from her pocket, she used a weapon to try and pry open the door.

I looked back up at the roof of terminal C, which appeared empty. *Did they run away?* There was a loud alarm from the plane, and I turned to face the now-opened door to the aircraft. Naziah lowered herself enough to get inside and then retracted the device.

"Catch!" she called, which I could only hear faintly over the engine. She tossed the device down toward us, which Kaylani deftly received.

Naziah disappeared inside the airplane, and Kaylani wrapped her arm around me. She aimed the device toward the door, and the hook latched itself onto the floor of the plane.

"Stretch your feet in front of you and don't lock your knees!" she ordered. I nodded in response, anxiously waiting for her to retract us toward the plane.

The device quickly pulled us, and we stopped the impact by pressing our feet against the side of the plane. Kaylani pushed me inside first and then climbed in next. I stood up to close the door and saw another figure standing on the roof of terminal C. They were aiming something toward me, and I hurriedly pulled the door shut. A loud sound pierced through the air, followed by something clanging against the door. Kaylani helped me pull the door all the way closed, and many of the sounds around us disappeared.

The alarm turned off, and the sound of the engine was much quieter. Both of us collapsed on the floor, exhausted from our incomplete endeavor.

"We have to help Naziah," Kaylani said. The airplane began to move, and we exchanged concerned looks.

"Let's go," I said, hesitantly rising from the floor. Kaylani moved past me, approaching the cockpit. We rushed down the aisles of the empty airplane, breathing heavily and ignoring the pain we felt from exertion.

After a few seconds of walking, we saw Naziah standing in the aisle, waiting for us.

"What's happening?" Kaylani asked.

"Riele got away," Naziah replied. She appeared angrier than I'd ever seen her. "Instead of fighting off the lady who came to free her, I stalled them both so I could get on the plane. It is currently in autopilot."

"At least one of them has a gun," I reported. "And they have a grappling hook of their own. They're gonna use the hook to get onto the plane, but probably after we're in the air."

The plane tilted backward, and we each held on to the seat closest to us. We were finally taking off.

I looked through the window to my left and saw the grass beneath us gradually getting farther. "We have to figure out where this plane is headed," Naziah said. Kaylani and I nodded to agree, though we had no idea as to how we would do so.

"We have until the plane flies over terminal C to do something," I said, recalling my idea of the plan that Michael's parents would carry out. They were probably waiting for the plane to get closer to the roof before they grappled onto it.

"This was obviously their plan B," Naziah noted. "We should assume that they have a plan C. Jessie, stay here and keep watch. Kaylani, follow me."

Kaylani followed Naziah down the aisle the way we'd come, and I slid into the seat closest to me. The speed of the plane practically glued me to the chair, and my hands were sore from gripping onto it when I was standing. Looking through the window again, I could see three figures standing on the rooftop of the terminal. Thinking about the possible plan C that our enemies had, I grew more nervous about how we would stop them.

The plane abruptly jolted, and I feared that the aircraft was falling. I heard Kaylani call for me and leaned into the aisle. She and Naziah were rushing back.

"What happened?" I asked.

"Someone shot at one of the windows," Kaylani replied, sliding into the seat across the aisle from me. Naziah held on to the top of my chair and steadied herself. She leaned forward and looked out of my window.

"If we go too high, the oxygen masks are gonna drop down," she said.

"Who was firing at us?" I queried.

"Probably people on our side," Naziah explained. "They may not know that we are on board." I sighed and slouched in the chair, subconsciously hyperventilating.

"It's all right. We found the parachutes," Kaylani said.

My eyes widened, and I looked at my friend. She'd spoken with such equanimity that I wasn't sure if she knew what she said.

"We're jumping out?" I asked.

"Possibly," Naziah said. "Although, I have another idea first."

She started walking, pushing herself forward against each chair she passed. Kaylani glanced at me nervously yet followed Naziah. I leaned into the aisle and watched the two go toward the cockpit.

Looking out the window, we were very close to terminal C. My heart was pounding as we grew closer to the terminal.

Down the aisle, a gunshot rang throughout the cabin. After a couple of seconds, glass crashed from where the cockpit was, and masks dropped from overhead. I debated whether or not to wear the mask or help the others but chose to do the latter. Struggling to steady myself, I worked my way through the cabin and toward the cockpit.

The door to the cockpit was open, and Kaylani rushed out. "They broke the windows in the flight deck." She sighed, leaning against the wall.

"Coward!" Naziah's voice echoed from the cockpit, and Kaylani and I rushed inside.

Upon entering the cockpit, it was almost impossible to walk forward. The wind was pushing us back, and my back was pressed against the wall. This was my second time seeing a flight deck trashed. There were two windows, each punctured by a couple of bullets, and glass on the floor.

"I hope the Browns aren't gonna try to come in," Kaylani said.

A siren sounded in the cabin, and Naziah cocked her gun before exiting the cockpit. "Actually, *Riele* is coming," she reported from the hall. "Kaylani, come on! Jessie, land this thing!"

With my face flushed, Kaylani gave me an assuring nod. "You got this, Jess," she said before rushing into the cabin. I turned to face the controls, which were nothing to me but levers, switches, and pretty lights. I brushed glass from one of the pilot chairs and took a seat.

"Naziah, I don't know how these work!" I called. Leaving me to land the plane seemed like the worst decision possible. Unfortunately, my cowardly response didn't sway her decision.

"Just lower us!" Naziah called back, followed by a gunshot in the cabin.

I nervously set my hands on the control wheel and saw that we were barely above the airport. Being so low made me terrified that we would hit the building at any moment.

"Get up," Naziah said from behind me. Relieved, I rose from the seat and Naziah took my place.

"Maybe I should help Kaylani, and you land," I suggested.

She sighed in response. "You know how to use a gun?"

"No."

"You know how to fight?"

"More than I know how to land an airplane."

"All right, listen closely." A gunshot followed by a crash sounded in the cabin, which caused both Naziah and me to turn around.

She quickly turned back to face the controls, and the urgency in her voice caught my attention. "Pull back on this throttle to reduce power, use that brake pedal *after* you land, push down this lever to deploy the wheels about twenty seconds before you land, and use the control wheel to direct where you go. Good luck." She quickly stood from her seat and rushed toward the cabin. I took her place and set my shaky hands onto the wheel.

Michael's parents weren't with us, which meant they were probably executing their plan C. I had an idea where that plan would take place, but we had to get there first.

Pull back on the throttle to reduce power...push forward to add power.

I hesitantly pushed the throttle forward with one hand. We flew above the airport and the plane tilted upward, pushing me further back in my seat. Using the control wheel, I attempted to guide the plane toward IFON as I'd know my way around from there.

Kaylani and Naziah entered the cockpit.

"What are you doing?" Naziah asked.

"Finishing the job," I replied. "You told me how to land this thing. Now tell me how to fly it."

it takes two: reprise

Michael's house
Garage
Tuesday
1850 hours

My phone had beeped repeatedly for the past three minutes. I had been too focused on looking out for Michael's parents yet finally decided to check the texts. The majority of them were from Olivia and Donnay asking where I was. The rest were from Finniake and River, who had originally typed in the *BFFs For Life* chat to ask what was going on but by now were having a full-blown conversation about Christmas.

"I still think they know that we're here," Kaylani whispered.

I powered off my phone and then turned to face my friend. "You're probably right. They know we left the airport."

We had landed a good distance away from Michael's house in an empty parking lot. Now, we were hiding in his garage with the guards who had escorted us to the airport. One of them had lectured us on how foolish it was to fly so far from the airport, and I was sure I'd get more lecturing when we returned to the academy.

"What if they don't come?" asked Kaylani.

"We know they will use the tunnels to get to California," Naziah said.

Kaylani and I turned to face her. "They wasted their money on plane tickets, and pretty soon their faces will be on 'wanted' posters in stations around the city. But there is no logical way for them to get to California without using the tunnels. Unless there is another opening big enough for a car to fit into, they most likely will come here."

We were seated on the floor at one side of the garage, with the guards and Riele on the other.

"What happened to the people in the tunnels?" I asked. "When the police came to investigate?"

"Police were never sent to investigate." Naziah shook her head. "Who told you that?"

"I was listening to some of Michael's inquisition yesterday. The woman said police were sent here to investigate the tunnels. Why would she lie about that?"

"Maybe to make him start talking about what it was like in the tunnels."

"But she told me that to my face. I asked her about it."

Naziah shrugged in response. "Maybe the woman misunderstood what she was told."

"So if nobody came to investigate the tunnels, that means that Michael knows the most about them?"

"If it is between IFON pupils, staff, and Michael, then yes."

"So shouldn't we call him? Maybe he knows if there is another entrance."

"The woman who talked to him would already know," Kay said.

"Not necessarily," Naziah replied. "Michael may be more lenient about what he says when talking to someone close."

"I can call the number for those in MSAC," one of the guards said.

"Mareschal Science Academy Care," Kaylani told me before I could verbally question the acronym. "The school helps out children in poverty or abusive situations through the MSAC program. The people in the program aren't a part of IFON."

I nodded my head in understanding, realizing that I'd been to the MSAC building. It was the first place where I met Naziah and what many had called the "refuge."

Naziah rose from next to me. "While we call Michael, I suggest giving another try at getting something useful from her," Naziah said.

"I'm not saying anything," Riele replied.

Naziah disappeared into the darkness across the garage, but I could hear them just as clearly.

"You are going to have to help us sooner or later," Naziah pointed out.

"I'm gonna be free from your custody by Monday," Riele replied. "You have no proof I was doing anything remotely wrong."

"Associating with the Browns is enough proof we need," one guard said.

"I just called the program, and they're transferring to Michael," another guard said. "I'll put it on speaker. Only Jessie talks."

Kaylani motioned for me to go to the guard. Apprehensively standing up, I carefully worked through the darkness as the figures across the room came into view.

"Hello?" Michael's voice sounded from my left, and I spotted the phone on the floor.

"Michael, it's me Jessie." I smiled, relieved to hear his voice.

"Jessie! Hi!"

"Hey! How are you?"

"I'm all right. I miss my house, honestly."

"You'll be back soon." I felt sickened by my own lie. "How are they treating you?"

"Surprisingly well. I felt like a prisoner at first, but now…"

"Stay on task. You can talk about other things later," Naziah whispered in my ear, shifting my attention from Michael. She then sat on the floor next to me.

"That's awesome!" I exulted, hoping that it was an appropriate response to whatever Michael had said. "Listen, I wanna ask…"

"Boo!" Riele's voice echoed in the garage, followed by her laughter.

"Who was that?" Michael questioned.

I turned around to make sure that the guards had restrained Riele.

"A video," I lied. "I forgot to put it on pause."

"Oh, okay. What were you gonna ask?"

"Something about the tunnels. Do you know anything about entrances to it?" Michael didn't respond for a moment, and I wondered if he didn't hear me.

"Why do you ask?"

"I wanna go to check on your friends and see it for myself," I said. Naziah nodded in approval. It felt good to have the closest thing to praise that I could get from Naziah but felt terrible to lie to one of my best friends.

"There was something about entrances, yeah. Oziril mentioned it. He said that some use cars in the tunnels to get around."

"Perfect! How would you drive through?"

"Well, he took me to watch the cars once, but only one came. It was a red truck."

I looked at Naziah, who motioned for me to keep talking. "I'm curious now...so you don't know how cars drive in?"

"He said some people get there from their garages."

"Do you think you could get there from yours?" Michael didn't respond, and I assumed he was thinking.

"I doubt it, honestly. My parents have this place that they never let me go near, though. It's a switch in the back of the garage that they said will cut the power permanently in our house if you use it. Maybe they lied, and it opens a portal to the tunnels!" He laughed at his comment, and I fake-chuckled along. Naziah stood up and went toward the front of the garage.

"That's really interesting," I said. The garage door gently screeched as it started to open. "I gotta go to bed—there's this rule at MSA that you have to be asleep at a certain time."

"Oh, that's the summer school, right?"

"Yeah, exactly."

"You think I could go there next year?"

"I think you'd be perfect. I'll put in a good word, okay?"

"A'ight. Tell Kay and Lion that I miss them."

"We all miss you too."

I hesitantly hovered my finger over the *End Call* button, but Michael ended the call for me.

"You have to be kidding me!" Naziah's voice sounded from the sidewalk outside of the garage.

"What happened?" I asked, rushing toward her.

"I knew she did it for some reason," Naziah groaned as Kaylani joined my side. "Riele was warning Michael's parents not to come in when she shouted. They were just here."

"How do you know?"

"I saw them." Naziah was looking at the house across the street.

"They're in there?" I ask.

One of the windows on the second floor opened, followed by Naziah shouting for everyone to get down. Dropping to the floor, three consecutive bullets flew our way. I scrambled to the wall of the garage with Kaylani, where everyone else was on the other side. Gunshots rang from the other side of the garage, and glass crashed across the street. Kaylani and I were covering our ears, trying to stay out of Michael's parents' sight.

In the heat of the moment, I stood from my position and quickly exited the garage. The guards and Naziah were still firing from our side, so I ran across the street toward the house. My heart was pounding from fear I would get hit in the crossfire. The firing ceased when I reached the other sidewalk.

I knelt down by the garage of the other house and heard heavy breathing behind me. Jumping at the sound, Kaylani was sitting on the sidewalk. "You followed me?"

"I wasn't letting you do this alone, Jess. And Naziah threw me her gun." She held up the weapon in a way that made me nervous to let her use it.

"Why didn't she just come with us?"

"She's Naziah. She does things that seem stupid but wind up helping out in the end."

"Right..."

Two shots fired from above us, and we lowered ourselves closer to the sidewalk, covering our heads. "When they respond, we move," I said, impressed by my own gallantry.

"That seems like a terrible time to move," Kaylani protested yet raced with me to the front door of the house when our guards began to shoot back.

At the front door, I had a terrible feeling that Michael's parents were aiming at us. Kaylani didn't have the same feeling. "You should take this," she said, handing me Naziah's gun. "I'm better at fighting. No offense."

"None taken."

"Just aim as you practiced in class. Only pull the trigger if your life is in danger and you have a close-range shot."

I wasn't sure how to cock the gun like Naziah did so instead simply held it with my index finger on the trigger. "When do we go in?" Kaylani whisper-asked. The streetlight would be enough for the guards to see us, so I waved my hands and pointed to the windows above us. They didn't seem to understand, so I motioned with my hands to shoot at the house. There was inconsistent firing from their side, and I hesitantly opened the door.

Kaylani stepped in front of me, and then we both carefully entered. The dark house was hard to see in, but nobody shot at us yet. Gunshots from the floor above us sounded, and Kaylani and I started to look for the staircase. I briefly worried about the others in the neighborhood who would be nervous about the sounds. Michael's neighborhood was relatively safe, and this could be a calamity for the residents. The thought pressured me even more to find Michael's parents.

The staircase was in the large foyer of the house, and the layout was fairly similar to that of Michael's house. We carefully went up the staircase, and I pointed Naziah's gun in front of me. The shooting continued, and it sounded like both of Michael's parents were firing.

"We have to go," a deep voice said from around the corner. Kaylani nervously looked at me, and I brushed past her, holding out my weapon. The firing in the room to our left stopped, but nobody had exited. I carefully walked down the hallway, sensing Kaylani's presence behind me. My hands were shaking, and I gripped the weapon tighter.

Shots came from Michael's house followed by glass shattering in the room. Ambivalently turning into the room, Kaylani rushed past me and moved out of my sight. I quickly followed behind, spotting a man hiding by the large bed. Kaylani lunged, knocking him down. His weapon clattered to the floor, followed by a gunshot from my right. I rushed toward the master bathroom where the shot came from and aimed my gun inside. The lady spotted me and cocked her gun. I prematurely fired my weapon, eyes closed as I did so.

I heard the woman's gun clatter onto the tile flooring. Quickly opening my eyes, I saw that the bullet had punctured the bathtub. After noticing that she was unharmed, the woman reached for her weapon. I rapidly moved forward and kicked her weapon out of her reach, carefully aiming my own weapon at her.

Now that I could see her face, I recognized the woman to be Michael's mother. Her eyes widened as she looked me up and down, realizing that her son's best friend was the one aiming a gun at her. I began to lower my weapon as footsteps echoed in the hallway outside the bedroom.

"What in the world are you doing?" Naziah's voice came from the front door of the room, and she walked toward me.

"She was going to fire," I told her, worried that I'd done the wrong thing. Naziah entered the bathroom and retrieved the woman's weapon.

"Make sure it was not a lethal discharge," she instructed, taking her gun from my hand as she passed me.

"How do I do that?" I asked, carefully approaching Mrs. Brown.

"Just let me know if you hit her torso."

I knelt by Mrs. Brown who made no effort to sheathe her vexation. "You idiot! You coulda killed me!"

"I didn't even come close," I said, then directly told Naziah that I had only hit the bathtub.

Naziah leaned against the bathroom wall. "Impressive that you missed such an easy shot," she noted.

I wanted to defend myself by stating that I had missed because my eyes were closed, but I decided it wouldn't help my case.

"You managed not to kill her in the process, though. I was unsure of Kaylani's faith in you," Naziah added, which seemed to be more of a compliment.

Both of us looked into the bedroom at Kaylani, who had tied Mr. Brown's hands to the bedpost with a blanket.

"The guards are coming inside to get the Browns and take us back," Naziah stated.

I nodded and leaned against the bathtub in front of me. The whole night had been exhausting and a lot to process.

"Good job," Kaylani complimented, entering the bathroom. Naziah exited into the bedroom while Kaylani came and sat by me. "You completed the mission. Lady Kate was smart for bringing you here."

"I completed *my* mission," I said. "And I needed you to do that. Now we get to take these two back for questioning."

"More like imprisonment," Kaylani corrected, flashing a sly smile at Mrs. Brown.

Mrs. Brown said something back at Kaylani, but I drowned out her voice. Finally having found Michael's parents was relieving, and I was more than pleased to share the credit with Kaylani. I thought it would be her and me against the world, but starting off with the Browns didn't seem too bad.

From the relief and comfort mixed with exhaustion, I drifted to sleep within seconds.

reassemble

I sat on the floor, waiting for the others to come by. After going through a unique school day, the professor asked me to meet with him. We'd just finished discussing what I did the night before, and what it was like finding Michael's parents. He praised me multiple times in the one session, saying things like "IFON is blessed to have a student such as yourself."

Though it was the middle of the week, Finniake, River, and my roommates had suggested that we hang out after school. The suggestion seemed so out of place that I wondered if they only wanted to ask me about everything that happened the evening prior. After such an overwhelming school day, I was willing to converse with people whom I recognized.

All throughout the day, people whom I didn't know were either staring me down or complimenting me. It didn't surprise me that the word had spread so quickly, but the attention would take some getting used to.

"There she is!" Finniake came from the hallway to my left, eagerly waving to me. I waved back, rising from the floor. River was just behind him.

"Where are we goin'?" he asked.

"I don't care. Just to have some fun," I told him.

"We could go outside until dinner. Is that them?"

I looked over my shoulder to where River had pointed and saw Donnay and Olivia climbing up the staircase. Both of them rushed over at the sight of us.

"So where we goin'?" Donnay asked.

"Outside," River said, looking at the rest of us to ensure we were fine with the suggestion.

"Could we visit someone first?" I asked.

The group looked at me, but a collection of nods and shrugs confirmed that my idea would be fine.

"Who are we visiting?" Donnay asked as I started to lead the group toward the staircase.

"Michael," I replied. "I wanna make sure he's okay."

We only went down two steps on the staircase before the intercom turned on. "Jessie Parker, please report to the principal's office." The voice that I couldn't recognize repeated the command, and my heart rate seemed to speed up instantly.

"We'll go with you," Finniake offered. "To the elevator, at least."

Now, it was Finniake leading us back up the stairs and toward the nearest elevator. Olivia set her hands on my shoulders. "Don't be nervous."

"There's a lot of bad news that Lady Kate could tell me," I fretted.

"I guarantee she just wants to congratulate you," surmised Donnay. I shook my head, too worried to believe my roommate.

We stopped at a different elevator than the one I'd used my first time going to Lady Kate's office. Thankfully, I had peers who would tell me how to get around. "You'll be close to the office," River said. "Go straight, then make your first left, then the first right after that left."

"That was confusing even for me," Finniake shook his head.

"Straight, left, right," I summarized. "Got it."

The elevator door opened, and I quickly stepped inside.

"Meet us by the front office," Donnay said. I nodded my head and pressed the button for the top floor. The group gave some waving *goodbye*s as the elevator doors closed. I leaned against the back of the elevator, feeling the wall vibrate against my back.

Please let this be good news.

When the doors opened, there were a lot of people walking through the halls. All of them were staff workers, but only a couple seemed to notice my presence. I stepped out of the elevator and started walking forward, trying to avoid the other people present.

Make the first left.

The hallway to my left was clear except for two staff members who were talking. One of them nodded at me, and I waved back. *Maybe they know who I am... Just make the next right.*

I didn't have to think much about where to go as the large familiar seating area directed me toward Lady Kate's office. I could see the hallway to Lady Kate's office from here and quickly walked toward it.

As soon as I turned the corner into the hallway, the guards in front of her office opened the doors.

I stepped into the entrance foyer and saw Lady Kate's office door electronically locked. The guards closed the doors behind me, and I was startled by the sound. *Relax, Jessie.* I took a deep breath and stepped forward to knock on the door.

Not even three seconds later, Lady Kate opened the entrance and greeted me with a smile. "Come in, Ms. Parker!"

"Thank you," I replied, carefully entering the office. She motioned for me to sit in the chair on one side of the desk. Lady Kate's office was more modern than Professor Jones, but somehow I found his office more comfortable.

"I'm sure you know why you're here," she said, sitting in her chair across from me.

"For finding the Browns," I said. She nodded and cupped her hands in her lap. "As many compliments as I am sure you have heard, I do feel inclined to give you praise of my own." Her voice was welcoming and honest, and I felt significantly more respected. She hadn't stopped smiling since I arrived and seemed genuinely proud.

"You've done the academy a *great* favor. The Browns were of much more value than we imagined. This morning I attended the inquisition, and the Browns are *strongly* connected to an agency that we have been trying to make contact with for about a year now. We're still far and don't know their exact location, but we're progressing.

This progress would've taken a lot more time without you and your bravery. You do know why you were brought here?"

The last sentence felt like a statement, but the overhanging ellipses required me to respond. "To find the Browns," I replied. She gently shook her head with a smile, and it was the most comforting reprimand I'd ever encountered. "You were originally brought to the academy to lead us to the Browns. We didn't expect you to actually bring them in, or even follow your brother and get to the refuge when you did. With all honesty, you've displayed bravery since that very moment. You flew a plane! Dare I say, it's harder explaining that to the airline, police officers, and press than it was to do what you did."

I couldn't help but smile, though I was sure there was another point she hadn't mentioned. "All that said, Jessie, I'd like to formally ask if you would lead one final mission."

"Final?"

"Well, I understand if you no longer want to attend IFON. We would trust you not to spread word of the truth behind what happens here, as you know there would be consequences."

"I wouldn't expect anything less. Though I think I'd be doing the academy a favor that they couldn't repay if I were to remain a student."

Being confident in front of Lady Kate was important, though Lady Kate seemed to take my words as more than simple confidence—she seemed to take them as merit.

"I agree with you, Ms. Parker." If you comply, I would like to send you to investigate the tunnels found at the Brown's residence. Even better, I'd like to send Michael Brown with you."

The offer was something I wanted, but it could be better. "I think the absence of guards would be beneficial," I said. "Though there is safety in numbers. Perhaps, you can allow me to bring two others in addition to Mr. Brown?"

"I doubt the committee would appreciate that. Furthermore, I'm not sure that I would. Safety is vital and the absence of guards on site could be arranged, but bringing extra people could be worse, especially ones who don't know anything about the academy."

"All due respect, Lady Kate, I have saved the academy months' worth of consistent research, planning, and expedition. I do think allowing me to explore this newfound area with trustworthy people would be among the least that the academy could do."

Lady Kate seemed hesitant, and I knew I'd have to push my case if she would comply.

"Also, both people have been in the vicinity of the academy. To one of which I honestly owe most of the progress in locating and capturing the Browns."

Lady Kate leaned forward inquisitively.

"Who did you have in mind?"

the friendly four

Somewhere underground
Wednesday
1730 hours

Okay, I knew you were rich, but not *this* rich."

"I don't think I am. My parents probably don't own this."

"But it's under your house! We literally got here from your garage."

"If my parents *could* afford all this, then they owe me a raised allowance."

"Be quiet, guys," Kaylani said. "We're almost there."

As for me, I could listen to Michael and Lion talk all day. I hadn't been with them in a long time, and it was amazingly relieving to know that they were safe.

We aimed our flashlights in the same direction, and I had yet to anxiously look behind me. Kaylani opened the first door we reached, leading us to a room that I recognized. There were two doors at the far wall just as I remembered, and Kaylani and I knew which one we would open.

"If anything goes wrong, we run back the way we came and meet the guards who are outside the house," instructed Kaylani. She opened the door to the right, which led to another hallway.

In just a few seconds, we entered the same place that Officer Cole had described as a circus. Had he been with us, he might've called it a dump.

There were glass bottles, wrappers, and abandoned jewelry all over the floor. Many chairs were lying on their side. The entire room felt a lot larger compared to our previous visit, mostly because we were the only people present. The best thing about the room was the lighting, and the fact that we wouldn't need our flashlights to get around.

"I hope the others are here," Michael said, seemingly not feeling that the dirty room was out of the ordinary.

"You know them?" Lion asked, pointing toward the left of the room. We looked in the direction that he pointed, and we saw a tall figure walking along the wall, dropping things from the floor into a bag as they went.

"No way." Michael shook head, starting to race after them. The rest of us quickly followed, assuming that this was one of his friends.

"Mariah!" he called, and the girl turned to face us. As we grew closer, I could see her a lot better. She was very tall and had hair extensions that reached to her heel. Her sparkling green dress was form-fitting and reached just above her knees.

"Oh my gosh!" The girl stretched out her arms for a hug as Michael was the first to meet her.

"I missed you," Michael told her. Kaylani, Lion, and I looked at one another.

"So…uh, Michael, you gonna introduce us to your girlfriend?" Lion asked.

Michael and Mariah separated their hug, and Michael stared at Lion sternly.

"His *friend* can introduce herself," Mariah said. "I'm Mariah. Let me guess, you're Jessie, you're Kaylani, you're Lion?"

"Switch the first two around, and yes." Kaylani smiled. "Nice to meet you."

"Likewise. Michael has said a lot about you. Good things, of course. Except for you, Lion."

Lion playfully rolled his eyes.

"Where's Ozi?" Michael asked Mariah.

"He's in his room. Harry's in his too. Would you like me to show your friends around?"

"It's all right. I don't want you getting in trouble for the area not being clean."

"Fair enough. But be careful. Some people are angry that others have been leaving."

"Who's been leaving?"

"Other than you, mostly adults and their children. They've been finding cheap houses to move into. A lot have been vacant, though they have to go a long distance."

"How far?"

"Some are going to Colorado, a few up to New York, and some to California."

"They can afford plane tickets?"

"Nah. Maybe some can, but I'm pretty sure most are taking the tunnels."

"I'm sorry, how many people have left?" I asked.

Mariah looked at me as if she'd forgotten I was present. "A few," she replied. "Less than thirty, but that might change soon. Summertime is the best time for travelling around here."

"Thanks, Mariah," Michael said. "I'll see you around." He motioned for us to follow him, just as my phone rang.

"You get service down here?" Lion queried. "I didn't think that'd work."

"Neither did I," I admitted, reaching for my phone in my pocket.

"Harry!" Michael exclaimed. I turned around and saw a recognizable face on the other side of the large room. The four people around me walked toward the boy, but I stayed where I was and answered the call.

"Hey, Miles."

"Jess, what's been goin' on?"

"A lot actually."

"Well, I coulda guessed that. You're kinda famous now."

"Like you?"

"Better, unfortunately for me. Dad told me that he and Mom want us to come for breakfast on Sunday."

"What time?"

"Just meet me in the school lobby at nine."

"Okay."

Miles loudly ate what sounded like chips, and I had to push the phone away from my ear. "So are you staying at IFON?" he loudly asked, a mouthful of food.

"I dunno." I carefully brought the device to my ear. "I don't think Lady Kate wants me here anymore."

"Trust me, she does. You're not even good at fighting, yet you brought in Michael's parents. You can't blind me like you do to her, though. I know you couldn't have done it alone."

"Well, Kaylani helped a *lot*."

"Oh, that reminds me!" He shoved more chips into his mouth, loudly chewing. "I need you to tell her something."

"She's here actually. You could just talk to—"

"No, I'm not gonna smack on chips in your friend's ear."

"Oh, but you'll do it in mine."

"Exactly," Miles said. "Now listen. There's this guy named Damian. He emailed me this morning saying that he's trying to leave California on his own. Some people are after him, and he can't afford to stay where he is any longer. So tell Kaylani that he's heading south and will be off-the-grid for a while. He doesn't want her to worry about him."

"I'll tell her."

"Good. Talk to you later."

He ended the call before I could, and a collection of laughter started from behind me. I walked toward the group, and Harry was the first to notice me.

"Who's this?" he asked.

"That's Jessie," Kaylani said, rushing toward me. She threw her arm around me, and the others started talking again.

"Miles wanted me to tell you something," I whispered.

She stepped back and raised an eyebrow inquiringly. "It's about Damian," I began. "Miles said that some people are after him so he's running south and will be...off-the-grid, I think he said. But Damian doesn't want you to worry about him."

Kaylani scoffed at the news. "He never does, does he?" Her words and tone disclosed an emotion that I couldn't quite understand.

"You ladies in?" Harry asked. We shifted our attention to the group.

"For what?" I asked.

"He wants to know if you wanna explore the tunnels with us," Lion clarified.

Harry shook his head. "I dinny say all that. I say we oughta explore the mess hall. It's pretty large. Only a few people there, and they all blocked. Won't see us comin'."

I looked at Kaylani wondering if she'd understood Harry better than me, but we both chuckled when realizing that neither of us were clear on his suggestion.

"Okay, let's go," Michael said, comprehending Harry much better than I had.

"You all have fun," Mariah said. "*Harma-sil.*" She ended with a slight bow before returning to the trash bag that she had been using.

"What's that mean?" Kaylani asked.

"It's a way people around here say *hi* and *bye* to each other," Michael explained. "I guarantee you a drunk made it up and it caught on." Harry and Lion laughed at the idea, and Harry started leading us through the large room we were in.

Being surrounded by friendly faces made me feel relaxed. Despite associating with a stranger who had a thick accent and unusual vernacular, being with my best friends was all that I could ask for. We hadn't been together in weeks, and I didn't doubt that my friends felt the same comfort and relief that I did.

IFON Academy: Reprise

IFON Academy
Library
Friday
1630 hours

The library was much busier on Fridays than throughout the rest of the week. Students would hang out together at the computers, while those with homework loved to study on the higher floors. Today, I was one of those students with homework. It was a relief that my friends had homework too, and we could study together.

"Donnay, you put negative three," Kaylani said from next to me. I looked over my shoulder at the desktop where Donnay was working and saw that she had, in fact, typed negative three.

"The equation says negative, Kaylani."

"Yeah, then you used the reciprocal. That makes it positive."

"Oh. Math isn't my strong suit anyways."

"Not mine either." Kaylani shrugged. "I'm more into science, but they go hand in hand."

"And I'm more into combat. Too bad we don't really get home-work in it."

I turned back to face the desktop in front of me, which was a black screen with green letters and numbers in it. *Loop the code and set each variable to increase by one*, I repeated the instructions in my head. Leaning back in the chair, everything we'd learned in computer class seemed to escape my head. *How do I write a loop? What type of loop do I execute?*

"Need some help with that?" I looked over my shoulder to see Olivia facing backward in her chair.

"Kinda," I admitted. "I don't remember anything Mr. Davis said."

Olivia nodded, squinting to see what was on my computer. I leaned back to allow her to read the entire screen.

"Aw, that's easy!" She laughed. "I'll email you how to loop the code like he said."

"Can you send me how to execute it too?"

"For sure!" She eagerly turned around to face her laptop and started typing quickly. I shifted back to sit correctly in my seat and minimize the page on my screen.

"So how are things looking?" Kaylani asked, her voice close to a whisper. It was almost impossible to hear her over the other students surrounding us.

"What do you mean?" I asked, typing in the search bar for my email.

"Well, you found Michael's parents."

"With your help, yeah."

"You still did it. And Michael's staying with Lion for the time being."

"So?"

"So…"

"I just sent it!" Olivia called as the page on my screen loaded in.

"Thank you!" I replied, clicking on the most recent email. The right side of my screen showed the fullness of the email, which was surprisingly easy to read. The topics were separated for me to refer to different parts of the email when working on different parts of the code.

"She's *really* good," I observed.

"Definitely the best in our computer class," Kaylani agreed.

"Oh, I'm sorry." I shifted to my right, facing my friend. "What were you asking?"

"I just wanted to know how you feel about this place. I love it here, a lot more with you, and I didn't know if you were planning to leave anytime soon."

"You still haven't asked your question." I smiled.

Kaylani laughed, shaking her head. "Are you staying at IFON?"

The screen to my left shifted as a new email loaded in. I glanced toward it briefly and then took a second look. Just seeing who the email was from told me the answer to Kaylani's question and confirmed my summer to be a once-in-a-lifetime experience.

"Looks like I'll have to."

From: Emircy Kate <ladyemircykate @msacademy.edu>
To: <undisclosed-recipients>
CC: Jessie Parker <jessieparker@msacademy.edu>

Good afternoon!

Within the past hour, I was informed that Riele Mana-Kahananui has eluded confinement from the academy's dedicated juvenile detention center. Jessie Parker was instrumental in bringing Ms. Mana-Kahananui to custody of the academy. As we all know, the Browns are still in custody and have gone through an inquisition. We should expect not to learn much about this recent escape from them.

Rather, I would like to supplicate Ms. Parker to lead the process in locating Ms. Mana-Kahananui. The escapade would last no more than four weeks as Ms. Parker is discerned to desire to part from the academy. With her cooperation, we will begin the search on Monday afternoon. Without, we will begin tomorrow morning.

Please permanently delete this email after reading, or reply with any concerns before doing so.

Sincerely,
Emircy Kate

From: Jessie Parker <jessieparker@msacademy.edu>
To: Emircy Kate <ladyemircykate@msacadelm.edu>

I am more than pleased to assist in the endeavor, and do intend on remaining at the academy. However, if I am to assist, I would like to request adding another student to the team. I am sure you know who that is.

About the Author

Emily Ross is the author of *IFON Academy.* A lover of music, she uses writing to make melodies and stories in which readers can indulge. Her adventurous disposition influences her creations, and her persistence makes them available to the world. She lives vicariously through her characters and shares their stories for all to enjoy.